Evil Above the Stars
Volume 3

Unity of Seven

Evil Above the Stars
Volume 3

Unity of Seven

Peter R. Ellis

Elsewhen Press

To Alison

Map of Gwlad

NORTH POLE

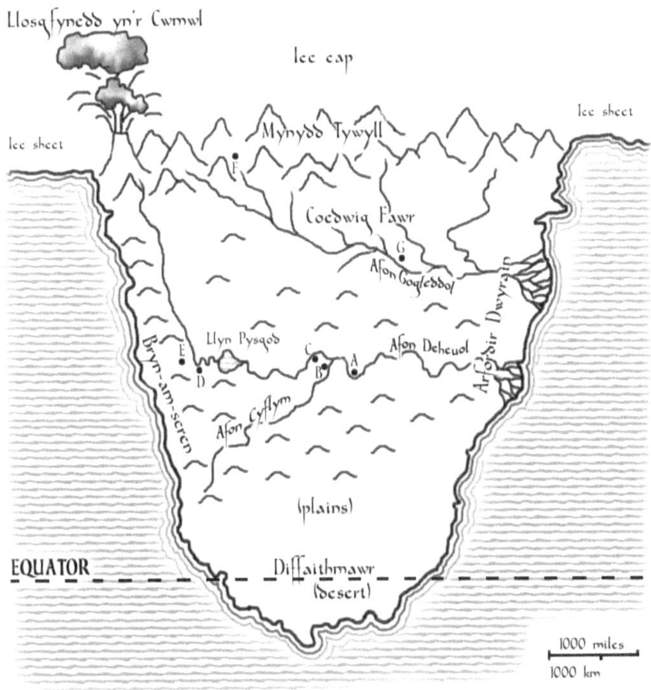

Towns and Villages:

A-Amaethaderyn

B-Abercyflym

C-Glanyrafon

D-Dwytrefrhaedr

E-Arsyllfa

F-Mwyngloddiau Dwfn

G-Trefyncoed

Pronunciation guide

The 'old tongue' used by the people of the Land is derived from Celtic languages such as Welsh. General guidelines on pronunciation are as follows.

- 'll' does not occur in English, in the glossary it is written as 'LL'. The sound is made by partly opening the mouth, pressing the tongue against the roof of the mouth and blowing gently.

- 'dd', written as 'TH' in the glossary, is the hard th sound in 'this' and 'that' but not as in 'path'.

- 'a' is always as in 'cat' and not as in 'ape'.

- 'e' is always as in 'pet'.

- 'f' is the v in 'van' while 'ff' is the f in 'fan'.

- 'c' is always the hard 'k' sound in 'kid'.

- 'ch' is similar to ck and pronounced as in the Scottish 'loch' and not the English 'church'.

- 'g' is always hard as in 'god' and not as in 'german'.

- 'o' is like in 'on' but not 'open'.

- 'i' and 'u' are pronounced 'ee'.

- 'r's should be rolled.

- 'si' is between the sh in 'shone' and the j of 'john'.

- 'w' is oo as in 'cool'.

- 'y' is sometimes the u sound in 'run', sometimes the i in 'bin' and occasionally the ee sound in 'been'.

- 'yw' is pronounced 'you'.

- 'ae', 'ai', 'au' and 'ei' are all pronounced 'eye'.

- 'eu' is the oy in 'boy'.

Glossary

Word	[Pronunciation] Meaning
Adarllwchgwin	[ad-ar-LL-ook-goo-in] giant eagle bearing red devil-like figures with tridents, air manifestations of the Malevolence
Adwyth	[ad-oo-eeth] The Malevolence, the evil from above the stars
Afon Deheuol	[a-von de-hoy-ol] Southern River, one of the great transport links of Gwlad
Afon Gogleddol	[a-von gog-leTH-ol] the great northern river
alcam	[al-kam] tin, a silver-grey malleable metal
Amaethaderyn	[am-eyeth-ad-er-in] Farm of birds, a village on the Afon Deheuol, the southern river
Arfordir Dwyrain	[ar-vord-eer doo-ee-rine] the coastal region on the east of Gwlad
arian	[ar-ee-an] silver, a rare silver metal
arianbyw	[ar-ee-an-byou] mercury, dense silver liquid metal
Arsyllfa	[ar-siLL-va] The observatory-cum-fortress in the Bryn am seren in the west of Gwlad
Aur	[eye-er] gold. A rare, maleable, yellow metal
Bryn-am-seren	[brin-am-ser-en] Hills of Stars, a range of low mountains in the west of Gwlad
cariad	[kar-ee-ad] love
Ceffyl dwr	[kef-ill doo-er] Water horse, a giant aggressive winged horse, a water manifestation of the Malevolence
Cemegwr	[kem-egg-oo-er] Creators, chemists, the Makers of everything
Cludydd	[klee-deeTH] bearer or wielder

Word	[Pronunciation] Meaning
Word	**[Pronunciation] Meaning**
Coblynau	[kob-lin-eye] dwarf-like creatures with rock crushing hands, earth manifestations of the Malevolence
Coedwig Fawr	[koy-doo-ig vow-er] The Great Forest south of the mountains
Cwn annwn	[koon ann-oon] fiery hounds, a fire manifestation of the Malevolence
cymysgwch	[cum-us-gook] command – mix
Cyrhyraeth	[kir-hir-eyeth] a moaning, disease-bearing wind, an air-manifestation of the Malevolence
Cysylltiad	[Kuss-uLL-tee-ad] The Conjunction, the lining up of all the planets
Daear	[die-ar] Earth, the planet at the centre of the universe
Dechreuwr	[dek-roy-oor] initiator, catalyst
Diffaithmawr	[dif-eyeth-ma-oo-er] The great desert at the southern end of Gwlad
Draig tân	[dry-g tarn] Fiery dragon, comet. A fire manifestation of the Malevolence
Dwytrefrhaedr	[doo-ee-trev-rheye-der] The two towns by the waterfall, on the River Deheuol
efyddyn	[e-vu-TH-in] copper, a malleable red metal
egwyddorpum	[egg-oo-eeTH-or- pim] the quintessence, the fifth element that forms the stars and the Maengolauseren
Gwener	[goo-en-er] Venus, the 3rd planet from the Earth in the geo-centric system
Gwlad	[goo-lard] The Land – the occupied continent on Daear
Gwlyb Hoedl Gwyrthiol	[Goo-lib hoy-dil goo-er-thee-ol] The 'miraculous liquid of life' or the elixir of life. The liquid that gives eternal life.
Gwyllian	[goo-iLL-ee-an] old women, earth manifestations of the Malevolence

Word	[Pronunciation] Meaning
haearn	[heye-arn] iron, a hard grey metal
Haul	[h-eye-el] Sun, the 4th planet from the Earth in the geo-centric system
Iau	[ee-aye] Jupiter, the 6th planet from the Earth in the geo-centric system
Iechyd da	[ee-e-kid da] "Good health"
Llamhigwyn y dwr	[LLam-heeg-oo-in u doo-er] giant flying frogs, a water manifestation of the Malevolence
Llanidloes	[LLan-id-loyce] Town in Mid-Wales
Llelluched	[LLe-LLee-ked] deserted mining town in mid-Wales
Lleuad	[LL-eye-ad] Moon, the 1st 'planet' from the Earth in the geo-centric system
Llosgfynedd yn'r Cwmwl	[LLos-g-mun-iTH un-er koo-mool] The fiery mountain in the clouds. A volcano
Llywelyn	[LLew-el-in] A Prince of Wales
Machynlleth	[Mak-un-LLeth] town in Mid-Wales
Maengolauseren	[mine-gol-eye-ser-en] stone of starlight or starstone, the stone of power held by September
Malevolence	[mal-ev-o-lens] the power of evil from above the stars
mamgu	[mam-Gee] grandmother
Mawrth	[ma-oorth] Mars, the 5th planet from the Earth in the geocentric system
Mercher	[mer-ker] Mercury, the 2nd planet from the Earth in the geo-centric system
Mordeyrn	[mor-day-ern] Leader
Mwyngloddiau Dwfn	[moo-een-gloTH-ee-eye doo-ven] mining town high in the Mynydd Tywyll
Mynydd Tywyll	[mun-iTH tu-oo-iLL] the dark mountains in the north of Gwlad
Penbryngolau	[Pen-brin-gol-eye] ridge above Llelluched

Word	[Pronunciation] Meaning
Word	**[Pronunciation] Meaning**
plwm	[ploom] lead, a dense, soft grey metal
prif-	[preev] chief, head
Pwca	[Poo-ka] a shape-changer, an air manifestation of the Malevolence
Sadwrn	[sad-oo-ern] Saturn, the 7th planet from the Earth in the geo-centric system
seryddwr	[ser-iTH-oor] observer of the stars and planets
symudiad	[see-mud-ee-ad] the ability to transport instantly from one place to another
tadcu	[tad-kee] grandfather
Toddfa Penbaladr	[To-TH-va Pen-bal-ader] The Alkahest or Universal Solvent. The liquid that dissolves and combines everything
toddwch	[to-TH-ook] command – dissolve
Tylwyth teg	[tul-oo-eeth teg] pale, fairy-like creatures, earth manifestations of the Malevolence
typyn bach	[tip-in baak] 'a little bit'
ymadaelwch	[uma-die-look] command – be gone

Dramatis Personae

Arianell	[a-ree-an-eLL] bearer of silver at Mwyngloddiau Dwfn
Arianrhod	[a-ree-an-rhod] Chief bearer of silver
Arianwen	[a-ree-an-oo-en] The cludydd o arian, silver-bearer, of Amaethaderyn
Aurddolen	[eye-er-TH-olen] chief bearer of gold and leader of the Land
Bechan	[bek-ann] one of Gwenda's sisters
Betrys	[bet-rees] Chief bearer of tin

Breuddwyd	[broy-TH-oo-id] September's mother
Cari	[kar-ee] bearer of copper at Mwyngloddiau Dwfn
Catrin	[kat-rin] The cludydd o efyddyn, copper-bearer, of Amaethaderyn
Cyfaill	[kuv-eye-LL] A 'Brain' of the omniverse
Cynddylig	[kin-THil-ig] older man, boatman and river guide
Cynhaearn	[kin-heye-arn] Chief bearer of iron
Dafydd	[dav-iTH] one of September's uncles
Dilwen	[dill-oo-en] the 2nd Cludydd
Doli	[Dolly] landlord of the Moon & Stars inn
Eirawen	[eye-ra-wen] the 5th Cludydd, September's great grandmother
Eluned	[e-lee-ned] The cludydd o arianbyw, mercury bearer, of Amaethaderyn
Emlyn	[em-lin] one of September's uncles
Falmai	[val-my] September's grandmother
Gruffudd	[grif-ith] one of September's uncles
Gwenda	[goo-enda] the 1st Cludydd
Hedydd	[hed-eeTH] astronomer's apprentice, female
Heulfryn	[hoyl-vrin] bearer of gold at Mwyngloddiau Dwfn
Heulwen	[hoyl-oo-en] daughter of Aurddolen
Heulyn	[hoyl-in] chief bearer of gold and leader of the land at the last conjunction
Ilar	[ill-ar] bearer of tin at Mwyngloddiau Dwfn
Iolo	[ee-o-lo] one of Gwenda's brothers
Iorwerth	[ee-or-oo-er-th] The cludydd o haearn, iron-bearer of Amaethaderyn
Isfoel	[is-voy-el] bearer of mercury at Mwyngloddiau Dwfn
Maerwen	[my-er-oo-en] the name given to Malice by her mother
Malice	twin sister of September

Nona   [non-a] one of Gwenda's sisters

Padarn   [pad-arn] bearer of lead at Amaethaderyn

Pedr   [ped-er] one of Gwenda's brothers

Rhiainwen   [rhee-eye-n-wen] the 4th Cludydd, grandmother of Sionen

September   The Cludydd o Maengolauseren

Sieffre   [jef-re] young man, lead guide to the Bryn-am-seren

Sionen   [she-on-en] Mother of Eirawen

Tudfwlch   [teed-voolk] young warrior and ironsmith, apprentice to Iorwerth

Wenhaf   [oo-en-hav] the 3rd Cludydd

Previously...

Parts 1 and 2
Seventh Child

Looking at the stars through a glassy stone September has found she is transported to the world of her dreams. She is greeted by the Mordeyrn Aurddolen, a bearer of gold. He names her as the Cluddydd o Maengolauseren, the wielder of the starstone, who will save the people of Gwlad from the Malevolence, 'the evil from above the stars'. September is told that she has this position of responsibility and power as she is the seventh child. September is confused, because she only has four sisters and a brother but nevertheless when she helps Aurddolen resist an attack by a Draig tân, a fire dragon, she discovers that the starstone does indeed have miraculous properties.

September returns home until the time when the threat of the Malevolence will be reaching its peak. At school she is bullied because of her weight, white hair and silly name and is considered lazy and dim, but she finds some answers to the questions her brief visit to Gwlad has posed. On her sixteenth birthday she learns that she had a twin sister who died at birth and that she is indeed the seventh of her mother's children. In the evening she looks through the stone at the stars and is again transported to Gwlad.

Her arrival in the village of Amaethaderyn is welcomed by the bearers of the other six metals but they tell her that she must embark on a long journey following Aurddolen to the fortress-observatory, the Arsyllfa. During the preparations for her departure the village is attacked a number of times by manifestations of the Malevolence and September realises that she is the focus for the attention of evil.

The metal bearers give her gifts of silver, copper, iron, mercury, tin and lead imbued with the powers of the six planets which, together with the Sun, orbit the stationary world of which Gwlad is part. She sets off on the river in a gold-powered boat accompanied by Tudfwlch, an apprentice warrior and blacksmith, and Cynddilig a boatman and guide. During the weeks that follow September learns more about her task but they are attacked by various manifestations. The starstone will protect September, but only when she is truly afraid.

Tudfwlch and Cynddilig are killed and September is rescued by Heulwen, the daughter of Aurddolen. She is taken to Dwytrefrhaedr, the twin towns by the waterfall. From there, September and Heulwen, assisted by warrior and guide Sieffre and four other guards, set off on the final stage of the journey, on foot, across the range of hills known as the Bryn am Seren. Climbing the highest peak with the Arsyllfa at its summit they have to fight through hordes of manifestations. At last they reach the great doors of the fortress but September is hailed by a woman in black who appears to be directing the besieging monsters. She has white hair and a face that September recognises as her own. The woman warns September that the Arsyllfa will become her prison and then unleashes her forces. September steps through the doors of the fortress, her journey complete, but her task barely begun.

Previously...

Parts 3 and 4
The Power of Seven

September has arrived at the Arsyllfa but has yet to find out how she can perform the task she has been given. While September and the other guests are being informed of the exact date and place of the Conjunction when the Malevolence will descend, they are attacked by Draig tân lead by the woman in black; Malice, September's twin sister who died before birth. September destroys the comets but reaches a stalemate with Malice.

Aurddolen gives September the Book of Heulyn which recounts what happened when September's mother, Breuddwyd, was Cludydd. September realises that she must cut herself off from the other inhabitants of the Arsyllfa in order to learn the skills of the Cludydd. She locks herself in her room and when she falls into a trance is carried on a journey through the solar system. At each planet she learns how to use the powers of the metal associated with that planet. After visiting Saturn, and confident of her new abilities she ventures beyond the sphere of stars into the realm of the Malevolence. While she is powerful she discovers she cannot overcome the spirits of evil and retreats to the Arsyllfa.

She discovers the Fortress has been breached and is in the hands of Malice and her servant, Heulwen. They fight and September escapes in the form of an eagle with Heulwen. Below the Arsyllfa's peak she finds Sieffre and in the form of a panther she carries Sieffre and Heulwen in pursuit of Aurddolen and others.

When she catches up Aurddolen and his companions she

offers to ferry each in turn to Mwyngloddiau Dwfn, the mining town in the Mynydd Tywyll, closest habitation to the site of the Conjunction. There Aurddolen starts to prepare for the coming battle while September travels Gwlad fighting manifestations wherever they appear. She becomes accustomed to her special abilities but worried that the power of the Malevolence controlled by Malice may be more than she can match.

At last the time has come to travel to the point on the icecap where she will meet the Malevolence as it descends. She and the army commanded by Aurddolen travel through the mountains. They are attacked by manifestations and their supplies destroyed. September decides to continue with just Sieffre and Hedydd, the astronomer, as guides.

At the Conjunction September attempts to hold back the descending hordes of evil spirits but she is overpowered by Malice. On the point of death the starstone takes her home.

September is overwrought to find herself at home knowing that she has failed. Her mother tries to comfort her. September discovers that she still has the starstone, which has split into two parts. She takes this as a hint that she can return to Gwlad, with her mother. They do so and find the Land devastated by the Malevolence. They find a few of the inhabitants of Amaethaderyn hiding in the wood protected by the remaining cludydds. September and Breuddwyd travel to Mwyngloddiau Dwfn, but find it deserted.

They are met by Heulwen, embodying Malice, who has imprisoned her father, Aurddolen. September manages to throw Malice out and release Aurddolen but Heulwen dies. The people are found hiding in the mines. September, Breuddwyd and the cludydds discuss how to defeat the Malevolence but they are lost for ideas. The Cemegwr, the fabled creators of the world are mentioned and, against Aurddolen's wishes (he doesn't think they exist), September goes off to search for them.

By luck or by guidance, September meets the Cemegwr in Coedwig Fawr, the great forest. They have the form of human woodspeople who claim to have the power to create worlds but are disinclined to rescue their creation from the

Malevolence. September argues and the Cemegwr finally agree to help her. They give her the Toddfa Penbaladr, the universal solvent which will help her to overcome Malice and allow the Maengolauseren's power to throw the evil off the world.

September re-joins Breuddwyd and they travel to the southern desert and draw Malice to them. The power of the Toddfa Penbaladr merges September and Malice removing her control of the Malevolence and at the final victory over the evil September and Breuddwyd are transported to their home. But what has happened on Gwlad and does the Malevolence still have power?

Part 5

~

Return

1

It was dark. Again. The darkness was silent, without heat, without substance. She had no memory as she had no sense of time but there was a feeling of difference from what had been familiar. Before, whatever that meant, the darkness had been boundless and she could reach out across limitless space. Here, she was confined. Instead of infinity she experienced the infinitesimal. She was constrained in the interstices of dimensions folded in on themselves, compressed by quantum entities that popped into existence and out again.

She had no recall of freedom and power. All that she retained was what she had in that other place – one emotion. Hate. Hate for everything, all that was or ever had been, because she was Malice, a servant of the Malevolence, a servant of the evil forces of hate. But something else was holding her here, confined in the darkness, something which she could not identify.

2

September stirred. She didn't want to wake up. It had been so lovely sleeping and she felt so comfortable wrapped in the duvet on the soft mattress. It had been so long since she had felt so relaxed and calm. It felt like forever since she had slept.

She jerked herself up and banged her head on the bottom of the top bunk. She fell back rubbing her forehead. Images slipped through her mind like a slide show on random – whirling rainbow lights; a struggle with someone who was herself but wasn't; huge birds with riders and flaming spears; fiery comets with tails that stretched across the sky; lurching crones and acid-spitting fairies. She stared up at the slats supporting the mattress above her. She was home. In her own bed. Those images were only in her head. But they were real, weren't they?

The door opened and she saw the bare legs of Julie, older sister number four. Julie bent down and looked at her. She was just in her bra and knickers.

"Oh, you're awake. At last. You can use the bathroom now. The rest of us have finished in there."

"Thanks," September mumbled. Was it actually only the day after her birthday? Was she really just sixteen?

"Are you feeling better now?" Julie asked in a tone of genuine concern. "You made enough fuss in the night. When I woke up you were rolling on the floor and screaming. What was it? Too much wine?"

No, it was the fight with her twin in the frozen wastes of Gwlad.

"Something like that," she said, "I feel fine now."

"Good. Mother seemed worried about you. Made me promise not to disturb you." Julie pulled on a pair of jeans and a t-shirt. "I'm going to see if there's any breakfast left. Gus may have gobbled the lot."

She left the room and September closed her eyes, again enjoying the peace and the quiet, except for the murmur of voices down below – and the comfort. Warm, not bitterly cold like the polar ice, or burning hot like Gwlad's barren desert. Safe, not constantly under attack from monstrous manifestations and the hate-filled spirits of the Malevolence guided by her evil twin.

A sudden shiver. What of the people of Gwlad, her friends? Had they survived? Had the destructive force of the Malevolence been lifted from them? She didn't know. She no longer held the starstone, the Maengolauseren, in her hand, so she had no way of finding out. It was real, wasn't it? The memories were too strong, the images too clear, the emotions too powerful to be just a dream.

There was a light tap on the door followed, without a pause, by it opening.

"Ember? Julie said you were awake. Are you alright, love?" It was Mother, entering the room, crossing to her, kneeling beside the bunk bed so that she could look in on her. September saw herself, or what she imagined she would become, thick white hair and pale round face, slightly lined.

"Oh, Mother," September cried, reaching out with her arms. They hugged. "Did it really happen? Did we stop the Malevolence from destroying Gwlad?"

"We've both been there Ember. I thought it was a vision, before you were taken there. Now I think it must be true. I think you did it, love. We're back and the stone has disappeared."

"And what about Malice? What happened to her?"

Mother frowned. "You said you thought Mairwen had become part of you. That's what the Cemegwr told you would happen."

September remembered her conversation with the strange people, the Cemegwr, who claimed to be the creators of the universe. They had given her the elixir that entwined her with Malice, named Mairwen by her mother when she was still-born. Terror filled her. She held her head.

"Is Malice part of me now? Do I really have all her hate inside me? What's happened to me?"

Mother hugged her more tightly. "I'm sure she's not in you

now, love. That was all in Gwlad. Things are different there."

They certainly were. Besides the monsters there, there was the magic of the metals and the planets and the friendly, mild, but resourceful people. Anxiety gripped September. What had become of them all?

"What about Aurddolen and Berddig and all the others? Do you think they're still alive, Mother?"

"I prayed for them this morning, love. I don't know whether they are God's children since they don't know Jesus, but I hope the Malevolence has left them." Of course, it was Sunday. Mother would have been to chapel this morning.

"I need to know. Did I, we, push the Malevolence back above the stars?"

"I don't know, love. Without the starstone we can't go back again. It was the same when I was called."

"But I've got to find out, Mother. The Cemegwr didn't seem too bothered about what happened to the Land or its people. I was the last Cludydd. They didn't expect the universe they'd made to last much longer."

Mother shook her head sadly.

"I'm sorry love. There's no way of finding out. Gwlad is another place. Praying is all I can do. Would you like me to bring some breakfast up to you? You still seem troubled by it all."

Is that surprising? September thought. *I've spent three months away in a place that is completely weird and strange and now I find myself back home with no time passed at all.*

"No. I feel fine. I'll get up and come down and see everyone."

Mother smiled and kissed her.

"That's good, love. We'll have a chat about it later when Julie has gone and Gus and your father are watching the football or something." She stood up and left September alone.

How could Mother just carry on? She was Breuddwyd, the sixth Cludydd, who had defeated the Malevolence last time and now had helped do it again. Perhaps it was her belief that it was just a test from God that helped her to accept it all. September swung out of her bunk and went to the bathroom for a shower. Getting dressed, she looked at her body sadly.

She longed to feel as slim and lithe again as she had felt in Gwlad. Here she couldn't look good in a pair of tight jeans like Julie did. She pulled on a pleated skirt that hid her big bottom and broad thighs and a loose top that covered but didn't cling to her. She brushed her short white hair wistfully, recalling the avalanche of shoulder-length tresses that she had grown used to for all those months.

Gus was still munching through a plate of toast when she entered the kitchen-diner.

"Oh, you're still alive then, Em," he growled. "You made such a din in the night I thought you were chucking your guts up."

"Thank you for your concern," September replied. "I'm fine." She collected a glass of orange juice and an apple and retreated to the lounge where Father was reading his newspaper and Julie was focussed on her smart-phone. Father looked up, Julie didn't.

"Hi, Em," he said, "Mum said you were better after that turn in the night. Bad dream was it?"

"Sort of," September agreed biting into her apple.

"Has Gus eaten all the toast? Is that enough for you?"

Restricting herself to just a piece of fruit was unlike her, September agreed, but she was determined to continue with her diet and transform this flabby body of hers into the svelte form she had relished on Gwlad.

The rest of the day was a bit of a blur. May and June turned up for lunch with their men in tow. Then Julie set off back to her university digs. It was evening before September was able to retreat to what was now just her room again. She'd been careful about what she'd eaten all day but now her stomach was rumbling. How could she go for weeks on Gwlad and not feel hungry at all, and yet here, at home, she couldn't go for a day without her appetite betraying her? She wanted the same control over her feelings she had as the Cludydd – the ability to wield the magic of metals and the starstone just by invoking feelings of compassion, hope, joy, sadness, surprise, love, anger and of course, fear.

She sat at her desk looking out of the window. The sky was full of stars, the same stars that had poured through the starstone and transported her to that other world. Terror had been a frequent companion there but she had also learned to wield power with confidence and wisdom. To be that person, both there and here at home was now her greatest desire. She would visit the Land again; she would meet the people she knew; and she would find out what had happened to Malice. But how?

3

The darkness was as complete but something changed. She was no longer separate from, but a part of, the universe. Time had meaning. She reached out and became a string that manifested as a quark. She spread to two more quarks and became a proton. She added neutrons and electrons and became an atom. She felt the jostling of other atoms and leapt across the bonds to feel the spiral structure of the molecule. It had order and carried information in its own language. There were other molecules around her. She was a cell with a nucleus. She possessed long, long dendrons and synapses – a neuron. She was a bundle of neurons receiving signals from the surroundings. Awareness grew. She was Malice also named Mairwen, and she was captive within her twin. She felt an outpouring of hate; hate for her sister, hate for the mother she never knew, hate for the people of all the worlds, hate for all the universes. She was the embodiment of Malevolence. She screamed her hate and cried for vengeance.

4

September opened her eyes. It was still dark, still night, but something had woken her. It was something in her – a dream, a thought, the merest inkling of an emotion. Darkness, hate, anger. It was a tiny corner of her mind but was like a spark in the dark or a breaking twig in the silence. It demanded that she take notice. The feeling in her head was unfamiliar but she had a memory. It was like when she had ventured beyond the sphere of stars around Daear, into the remote darkness that was the realm of the Malevolence. Then the hate-filled spirits had surrounded her. She had felt their hostility but then it had been outside her, directed at her. This was within her, somewhere in her mind. There was a familiar itch too, in the birthmark on her right hip. It hadn't troubled her until she had been taken to the Land. There she had learned that the itch was a signal of an impending attack by the Malevolence. Did it mean that the Malevolence was here?

She shook herself, trying to force the feeling out. The abhorrence became a memory, an echo of a feeling, something she didn't want to remember but could not forget. She looked at her alarm clock. It was four o'clock. Still two or three hours before she had to get up for school. That realisation felt strange. It seemed like she'd been absent from school for more than three months, not a weekend. How could she go back to sitting in a class surrounded by the people who ridiculed her and were disgusted by her appearance? She, who had been the Cludydd o Maengolauseren, with magnificent powers that saved people and whole universes.

She snuggled under the duvet. At school she would have to face all her persecutors and her friends. 'Try to be normal', that's what Mother would say. What did that mean? Normal was the fat, dim, clumsy self she had always been, but she wanted to be the slim, fit, powerful Cludydd. She would be.

She would make herself into the person she knew she could be.

The alarm disturbed the sleep she had fallen back into. The routine tap on the door and call from her mother followed. She hauled herself from the top bunk and beat Gus to the bathroom. Although her stomach cried for more she restricted herself to one thin slice of bread with spread and a glass of orange juice for breakfast. Mother noticed her empty plate.

"Have you had enough, Em?"

"I'm going to lose this," September replied pointing to her waist.

"But you mustn't starve yourself, love. You should follow a proper diet."

"I know what I'm doing."

Mother's eyes showed her love.

"I understand but it will take time you know."

Gus looked up from his heaped bowl of cereal.

"Bet you can't keep it up."

"I will," September replied, leaving the table and grabbing her blazer and bag.

Her tormenters were in their usual places by the gates and doorway to the school but she strode past them before they had a chance to hurl any of their regular insults regarding her shape, hair colour or name. She went straight to her classroom, flung herself into a chair and pulled a file from her bag. She was going to check her homework, make sure she got better marks than usual. Unusually, the subject soon took all her attention and she didn't hear the door open.

"Hey, Ember. What are you doing?" Poppy said, skipping up to her and staring at her work as if she'd never seen such a thing before.

"You're not doing homework, are you?" Emma, her companion, added.

"Yes, I am. No time over the weekend," September mumbled, avoiding looking at her two, her only, friends.

"You had your big family party did you?" Poppy asked.

"Yes."

"Are we still going to celebrate your sixteenth on Wednesday evening?" Emma asked.

"I suppose so," September said. Of course she couldn't possibly think of eating a whole pizza now. When they'd planned the grown-up expedition to a restaurant there had been nothing that she would have liked more than guzzling a twelve inch circle of thick dough covered with cheese and sausage and all sorts of other fattening goodies.

"Good. We can talk about all the things you're legal to do now," Poppy said with a wink.

Nothing she was permitted to do now would be as amazing as flashing from one place to another in a moment or flying across the Land or running faster than a high-speed train in the form of a panther. September didn't say anything and luckily the bell went for the start of school before she had to find a reply.

It wasn't a good day. She tried so hard to concentrate, to be intelligent, to participate, but her rumbling stomach kept on reminding her that she hadn't eaten much. There were too many questions that she didn't know the answers to and teachers passed her over because they didn't expect her to have anything useful to offer.

Back home she slumped into the sofa in the lounge feeling exhausted and hungry. Gus came in slamming doors and went straight up to his room. Various noises reverberated through the house. Then Mother arrived.

"Oh, hello, Em," she said, looking around the door. "Are you OK?"

September mumbled something. Even she wasn't sure whether it was a yes or no.

"Problems?" Breuddwyd asked.

September shrugged. "No, not really. Just that I'm useless," she said.

Breuddwyd came into the room, sat beside her and put an arm around her shoulders.

"No, love, you're not useless. You've just defeated the Malevolence."

"That was there. Here I'm fat and dumb and useless."

"No, Em. Don't say that. You're the same person who defeated all those manifestations, who helped the people of Gwlad and demonstrated all the powers of the

Maengolauseren. It's just going to take a little time to get you how you want to be. If you want to diet, you've got to do it properly. I bet you missed lunch today didn't you."

September nodded.

"Well, that's not the way to do it. I'll help you, but you need to eat so you can concentrate on your school work."

"I don't care about school," September said, surprising herself.

"Yes you do, love. You want to pass your exams."

September shrugged again.

"Yes, but I want to know what's happening there, in the Land. Has the Malevolence really gone? How are the people who are left doing, and how did it all start?" Suddenly, the worries about what she had left behind were the most important things on her mind.

"What do you mean?"

"There's so much I don't understand. Why us? You're the sixth and I'm the seventh Cludydd. What about the other five? They are our ancestors, but who were they? Why our family? Why were we picked to bear the starstone and fight the Malevolence?"

Breuddwyd sighed.

"I know how you feel, Em. When it was just my experience, my vision, I didn't have any questions. It was God's will that I should experience those things. Now I see that there is more to it. You and I have both been chosen and we know it is something to do with our family."

"I want to find out more."

"Yes, Em, I understand. Perhaps if we speak to your Gran, she might be able to tell us something."

"Do you think Gran was the fifth Cludydd?" September asked.

"I don't know," Breuddwyd acknowledged.

September pondered for a moment. "She can't have been."

"Why not?" Breuddwyd was mystified by September's certainty.

"She's not a seventh child like you and me, and she never had hair like us." September was sure that their snow-white hair was important and she'd seen photos of Gran when she was younger when she had hair as dark as coal.

"But *her* mother had lots of brothers and sisters," Breuddwyd said, "and I remember seeing a picture of her taken when she was young. It was a black and white photo but her hair looked as white as ours."

"You mean your grandmother?"

"Yes, Mamgu Wen. Her full name was Eirawen. But I hardly knew her. She died when I was about four."

"Eirawen? Another Welsh name."

"Yes. I think she actually spoke Welsh. My mother doesn't though."

"She must be the fifth Cludydd. Perhaps Gran knows something."

Breuddwyd looked thoughtful.

"Perhaps. I don't remember her mentioning the starstone or the Malevolence or anything about the Land. If she had I might have talked about my experiences."

"Can we go and see Gran?"

Breuddwyd paused to think for a moment, checking a mental calendar. "We could go this Saturday. It's been a while since we visited her and she would love to know all about your birthday. I'm not sure we'll get much out of her though. You know what she's like."

September wished it was a few years earlier when Gran Falmai was active and bright. Now she sat in a chair in the nursing home most of the time, staring at the television even if it was turned off and not always sure who her visitors were.

"We've got to try, Mother."

"Yes, I know. Talking about her mother might bring some memories back. I'll see if I can find the old photos before we go. Something to jog her memory."

The next four days couldn't pass quickly enough for September. The thought of finding out something, anything, about the earlier Cludydds gave her something to aim at. She attacked her schoolwork with renewed determination and even drew some praise from her teachers when she showed knowledge and insight that she had not apparently had previously. Mother produced meals that filled her up but which she promised would help her shed the kilogrammes she wanted to lose. She didn't feel hungry all the time and trusted Mother's insistence that the fat would fall away, albeit slowly. She even continued with her after school jogs. She didn't go far – she was puffing like an old steam train after a few hundred yards – but she kept at it. By the end of the week, even Gus had stopped joking about her running style and offered encouragement.

The evening out with Poppy and Emma proved to be an anti-climax. She had tried to dress up but was disgusted by her appearance in the mirror. A short skirt and sparkly top had clung and shown off all her bulges, while a long dress looked like a sack. She'd settled at last and without enthusiasm for a blouse, skirt combination that was drab but at least ensured that she wouldn't stand out. Her two friends looked like two fun-loving young women, in outfits that showed bits of flesh and accentuated their figures. They looked as if they spent every night living it up in the town centre.

Father had driven the three of them into town, dropping them off outside the restaurant. She had chosen a small bowl of pasta with a green salad while her friends, stick-thin both of them, munched through massive pizzas. She never understood why they could apparently eat anything while she ballooned just by looking at an ice cream or a cake with longing eyes. Poppy and Emma applauded her new objective to become slim but they thought that the aim was to attract the boys now that she was over sixteen. September didn't explain her purpose and found herself losing interest in the conversation as her two friends nattered about fashions and celebrities and things they'd seen on their smart phones. A week earlier she would have been as involved in the chatter as the other two. Now she was relieved when Father returned by nine p.m. to pick them up.

Back in her bedroom she felt sad and lonely. Her experiences in the Land and her dramatic battles with the Malevolence had driven her apart from her friends. Previously she had been delighted by the same topics but now she felt she had more important matters to worry about. Poppy and Emma were her closest friends but now it seemed she had no one in this universe who understood her, other than Mother.

It was the nightly flashes of anger and hate that worried her most. Each night she awoke and jerked upright wondering what it was she hated so. It wasn't the same time each night but the length and intensity of the memory, or whatever it was, seemed to be increasing. At first a spark, by Friday night it was a lightning flash of raw emotion. Was it Malice? She recalled the Cemegwr telling her that the elixir would unite her with Malice and make them one. When the elixir had mixed the seven metals and starstone together she had wrapped Malice in her arms and they had left the Land together, but where was Malice now? There had been no other hint of what had become of Malice other than these brief outpourings of hate in her head. September worried that she was going to have a stroke, like Grandad Stan, Father's father. He'd died after suffering a sudden blinding headache.

On Saturday morning, September was up earlier than a normal school morning. Mother was already bustling around the kitchen of course, preparing breakfast and putting together supplies for the journey. Father was there too but Gus had yet to emerge from his den. It was a family trip, one of the three or four they made annually to visit Gran Falmai in her Swansea home.

"Why have we got to see her today?" Gus complained as he slouched into the kitchen. "You didn't mention it until yesterday."

"Your mother decided it would be nice for Gran to see September soon after her birthday," Father answered.

"Why do I have to come, then?" Gus said sitting down in front of a large fry-up placed there by Breuddwyd.

"You don't see Gran very often. We probably won't be going again before Christmas," Breuddwyd said.

"She probably won't even know who I am," Gus grumbled on, stuffing his face with bacon and toast. "Last time she thought I was what's-his-name, cousin thingy."

"She does get a bit confused," Father said, "but so would I if I had all those grandchildren as well as seven children."

"Well, you and your father will be able to go for a walk on the beach after you've said hello," Breuddwyd said, "Em and I will stay and chat to her."

Gus grunted some semblance of satisfaction and September noted how her mother had cleverly manoeuvred to get a private chat for them with Gran without Gus and Father being any the wiser.

The drive, though three hours long, was relatively painless. Saturday morning traffic was light and the late September weather was pleasant. Father concentrated on driving; Mother dozed at his side; Gus was immersed in his smartphone with his headphones insulating him from the surroundings. September watched the motorway verge go by while reliving her experiences of fighting monsters and wondering how she had managed to keep calm enough to control her emotions and wield the various powers of the Maengolauseren. She recalled the thrill of swooping over the Land in the form of an eagle, travelling far faster than the car was.

It was gone eleven-thirty when they pulled up in the nursing home car park. They trudged the familiar corridors until they came to Gran's room. She was sitting in her chair beside her bed looking at nothing when they entered.

"Hello, dear," she said as Breuddwyd stooped to kiss her cheek, but looked blankly at her other three visitors.

"Hello Falmai," Father said, also bending to place a kiss on Gran's cheek. Gus held back but September approached the old lady, wondering how close she dared come. At least she only smelled of talcum powder.

"It was Em's sixteenth birthday last week," Mother said nodding to September to get her to kiss her grandmother.

"Oo, there's lovely," Gran said, "I remember when I was sixteen and never been kissed. Have you been, love?"

September thought of Sieffre, her guide and protector, who had once kissed her tenderly.

"No, Gran," she said. The old lady giggled.

"I expect it won't be long."

Breuddwyd began the customary questioning to elicit the real state of her mother's health. It soon became apparent that although Falmai recognised Breuddwyd she thought she was her own sister instead of her daughter and had little idea of who Gus, September or her Father were. Breuddwyd sat on the bed beside her with September standing close by while Gus and Father stood awkwardly by the window looking out at the lawn and the mountains that rose up behind the city.

After a long, complex and circular conversation Breuddwyd looked up and addressed Gus and Father.

"You go off if you like. Em and I will stay and have a chat with Gran and give her lunch when it comes."

Gus was already heading for the door.

"How long?" Father asked, following Gus.

"An hour or two will be enough I think. She'll want to sleep after she's eaten."

The two men slipped out without Gran noticing.

"Pull up a chair, Em, while I make us all a cup of tea," Breuddwyd said. Gran smiled at the mention of tea. September collected an old dining chair from the other side of the bed and placed it beside Gran's armchair. Both chairs were remnants of Gran's own house in Swansea which she had moved out of when she became incapable of looking after herself.

"Now Mum, Em and I have some questions for you," Breuddwyd said as she set down a cup and saucer on the bedside table by Gran's side. Gran frowned. Breuddwyd dug in her handbag and pulled out a couple of small photographs. The edges of the prints were ragged and worn. The photos had been in and out of albums for many years, most recently languishing in an old shoe box of photos.

"Do you know who that is?" Breuddwyd asked. Gran peered at the photos with her rheumy eyes.

"My Mam!" she said, smiling broadly.

"That's right. What do you remember about your Mam?"

Gran stared for a while, then looked up with an expression of discovery.

"She had hair, whiter than white. Just like you do." She looked from Breuddwyd to September.

"That's right Mum. You must have passed it on to us from your mother."

Gran nodded as if understanding.

"Did your Mam tell you anything about when she was young?" Breuddwyd asked.

Gran looked blank, then brightened.

"She told me nursery rhymes. Ring a ring a rosies…" She paused, searching for the words, then adding, "and fairy stories."

"Can you remember any of the stories, Mum?" Breuddwyd asked. September wondered why she was asking about fairy stories when they wanted to know if Eirawen had been to Gwlad.

"Oo, let me see. She told me lots of stories. There was Little Red Riding Hood and the wolf in the forest, and Cinderella and the ugly sisters, and the story of the fairy who came out of the lake and married a man but he hit her three times so she went back into the water."

"I remember," Breuddywd said, "that's an old Welsh story isn't it. Did your Mam tell you other Welsh stories?"

"Oh she had lots of stories did our Mam," Gran replied. She was enjoying retelling the tales she learned in her childhood. September realised that Mother was trying to guide Gran's memories. She leaned forward to listen carefully.

"There was the story of the man with the golden sword," Gran continued, "which he used to kill horses that came out of the water and giant birds that dived down from the sky."

"She's describing Ceffyl dwr and Adarllwchgwin," September said, jumping up in excitement. Breuddwyd put a finger to her lips to calm her down.

"…and there was a magic jewel that gave out a blue light that made everyone well," Gran went on as if in a dream.

"That's the Maengolauseren," September said. "She was a Cludydd. Eirawen was the fifth Cludydd."

"What's that, love?" Gran looked questioningly at September.

"Em's saying that your Mam knew lots of wonderful stories," Breuddwyd said, frowning at September. "Did your Mam always live in Swansea, Mum?" she asked.

"Oh, yes," Gran nodded." She lived her whole life in Swansea. Her father worked in the foundries."

"What's a foundry?" September asked.

"It's where they make metals, I think," Breuddwyd said. "Swansea used to be an important metal town."

"Oh, he knew all about metals, did Mam's father," Gran

went on, "iron and copper and tin and I don't know what else."

"That's interesting," September said, "I wonder if that has anything to do with the metals being so important on Gwlad?"

Breuddwyd nodded. "Did your Mam's family always work in the Swansea foundries, Mum?"

Gran frowned and shook her head, "No, her Mam came from somewhere else. I don't know where." September sighed. Just when they seemed to be getting somewhere the trail had gone cold, but at least they knew that the trait of the Cludydd, the white hair, went back in the family.

There was a tap on the door and a care assistant came in carrying a tray with Gran's lunch. Stories from her childhood were quickly forgotten as she tucked into the food. Once her spoon was laid down in the empty dish, Gran rested her head on the back of her chair and her eyes swiftly closed. Soon she was emitting soft snores.

"Well, that was interesting wasn't it, Em?" Breuddwyd whispered.

"Yes," September agreed. "We know your grandmother was the fifth Cludydd and that she resembled us."

"So, presumably the others are also seventh children going further back in the family line."

"But how do we find out about them. Where did they come from if Swansea wasn't their home? Did they have something to do with metals?"

"I don't know," Breuddwyd said.

"We need an expert in family trees," September said.

"Ah, now. That's given me an idea."

"What?"

"I'm sure one of my brothers started looking into our family tree. What's it called? Genealogy, that's it."

September leaped up. "Why didn't you say that before, Mum? Who is it?"

Breuddwyd appeared confused.

"It didn't occur to me until Mum started talking about her Mam's father. I hadn't realised how far back this must go."

"Of course it does, Mother. There are four more Cludydds before Eirawen. When did she go to the Land do you think?"

"I don't know Em. She must have been born around 1900, she was only sixty something when she died, and that was in the early 1960s."

"So which of my uncles do we need to ask to go back even earlier?"

"I'm sorry, Em. I can't remember. Is it Dafydd or Emlyn, or Gruffudd?"

They were just vague names to September. She couldn't remember when she had last seen any of her uncles, or any of her three aunts on Mother's side of the family. They never came to visit Mother and she rarely set out to do the rounds of the large family.

"Can you find out, Mother?"

"Yes, of course I can Em. I'll ring them when we get home and see what they can tell us."

The door opened and Gus and Father walked in.

"It started to rain so we thought we'd come back," Father said. September glanced out of the window. She hadn't noticed the clouds building and covering the Sun. The bright morning had been replaced by a dull, wet afternoon.

"Well, we can leave in a few minutes," Breuddwyd said. "She's had a good natter and eaten her lunch so I expect she'll doze now until it's time for tea and telly."

5

She flowed along neurones. Brightness, colour, sounds, pressure, heat, texture, tastes, odours filled her. Gradually she interpreted the impulses and built up a view of the world as a passenger on her host's senses. There was life, scented flowers, leaves rustling, a buzzing fly, dogs barking and people. Many people. She hated them all. They all had the life that had been denied her. Even now she was trapped, able to observe but not to manipulate.

She stretched and slipped into new cells, finding the nerves that operated the body she occupied. She would have control and then she would destroy all that she could see and hear and feel and smell and taste. But there was something resisting her, another personality, close by. The owner of the body that she shared unconsciously pushed back, excluding her. She felt echoes of emotion spilling over from the other, unfamiliar feelings which she did not understand. They seemed to give this other person pleasure and satisfaction, but they weren't the hate and grievance that Malice felt. Knowing that she had little power, Malice pushed out, striving for even a little influence on her body.

6

Her head ached. Actually it did more than ache. It felt as if her brain was trying to break out of her skull. If it hadn't been a school day, September would have curled up under the duvet and just hoped the pain would go away, but she didn't want to miss school; she wanted to show that her new-found determination to succeed wasn't just a brief passing phase. Then her birthmark began to itch, just a tiny irritation but enough to worry her. Images of attacking Adarllwchgwin filled her memory. Perhaps that was all it was, a memory of past battles.

She dragged herself from the bed and into the bathroom, her head pounding. It was a struggle but she washed and dressed in her uniform. As she went down the stairs, Gus appeared at the bottom and started to climb. When he passed her he jostled her. September dug her elbow into his ribs.

"Get out of my way, you idiot," she growled.

"Hey, temper," Gus said.

"I hate you," September said hurrying on down the stairs. She entered the kitchen and slumped into a chair.

"What was that all about?" Mother said from the cooker.

"What?" September replied, cradling her head in her arms.

"What you just said to Gus," Mother said.

"What did I say?" September couldn't recall a conversation with her brother.

"You shouted something at him. You sounded angry."

"Oh, I don't know. I've got a headache."

Mother showed concern, urged September to take a painkiller and placed fruit juice and cereal in front of her. September drank the juice but left the bowl untouched.

The headache faded during the morning and September was fairly satisfied with her day. She'd got good marks in a maths test, surprising her teacher, and herself. When she arrived home, Gus was in the kitchen drinking milk directly from the carton.

"Hi, Em. You in a better mood now?"

"Better mood?" September was mystified.

"Yeah. You literally bruised me with that elbow of yours and you said you hated me."

"Did I?"

"Don't come over all innocent. You can't have forgotten."

"Can't I?"

Gus drained the last drop of milk and chucked the container into the recycling bin. He stalked from the kitchen.

"Now you're just being weird," he said, pushing the door violently open.

September watched him go. What was he talking about? She had no recollection of the incident he mentioned. She couldn't have said she hated him. OK, brothers could be a nuisance at times, but Gus was generally ignorable or liveable-with. She couldn't have said she hated him. A feeling of hate wasn't something she had considered or experienced until she was taken to the Land. Now she knew it was the emotion of the Malevolence. She had seen the violence rendered to the People by manifestations of the Evil and its servants. Three months of fighting the Malevolence had shown her that hate was a negative, detestable emotion that could only bring harm. She wouldn't hate anyone or anything. She couldn't have said that to Gus, could she?

"It's Emlyn," Mother said, on Wednesday evening. Gus and Father were watching a football match on TV so September and Breuddwyd had evacuated to the kitchen.

"What is?" September asked.

"The genealogist."

"Oh, good. Have you been in touch with him?" Uncle Emlyn was the second oldest of Mother's siblings and already retired from whatever work he had done. September only saw him about once a year but she remembered him being a lot of fun when she was younger.

"Yes, I had a chat with him earlier this evening, and guess what?"

"What?"

"He's calling in on Sunday."

"He's visiting us this weekend?" September was excited.

"Yes. He's coming this way to do some family history research."

"Why here? Your family have never lived round here, have they?"

"No. It's for his wife's family tree. Apparently Aunty Kath's father was born near here."

"Oh, I see. Is Aunty Kath coming too?" September recalled a large woman who kept on wanting to hug her.

"No. Emlyn says she finds his research boring so she's staying home."

"What did you tell him? You didn't tell him about the Cludydds did you?"

"No, of course not. I just said we'd been to see Mum and that you'd got interested in who's who in the family."

"What did he say?"

"He was delighted. I think he's glad that someone, anyone, is showing an interest."

September was excited. How much did Uncle Emlyn know about his large family? How far back did his family tree go?

"How can we talk to Uncle Emlyn, just the two of us?" she asked.

"Oh, I don't think Gus will be interested and your father will keep out of the way."

On Friday morning, September awoke with another throbbing, excruciating headache. As well as her brain pounding there were tingles down her spine and arms and her hip felt inflamed. Although her vision was clouded she struggled up and got to breakfast without encountering Gus.

"Have you got another headache?" Mother asked.

"Yes," September whispered. Even speaking was an effort.

"Are you sure you want to go to school? Wouldn't it be better to lie down with a tablet?"

"I'm going," she hissed feeling her neck and cheeks heating up. Why was she so determined to get to school? It was a normal day of lessons; the same people to encounter and either be friendly with or to avoid; the same struggle to show that she was not the old fat, stupid September. She went anyway. Her tormentors were at their usual stations by the entrance, watching out for their regular victims to harass, steal from or simply shout abuse at. September walked quickly past them ignoring their catcalls – she'd heard it all before.

During the first few lessons the headache grew worse. She could hardly think, barely see, and felt as though her limbs had become too heavy to move. Her hip was burning. The bell for morning break went and she hauled herself from the classroom ignoring the calls of Poppy and Emma. She headed slowly to the school's main foyer where there was a water point. Perhaps a drink would help the headache. She pushed through the crowd of students.

"Oh, look, it's the snowball or is it a fatball?" There was a chorus of giggles around the speaker. September didn't decide to face them but she found herself doing so. The blurred image of the speaker and his henchmen moved to the centre of her view.

"You are the most detestable, loathsome piece of shit I have ever seen." She heard the words emerging from her mouth as if they were spoken by someone else. "I hope your body rots in hell with your guts spilling out after I've torn you apart." She leapt forward reaching for the boy's throat. "I HATE YOU."

He stepped back, his face showing astonishment, but he didn't move quickly enough. September fell on him, pushing him over with her hands grasping at his jacket. Together they fell to the ground, and there was a loud crack as his head hit the tiled floor. Lying on top of him, September pummelled his chest, screaming, "Hate, hate, hate!"

Arms wrapped around her waist, her thighs, her chest. Hands grabbed her arms. She was lifted, dragged away, dropped. She flailed her arms, tried to get up, found that she was held immoveable on the floor.

"What is going on here?" The arrival of the duty teacher caused the crowd to dissipate. Through September's bleary vision she saw the boy being lifted from the floor by his friends. He rubbed his head. What had happened to her?

"Please explain what was going on, September."

September looked into the face of Mrs Philips, the deputy head-teacher, frowning at her across the desk.

"I don't know, Mrs Phillips," September said truthfully. There was little memory or awareness in her mind of why she was standing here being questioned. She recalled being held by a couple of boys and seeing her number one bully, Sam Bedford, glaring at her while holding a hand to his head. What had happened? Why?

"Now come on, September, you must know what you did. You launched yourself at Sam, knocking him over and then you thumped him repeatedly while screaming the most vile and hateful threats."

"Did I?" It was as if she had watched the events on TV news. She recalled the events described by Mrs Philips but as if they had been carried out by another person, someone with feelings unlike her own. Mrs Phillips inhaled noisily and glanced at the screen to her right.

"I know you have had trouble with Sam before. There is a record of a complaint of bullying against him and we have been keeping an eye on his behaviour. We don't tolerate bullying here, September, but neither do we tolerate someone taking matters into their own hands. Attacking him as you did was uncalled for."

She looked at September as if expecting a response. September stood still not knowing what she should say. She had never confronted any of the boys or girls that taunted her, never having had the courage to do so before and preferring to keep out of their way. Mrs Phillips shook her head.

"I don't understand, September. You have always been well-behaved, not particularly responsive, but some of your teachers have said you seem to have been more motivated recently."

September was surprised at that – her teachers had noticed that she was trying.

"So why did you attack Sam today, inside the school building?" she said it as if the place was the most important aspect of the incident. Perhaps if it had happened outside, out of sight, it wouldn't have been a big deal.

"I'm sorry Mrs Philips." September didn't really feel contrite because she could not accept that she had done the things Mrs Philips described.

"Sorry is not enough, September. I'm going to have to suspend you for today and I will have to speak to your parents. I trust Sam's parents will not take the matter to the police but will leave it with us to deal with."

"He's been getting at me for years," September said, deciding that she needed to defend herself even though she had no recollection of what she had done.

"Yes, September, we have that on record but violent retaliation is not an acceptable response. Now wait outside until your father or mother come and pick you up."

"They'll be at work, Miss."

"In that case you might have a long wait until they are free to collect you. You can spend the time thinking about what you have done."

September sat for an hour in silent, lonely contemplation. What had happened to her? Why did it feel that she had not been in control? She couldn't have brought herself to face Sam Bedford as she had apparently done. What hateful things had she screamed at him? There was only one possibility. Only the servants of the Malevolence were so filled with all-consuming hate. She had seen it in the Land when people became the tools of the Evil and, overcome by hate, attacked anyone who stood in their way. Had the Malevolence got into her or was it Malice exerting her control from within her instead of from outside?

Eventually, Mrs Philips appeared again with Mother by her side. The sadness in Breuddwyd's eyes filled September with guilt and self-disgust. She stood up and faced Mrs Philips.

"You will go home now, September. Come to me first thing on Monday morning and we'll discuss what we are going to do about this." She turned to Breuddwyd. "Thank you for coming in Mrs Weekes. I'm sure we can smooth things over."

Breuddwyd showed a thin smile and took September's hand. They walked out of the building in silence. They were in the car before Breuddwyd spoke.

"What happened to you Em? Mrs Philips described what you did."

September had been stifling tears but now they poured.

Between sobs she tried to explain.

"Oh, Mother. I don't know what happened. It wasn't me. It was as if a spirit of the Malevolence took me over and made me do and say those things. I wasn't really there."

"I knew it wasn't like you, even if that Bedford boy has been bullying you for years and they've done nothing about it." Breuddwyd drove, staring ahead with her hands gripping the wheel. "Do you really think it's the Malevolence?"

"I think it's Malice. She's in my head and now she's starting to control my body."

Breuddwyd glanced at her before resuming her concentration on the road.

"Are you sure, love?"

Certainty had come to September, along with dread. "Yes, Mother. The Cemegwr said we would be united and the headaches and strange feelings of hate must be her moving around in my mind. My birthmark was hurting too and you know that was a sign of the Malevolence being close. At least it was on Gwlad."

"Oh, my darling. It must be awful for you. What can we do?"

"I don't know." How September wished she was in the Land with Aurddolen and Berddig and the others to talk to. They would understand even if they did not know the purposes of the Cemegwr or even believe that they existed. Here there was no-one who could assist her.

"Perhaps Uncle Emlyn can help," Breuddwyd said.

"How? You're not going to tell him about the Cludydds are you?"

"No, but I can't think who else could tell us anything."

7

She was disappointed. She had gained control of the body and vented her hate on a boy. She had knocked him to the ground but her powers were weak. The energy she had expected to wield had not been at her command nor had she been able to summon any of the elemental manifestations of the Malevolence. She had been pulled from the boy before she had been able to turn him to evil.

The other presence in this body had pushed back and regained control so now she brooded. What was this place? She had no memories of her past but this world felt different. None of the skills or powers she knew she should possess were available to her and she only had fleeting influence over this body. She was still trapped in the dark.

She was determined to explore, to find out where she was so she could regain the position she had once held as the Malevolence's guiding hand. Tentatively she edged along nerve dendrites. She found the areas which gave access to the muscles and senses of this body. She ignored them for now, moving on. Images, sounds, smells and tastes came to her, but these weren't immediate sense impulses, they were memories. She looked at past events with the eyes and ears of the owner of this body. They were mysterious, incomprehensible to one who had never lived. Time was unimportant to her; she had existed without time before, so she settled to reviewing these memories, to understanding what they meant.

8

Friday evening was miserable. Breuddwyd had to make a pretence of being angry at September in front of Father and Gus. Father was upset because he too knew of the bullying September had suffered but he couldn't condone her violent response. Gus was different. She had gone up several steps in his estimation. He congratulated her on standing up for herself and taking down that 'dickhead'. September spent most of her time in her room, doing school work she'd received by email and scanning through the internet, searching for reports of possession by evil spirits. Apart from diagnosing herself with various mental illnesses she didn't find anything that matched her experiences on Gwlad and the encounter with her twin. Thankfully the headache had receded.

Breuddwyd joined her in her room just before bedtime. She saw the computer screen shining on her desk.

"Have you found anything, Em?" Breuddwyd said, looking over her shoulder.

"Tales of demonic possession, schizophrenia, multiple personality disorder. Perhaps I'm ill, Mother. Perhaps my memories of the Land and fighting the Malevolence are false and I'm really sick in the head.

"No, Em, you know it's not that. I was there too, by your side as well as on my own years ago. We share those experiences."

"Perhaps we're both mad."

Breuddwyd put her arms around September's shoulders.

"That's not the answer, Em. We know that what happened to us is extraordinary but it happened."

"In that case there is nothing about it on the internet. It's only the women from our family that have been taken to the Land to be Cludydds."

"You're right, Em. It is just us and our ancestors. No one

else can go there and no one else has any knowledge or understanding of the existence of that other world. We were chosen."

"Who by? Don't say God."

Breuddwyd was silent and September knew she was going to say exactly that.

"I don't know," she said finally. "But what I do know is that if Malice is inside you because of the elixir the Cemegwr gave you then they expected you to be able to fight her or at least join with her and stop her from doing hateful things."

It was September's turn to be silent. Mother was right. They didn't know enough about why they were the chosen saviours of the universe of Gwlad but no-one in this universe would be able to help her oppose and subdue Malice.

"It's down to me then," she said, "I have to find a way to keep Malice bottled up somewhere inside my head and not let her get out and attack people."

"I'll help you any way I can, Em. You know I will. If you can, warn me if you think Malice is getting powerful and I'll protect you and stop you – I mean, her, doing evil things."

"Thank you," September said with a tear running down her face. "Is this how it's going to be? People thinking I'm round the bend; you watching out that I don't go crazy like a suicidal terrorist. Can I have a life?"

"I'm sure you will be able to control Malice, my love." September wasn't taken in by Breuddwyd's confident talk. "Rest well and sleep. I'm sure things will look brighter in the morning." She kissed September on the cheek and left the room.

September undressed and got into bed. She lay with the bedside lamp on trying to look inside herself. How could she examine what was going on in her own brain? You couldn't do it. You could feel other parts of your body, poke your stomach, squeeze an earlobe, rub your nose, but you couldn't do anything for what was inside your head other than bang your skull against a wall. She didn't want to do that. She tried to think inside her head, but all that came to her were memories; pleasant ones like holidays and days out with family and friends; unpleasant ones like standing in front of Mrs Philips; powerful ones such as any part of her time in the

Land. If Malice was inside her head it wasn't something she could feel or be aware of. Perhaps if she could remember what had happened when Malice had exerted control she would gain some understanding of what Malice could do. Pictures came into her head.

Crossing the school foyer in search of water, hearing Sam Bedford's shouted jibe. And then…?

Nothing. It was as if she had blacked out. Her next memory was of being on the floor with a few boys and girls holding her down and the teacher standing over her. But, if she had done what Mrs Philips said she had, and she had no reason to think Mrs Philips was lying, then there must be a memory of what happened somewhere in her head.

Over and over again she recalled the moment leading up to the incident, but each time she came to a wall – a dark, black wall that she could not pass. She reached out and put the lamp off and lay back in the dark. With her eyes closed she looked at that black wall. What was beyond it? What was Malice doing inside her head?

She didn't sleep. She'd wriggled and stretched and sweated with, all the time, the worry of what might happen to her if she slept. Would Malice take over, leave the bed and murder Gus and Mother and Father? By morning she was exhausted but still full of terror.

She spent the day largely in her room so that the others didn't see her bloodshot eyes and puffy face. She tried to work but couldn't concentrate; she tried to read but the words kept dancing across the page. The only thing she could do was to continue her internet searches for anything she could find on possession or on alternate universes or ancient cosmology or alchemy. Some articles illuminated her recall of the seven metals used by the cludydds on Gwlad and the four elements that made up matter and the manifestations of the Malevolence but nothing described her experiences. No-one seemed to know about the other world, its people or the dangers and evil it had faced.

Night came and again she was scared of what would become of her. She fought sleep for a couple of hours.

She awoke suddenly and sat upright. Was it a dream? No, she could not recall dreaming. Was it a headache? She felt her head, but no, there was no pain caused by Malice or any other source. It was just her wariness that had brought her out of sleep to abrupt wakefulness. She had slept and Malice had not taken control of her body. She breathed, relieved that she was still herself and that she was partly rested.

Breakfast was a staggered affair on a Sunday. Mother went to chapel early; Father got up a little later, put coffee on and cut bread. Gus did not appear. September went down stairs after Mother had returned and Father was sitting in the lounge reading his newspaper.

"You look better today, love," Breuddwyd said.

"I slept," September replied.

"That's good."

"Is it? What if Malice possessed me and did horrible things with my body while I was asleep? You know she wants to destroy everything and everyone."

"I don't think she would find it easy to push you out of your own body, Em."

"No? She's done it once, no twice. There was that time when I said I hated Gus."

"But both times only lasted moments."

"The first time was only a second or two but at school it must have been longer. I ran at Sam Bedford, knocked him down and was hammering him into the ground before they pulled me off. That was minutes and I don't remember any of it."

"Yes, but…"

"She's getting stronger, Mother. She's learning how to control me. What might happen next time?"

"I'll be with you."

"In bed? In school?"

"We'll think about what you can do to let you sleep. At school there are always people around watching you – teachers."

"And what will they do if I go bananas again? Throw me out for good?"

"Hmm. Perhaps you'd better have a few days off until you learn how to keep Malice under control."

"I don't know if I can."

"You can. You will. You're the Cludydd o Maengolauseren. Remember that."

Mother's reminder was encouraging. September recalled standing clothed in blue light, her long white hair streaming out behind her and the starstone raised in her right hand. Blue beams shone out destroying Adarllwchgwin, Llamhigwyn y dwr, Pwca, Tylwyth teg and the other manifestations that besieged the Land. She felt again the emotions that gave her power and became strong.

"Yes, Mother. You're right, I was, we both were, that person. But…" another thought conflicted with her feeling of power, "that was there. Here we do not have that power."

"And neither does Malice. She is the stranger in your body, Em. And she is a stranger to this universe. You have the experience and the power to defeat her."

September had to hand it to her mother. She knew how to deliver an uplifting speech.

"I'll try."

"I know you will."

"When's Uncle Emlyn arriving?"

"Oh, sometime this afternoon. He's got to do his family tree research first."

September was restless while she waited for Uncle Emlyn's appearance. She paced the house, took herself for a jog, showered, read bits of the newspaper, failed to do any school work, helped or rather hindered Mother's cooking. She was kneeling on the sofa looking out of the window when a car drew up. The familiar, if not very well-known, figure of Uncle Emlyn got out of the driver's seat; he opened the rear passenger door and lifted out a heap of box files. He pushed the doors closed with his hip and walked up to the front door. September hurried to open it for him.

"Hello there, my girl," Emlyn said in his south Wales lilt. "Thank you. Can you take these from me? They're a bit heavy." He passed the armful of files to September. Her arms nearly gave way with the weight but she stiffened her back, staggered into the lounge and lowered the pile to the floor, grateful that she hadn't spilled them.

Still in the hallway, Emlyn was greeted by Breuddwyd and Father and then by Gus leaping down the stairs. All four of them came into the lounge and they continued to exchange pleasantries occasioned by the infrequent meetings. September looked at Emlyn, comparing him with her mother. He was considerably older, fourteen years or so. He was the second child and son of Falmai, born just after the Second World War ended. There were a few tiny similarities, around the eyes perhaps, but they didn't look very alike. Emlyn had curly hair that was still dark and he had prominent front teeth. He wasn't a lot taller than Breuddwyd but was slim and wiry.

"Well, it is lovely to see you all," Emlyn said at last as they all settled into seats. "Mam was pleased to see you last week."

"Really," Breuddwyd said, "I'm surprised she remembered we were there."

"Ah, well she didn't really. When I dropped in on her on Monday, she had this thing about having had visitors. Of course we'd had that chat on the phone so I knew she meant you."

"Just as well Breuddwyd rang you," Father said. "You might have wondered who these strange visitors were."

"Yes, especially as Mother was convinced her Mam was one of them," Emlyn said. Everyone else laughed.

"I had a picture of grandma which I showed her and we talked about her," Breuddwyd said. "She commented on how alike we are."

Emlyn looked from Breuddwyd to September.

"You are indeed. She had the white hair and I think if you each had it styled the same way you could be sisters, twins, triplets. I'm not surprised Mam thought she was seeing her Mam."

"That's what started us off thinking about the family tree and wondering if there were any more of us with the white hair," Breuddwyd craftily explained.

"Ah, yes. Well, I'm glad you gave me a call," Emlyn said.

"I'll make the tea," Father said, rising to his feet.

"And I have a football match to watch," Gus said, following his father from the room.   September and

Breuddwyd huddled closer to Emlyn as he reached for the stack of files.

"You've done a lot of research have you, Uncle?"

"I suppose so," he replied picking up one box, "I got into it when our kids got grown and I had a little time on my hands. I must say it's taken over a bit since I retired last year."

"Did you find what you were looking for today?" Breuddwyd asked.

"Pretty much. I've been prowling round the graveyard where Kath's family are buried. I found her great grandfather's grave and those of a few other close relatives of that vintage."

"It must be easier looking into our side of the family down in Swansea."

"Yes. It's not far from Porthcawl. I drop in on Mam at least twice a week so I have a good excuse for doing some exploring."

"Didn't Gran say that her mother's mother came from somewhere else?" September asked. Emlyn looked at her with respect.

"That's right, my girl. That would be Sionen. She and her mother and father moved to Swansea in the 1880s. She married soon after and had her first child. Eirawen was her seventh." Emlyn took a breath and looked again at Breuddwyd. "That's a bit of a coincidence isn't it. She and you, Breuddwyd, having white hair and being the seventh child."

"And me," September blurted out. Emlyn looked shocked.

"You know you're the seventh?" He looked at Breuddwyd. "She knows about the other one?"

"Yes," Breuddwyd said, "I told her on her sixteenth birthday." September was pleased that her mother had altered the story. Actually it was her oldest sister, April that had let out that she had a dead twin. The twin who had become Malice.

"That was some birthday present," Emlyn said, not really joking.

"I was glad to know about my twin," September said as jauntily as she could. She couldn't really feel relaxed and carefree about her sister. Perhaps she was listening in on this conversation, there in her head.

"Ah, well, it is an amazing coincidence that the three of you look similar and are your mothers' seventh child."

"Are there any others like us in previous generations?" September asked.

"I don't know," Emlyn said shaking his head, "I don't know of any on Eirawen's father's side."

"No, it must be her mother's," September insisted leaning forward in her seat.

"It is difficult to follow the female line back," Emlyn said, "and of course there are very few photos of working class folk in the mid-nineteenth century and hardly any descriptions or letters."

September sat back feeling despondent. That was it then, they couldn't know of any other cludydds.

"Do you know where Sionen came from?" Breuddwyd asked.

"Yes, actually I do," Emlyn said. "Hers was a mining family, not coal, but metal ores. It was up in mid-Wales, a place called Llelluched."

"What does that mean?" September said, her interest rekindled.

"It's a strange name. It means place of lightning." September's eyes widened. "I suppose it must get a lot of thunderstorms," Emlyn continued, "being high up and in a broad valley."

"You've been there?" September asked, almost jumping up and down on the sofa.

"Yes, I did visit once. Desolate place. Nothing much there now, of course, since the mines closed. There was a church, which has been flattened; it had a graveyard, and there's a Methodist chapel which is a ruin. It once had a graveyard too and there a few headstones still standing."

"Did you find anything?"

"Well, I'm not sure. I knew that Sionen's father was a Williams and her mother was an Evans and she was apparently an only child born in the early 1840s. There were a few Williams and Evans in both graveyards but I recorded a gravestone at the chapel to a Rhiainwen Evans who died in childbirth in 1842. She was born in 1824."

"She was only eighteen, poor girl," Breuddwyd said.

"Rhiainwen? Surely, the 'wen' means white, doesn't it?" September was eager to ask.

"White maiden it means, actually," Emlyn said.

"There we are," September shouted as she jumped up, "she must be another one."

"Another what?" Emlyn asked with a look of incomprehension on his face.

"She means another member of the family with white hair like us and Eirawen," Breuddwyd said calmly although September could see that her face was flushed with excitement too.

"I suppose so," Emlyn said. "Is it important?"

Breuddwyd mumbled while September struggled to think of an answer.

"It's for school," she said at last, "we've been studying genetics. The white hair must be a special gene. We've been wondering how far back it goes."

"In the female line?" Emlyn said, nodding as if he understood. "Well, I'm sorry, that's as far as I've got on that side of the family. Early nineteenth century. It's not bad at all for a working class family. Actually it's lucky that Rhiainwen had a gravestone if she is one of your great-grandmothers."

"Why?" September asked.

"Marked graves were expensive. Rhiainwen must have been a bit special for her family to put up a special gravestone. The mines must have been paying well then."

The door opened, and Father appeared with a tray laden with cups and saucers and tea pot. Gus followed behind with another piled with sandwiches and cakes.

"Well, this looks lovely," Emlyn said beaming with delight at the appearance of the food. Tea was served and each piled their plates with sandwiches and cake.

"Iechyd da," Emlyn said before tucking in.

"You speak Welsh, Uncle," September said.

"Well, just a little. Typyn bach, as we say."

"Did you learn it from Gran?"

"Not really. Speaking Welsh wasn't exactly encouraged when I was a kid. I've learned more since I got into genealogy. It helps for reading old documents."

"So Gran doesn't speak it."

"Well, she doesn't admit it, but she was taught it by her mother, Eirawen, which is why she gave us all Welsh names. Eirawen was unusual for her time. In her childhood speaking Welsh was practically banned in places like Swansea but something made her want to keep it alive."

September and Breuddwyd exchanged winks.

While they concentrated on tea, September started to make notes of all the dates and names that Emlyn had told them about. As she jotted down the facts she felt an ache start in her head and an itch in her hip. She ignored it for a minute or two but the pain increased. She held her head and rubbed her birthmark through her skirt. Understanding came with a sharp intake of breath.

"What's the matter, Em?" Breuddwyd said pausing in a conversation with Emlyn. September put her notebook down and got up.

"I've got to go," she said.

"Where, love?"

"I don't know. Anywhere. My room." September got up and blundered from the room. Her head was throbbing and her hip was burning. She must get away before Malice took control. She mustn't do to Emlyn and Mother what she did to Sam Bedford. She clambered up the stairs, one hand on the banister the other reaching for the treads to steady her. She tried to concentrate on the thought, <Get out of my head, Malice>.

She reached her room as her vision began to blur and flung herself to the floor curling up in a ball. Her hip was on fire, the burning spreading down her leg and up her spine. Her head was bursting, her shoulders numb. She fought to control her limbs and stay curled but her muscles flexed involuntarily. No, that was wrong. They were under the control of the other person in her head.

Malice was hidden from her as if behind a screen like a puppet-master pulling strings that made her arms and legs work. She tried to visualise tearing down the black curtain but she couldn't reach; it receded from her as she was taken over by pain.

"What's the matter, Em? Oh, why are you lying there?" Breuddwyd's voice barely penetrated through the torment.

"Get out! You disgusting creature. I hate you." September felt the rasping in her throat, her lips moving, heard her voice.

"Em! It's me. Your mother."

"I have no mother. You abandoned me thinking my spirit dead. I will have my revenge."

<No, No, this isn't me,> September cried inside her head. Her legs uncurled, her hands pushed against the floor lifting her to her knees.

"Mairwen. Listen to me," Breuddwyd said. "You were loved. You died and we didn't know where your spirit went, but we loved you all the same."

"Don't use that name. I am Malice, servant of the Malevolence and I shall wield my hate to destroy you all." She staggered upright.

"September! Don't let her control you."

<I can't help it> She screamed silently in her head.

"You're not in Gwlad now, Mairwen. The Malevolence isn't here."

"Evil is everywhere. I will have my power."

How could she oppose Malice while trapped inside her own head? She couldn't see, could barely hear her own voice and Mother's appeals to her. The pain made it so difficult to think. But she must.

Her body lurched a step; her right hand began to rise.

How did she fight Malice on Daear? She used her emotions and the Maengolauseren responded – hope for gold to unleash the energy of the Sun to defeat evil manifestations; anger to release the strength of iron; joy to give the reinforcement of tin, and of course, fear to call on the power of the starstone itself. She recalled how she had learned to summon up each emotion. The pain hammered against her but she had summoned the emotions so many times when fighting the manifestations of the Malevolence that it was almost a reflex, a skill that had become programmed into her brain. Hope, anger, joy, fear, each different but each an aspect of herself. She felt each emotion wash through her.

<Stop! Be gone, Malice. I am in control.> In her mind she

visualised her right hand grasping her sword of iron, tin and gold. She swung it and it tore through the black curtain. There, behind it was the black clothed figure of Malice, her twin, an image of herself. Malice glared at her. From her left hand she flung a bolt of violet light. It hit Malice in the chest and she staggered back.

<No!> Malice cried, <You shall be mine.>

<Never! Go!> September threw one blast of violet light then another and another, pushing Malice back into the shadows. Malice tried to fend off the onslaught but she was beaten down, shrinking and receding until she was out of sight. The image faded. September felt feeling return to her body and she collapsed to the floor.

"Em! Are you alright?"

The pain was a memory; she could see again, move her limbs herself, make sounds. She sat up.

"Yes, Mother. I think so." She rubbed her head feeling a cooling slick of sweat.

"You defeated Malice."

"For now. She's gone but not forever I think. She's somewhere in here." September tapped her head.

"How did you do it?"

September recalled the brief struggle, the thoughts that had surfaced.

"I think I thought I was back in the Land, fighting the Malevolence so I summoned up the emotions to give me the power of the metals and the starstone."

"It worked." Breuddwyd knelt and hugged September.

"Perhaps, but when the Cemegwr said we would be joined I didn't think they meant that the two of us would be fighting over my body."

"But you've learned how to keep her down."

"Yes, but I think she's learning too. I don't know if I have the strength to keep fighting her."

"You do, my love, and I can help you."

"How? You can't get inside my head."

Breuddwyd didn't reply for a moment.

"I'll protect you. If Mairwen surfaces I can stop you hurting yourself – or anybody else."

"Thank you." September was grateful but sad. Was this

going to be her life from now on? Forever scared that Malice will attempt to control her and Mother always at her side to stop her committing atrocities. What kind of life was that?

"Emlyn will be leaving soon. Are you going to come down?"

Exhaustion swept over September.

"I'm tired Mother. I just want to sleep. Can you thank him for me and say I'm sorry."

"Of course, Em. I'll say you're not feeling too well – female things. He'll understand. Well not understand but you know what I mean."

September smiled. Breuddwyd released her and stood up. September crawled to the bunk bed and climbed onto the lower bed.

"Have a sleep love. I'll look in when Emlyn has gone."

The door closed leaving September in peace. She curled up, closed her eyes and drifted into sleep.

9

She was confined to the dark once more. How she hated the one that called herself her sister. She had no sister. She had no family. The terms held no meaning for her. She was a servant of the Malevolence and only existed to destroy all that opposed the Evil. But, September's memories were familiar to her; they were hers now. She had observed how September and the one known as 'Mother' behaved to each other and to the other 'family' and friends. She had watched September's memories of her time in the Land including how she had fought against her and the manifestations of the Malevolence. September's control of the emotions that gave her the powers of the Maengolauseren was a mystery to her; she had but one emotion, hate, but she wanted more of them for herself. She would have them and gain for the Malevolence victory over these rivals.

She sulked in her closet, miserable at her defeat by September's rediscovery of the strength of her emotions. But she would learn. Her hate was all-powerful; it could overcome everything that opposed evil. She had confidence in her superiority. She had gained access to September's senses and limbs and memories before and she would again. Next time she would be stronger and better prepared and she would destroy this one who said they were twins. She would not be kept prisoner.

10

It was Monday morning. School was about to start but September was sitting outside the deputy headmistress' office. She hadn't wanted to come to school at all. What if Malice re-surfaced and she attacked other students or teachers? Mother was confident that her victory last evening had banished Malice but September worried that her twin still lurked deep in her brain. She had given in to Mother's insistence however, because she didn't want to be confined to her room forever. She wasn't looking forward to facing Mrs Philips though. It wasn't usually her that was picked out for punishment or praise. In the past she had hidden in classes, neither sitting at the front where the nerds sat nor at the back where the troublemakers disrupted lessons. She tried not to draw attention to herself although her white hair and rolls of fat attracted the bullies. School work had been a low priority compared to surviving and avoiding being picked on by pupils or teachers.

The discovery of her powers as the Cludydd o Maengolauseren had given her a new confidence, a determination to succeed and to improve her fitness. That seemed to be a foolish dream now that she had to fight Malice for control of her own body. How could she concentrate on school work if she had to spare no effort to keep her twin from taking over?

Mrs Philips was busy, so after a brief admonishment September was sent to re-join her class. She slunk into the English room just as the lesson was about to begin and sat beside Poppy.

"Hi, Em. Philly let you back then?"

"Yes." September dug her file out of her bag and opened it on the table while keeping her head down. She didn't want to see if the eyes of the rest of the class were on her.

"What you did to Sam was real wicked. That'll stop him

having a go at you."

"Do you think so?" September was surprised that Poppy thought her assault on her chief tormentor had been a good move.

"Yeah. Real brill."

The lesson proceeded quietly, September only contributing when the teacher asked her a direct question. At least she had done her homework and had read the part of Macbeth that they were studying so she didn't give any stupid answers. In fact she was intrigued by the conflict of good and evil in the play. Macbeth succumbed to greed and the attraction of power. He was like the people of the Land who had become servants of the Malevolence. The witches reminded her of the Gwyllian, the manifestations of the Malevolence that turned everything they touched to dust.

The following lessons and the lunch break passed quietly and September began to feel a bit more relaxed. She joined in chat with Poppy and Emma and began to wonder if she could be normal again. For the last lesson of the day they were in the biology laboratory studying diseases caused by faulty genes. September was more interested in genetics now that it was clear that she shared her white hair and pale complexion with six of her ancestors. Perhaps she got too involved in the lesson and neglected her mental defences.

The pain arrived like a jumbo jet roaring into her brain. Her hip burst into fire. She arched her back and found herself leaping to her feet. Her stool fell back with a crash. She flung her books and files across the table and shoved Poppy on to the floor. She watched herself do these things through the frosted glass of her vision. She heard the muffled cries of the class and teacher as she strode around the room pushing tables, punching boys and girls, screaming, "Hate, hate, hate," as loud as her voice and lungs could manage.

The pain made it almost impossible to think. The only thought going through her own mind was <No, this can't happen! I must get out!> With vision reduced to shadows in the dark she saw herself grab a tall glass measuring cylinder from the side bench and approach the teacher swinging it wildly.

With nails being hammered into her brain she struggled to

find an emotion. Somehow she must oppose Malice and regain control over her limbs. She found sorrow; sorrow at her failure to prevent Malice escaping, sorrow at her twin sister's continuing hate, sorrow at the harm she was doing to her fellows. Sorrow was the emotion of plwm. She threw a cloak of mental lead around herself. It defended her from the agony that Malice was inflicting on her. The pain and the burning diminished. She could think.

Time seemed to slow as she bore down on the teacher. Miss Hargreaves stood by the whiteboard as if frozen. September could not see her expression through her clouded eyes but wondered whether she was angry or frightened.

On one of Malice's slow motion swing of her arms the glass cylinder caught the edge of a table. The end shattered leaving her with a tube with an end of sharp, jagged, glass. Malice would kill Miss Hargreaves if September didn't stop her. The fear gave her the power of the starstone. She projected a violet blanket of light through her mind. Malice fended it off but revealed herself. September saw her as if on a hilltop commanding unseen hordes to do her bidding. The hordes were her nerve and muscle cells.

September tried again with a beam of violet light directed at Malice. Her twin deflected it with a flick of her hands.

<I'm prepared for you now. You will not defeat me again with your energies,> Malice said.

<Stop, what you are doing, Malice. If you hurt her they'll lock you up and then you and me will be trapped.>

<I will not listen to your stupidity. I am regaining the power of the Malevolence.>

<But it doesn't work like that here. The powers we both had on Daear don't work in my world.>

The slowly whirling glass tube was closer to Miss Hargreaves now. She had begun to cower. September tried another burst of the starstone energy but Malice fended it off as easily as before. She needed another way of stopping her. She summoned up compassion and love. Despite everything she loved her sister and had sympathy for her. They were born together out of the same egg. They really were so alike though driven apart by life and death. Her life and Mairwen's death. The healing power of arian was hers to bestow and the energy of efyddyn would enable her to communicate with Malice. She broadcast her love as copper threads that wrapped around her sister and showered her with silver rain that would trickle and seep into the wounds that had damaged her so.

She felt Malice pause; her body stopped, the broken cylinder held aloft but unmoving.

<What is this? Love?> Malice thought haltingly. She strained against the copper bonds, cringing from the silver rain.

<That's right. Love and compassion is what Mother and I feel for you.>

Malice's domination lessened and September saw how she had spread through her nervous system from a spot in an egg shaped structure deep in her brain. While Malice was distracted by the unfamiliar feelings of love and sympathy, she needed to cut her off from her sense and motor nerves. September called up surprise. With the unpredictability of arianbyw she flowed like mercury into the origin of Malice's identity. She found the organ, the nerve cell, the atom that harboured her. She became a blocker preventing Malice's nerve impulses jumping across synapses, formed anaesthetic molecules to slow down the metabolism of the cell, and projected an array of laser beams to hold the atom in its grasp.

Her body was hers once more. She found her arm swinging the broken tube down towards Miss Hargreaves' face. September flinched and the tube slipped from her grasp crashing into the board beside the teacher. There was shouting all around her, chaos, bedlam. She had to get out. She ran from the room, along the corridor, down the stairs, across the foyer and out, away from the school. She ran along the familiar streets which suddenly felt unfamiliar. Streets where people would look at her and wonder why she ran. What was she running from?

She slowed to a walk, her heart beating, her breath coming in short pants. What would they think back at school? As far as they were concerned she had attacked a teacher, disrupted a class. She wouldn't just be suspended for a day. This would be serious. She would be marked down as unstable, perhaps even mentally ill. What would they do to her?

September made her way home, her breathing returning to normal. At least she had defeated Malice again, but her twin was still there deep in her brain. She didn't understand how Malice's whole person could be trapped inside a single atom but there was one thing she was certain of. Malice would find a way out. How many more times could she beat her back and regain control of her own senses and muscles?

Having Mother to look after her was not enough. She had to find help from the people who had placed Malice inside her – the Cemegwr. But how could she reach them? They were on Daear and without the starstone she could not go there.

She reached home. Her bag was still at school probably scattered across the biology lab floor but she felt in her blazer pocket. There was her house key, dropped there when she left in the morning. She let herself in. The house was quiet and unoccupied. Gus might be home soon when school finished unless he hung out with some friends. Mother would be back at tea time and then Father a little later. She had a short time to decide what to do. She knew she had to get away from everyone that knew her. Only Mother would understand her behaviour and she couldn't face the consequences. Where could she go? Where on Earth was the solution to her problems?

Only what Uncle Emlyn had told her yesterday seemed to provide anything like an answer. Her family, or at least her great-grandmothers had come from LLelluched. The place of lightning. Even its name suggested somewhere strange. A place where girls with snow-white hair were born; seventh children; special girls. Girls that deserved their own gravestones. Perhaps she would find answers there.

She hurried up to her bedroom and pulled her little-used rucksack from under the bunk beds. She stuffed knickers, bra, t-shirt, jumper, jeans inside. She added her toilet bag with toothbrush, toothpaste, flannel and soap. After a moment's thought she dropped in a lipstick. She didn't wear make-up usually but perhaps the lippie would help her look more mature and not just a fat kid. She changed out of her school uniform into a tunic/leggings combo with her most robust trainers on her feet. She stuffed the papers with the notes she made from Uncle Emlyn's work into the rucksack and went down to the kitchen to raid the fridge. She returned to her bedroom with an armful of snacks and fruit. She put them in the rucksack too. Lastly she pulled the drawer of her desk open and took out her purse. She was thankful that she had listened to Mother's warnings about theft at school and left it at home. It could have been scattered across the biology lab floor but here it was safe. It contained her bank card and some cash, nearly a hundred pounds, largely birthday presents from her sisters. That too went into the rucksack.

She hauled her rucksack downstairs. She would probably have to sleep rough where she was going. There were sleeping bags somewhere weren't there. She went out to the garage where Father had a stack of plastic storage boxes. In one she found a number of compact sleeping bags, relics of family camping holidays which had been endured rather than enjoyed. She took one and made sure everything else was put back as it was. Back in the kitchen she tied the sleeping bag to her rucksack then collected an anorak from the hooks in the hallway. The phone rang but she didn't answer it. It was probably school trying to contact Mother. They'd try her at work next and then she would rush home. Well she wouldn't be here. She scribbled a note – *Gone to find a way to stop M.* She went back upstairs and hid the note in Mother's book beside her bed. Her mobile phone was somewhere in the biology lab which was probably a good thing. It would be too much of a temptation to ring home if she had it with her and anyway the police could track phones couldn't they.

Downstairs again, September hoisted the rucksack onto her back and with her anorak over her arm looked in the long mirror. She was running away from home. That wasn't it. She wasn't running from her problems. She was going to find answers. Sadness filled her as she looked around the hall. It felt as though she had already been away for three months in Gwlad. That had only been an instant in time here. How long would she be gone now?

She took a deep breath and stepped outside the door, pulling it closed behind her. With the weight of her rucksack dragging on her shoulders, she set off up the road to the main street and the bus routes. She didn't know exactly where she was headed but Uncle Emlyn's description had told her enough to give her a start. She was off to Wales.

11

Malice brooded. Her confinement may be tiny in three dimensions but spacious in eleven so she spread herself out laying out her memories and those of September that she had copied for examination. From time to time, though time meant little to her, she tested the defences September had erected using the power of mercury. The bars of laser light, the nerve blocker and anaesthetic stopped her from invading the body's neural network immediately, but she would find a way she was sure. For now she was intrigued by this feeling of love and compassion that the shower of silver had infiltrated into her.

She had never known love, only hate. She had been alone, surrounded only by the hate-filled spirits of the Malevolence for all of her existence till now. Destruction and death had been the only outlet for her hate. She had loathed those that professed love. Love had been a meaningless concept but through the power of September's compassion she felt it for the first time. It gave her warmth where she had only ever felt cold, comfort where there had only been torment, happiness where she had only felt anger. She explored the feeling tentatively. It was unfamiliar and she viewed it with suspicion. It promised joy and companionship, two more emotions that she had not experienced.

These feelings were alien to the Malevolence. Malice felt that her loyalty to the Evil was under threat. Loyalty – another idea she had not known before. It was the Malevolence that gave her power, a reason for being. Hate was her power. Hate was her destiny. Hate would overcome love. She had no doubt of her superiority – did she?

12

It was dark as the train trundled along the valley. September could barely see the river and the hills beyond the pool of light outside the window. The carriage was almost empty as the train approached Machynlleth. She enjoyed the isolation.

This part of the journey had been easy. She knew from Uncle Emlyn's description that Llelluched was in the mountains between Machynlleth and Llanidloes. When she had got to the central railway station in town she was pleased to find that there was a direct train to Machynlleth. She handed over a sizeable chunk of her cash to purchase a return ticket – she hoped she would be returning when this was all over. A worry was that she had over an hour to wait for her train. What if Mother went looking for her and guessed she had headed to the station? She decided not to hang around the platform where a white-haired fat girl would look pretty conspicuous. The problem was that outside the station there was nowhere to go as it was surrounded by a car park and roads. She moved away from the entrance trying to find somewhere she could wait out of sight but having done a circuit of the car park she gave up and returned to the station. She hid for a time in the shop, behind the racks of magazines and books. She was relieved when eventually her train was called so she could get on board and curl up in a seat, except that she couldn't curl up. A man in a suit sat beside her and took out a tablet. Most passengers, mainly people commuting from work it seemed, got off at Shrewsbury after which she had the pair of seats to herself. Other people left at the towns and villages that they stopped at as they crossed mid-Wales. She ate some crisps and fruit from her rucksack then gazed out of the window into the darkness. She felt a mixture of anticipation and anxiety. She had never travelled on her own – well not in this world.

The train began to slow so September picked up her

rucksack and made her way to the doors. The train drew into the station and September saw the boards saying Machynlleth pass by ever more slowly until the train stopped. The doors opened and she stepped out alone onto the platform. The station was dark and grey with just a few yellow lights. The doors beeped and closed behind her and soon after the train began to move again.

September followed the directions given by the exit signs. Outside the station was a small, empty car park and a road that bent and sloped down from the elevated railway station. She followed the pavement and soon found herself at a junction with a main road. The darkness was broken by the street lamps and there was a sign showing that there was a bus stop at the corner. An old lady stood there illuminated by the beam of a street lamp, with a shopping bag on wheels. September approached her.

"Hello. Can I get a bus to Llelluched from here?" she asked. The old lady looked up in surprise. September wondered if she had said the name correctly.

"Llelluched?" The pronunciation was similar if not exactly the same.

"Yes, that's right."

"Oh, you won't get a bus there from here or anywhere, cariad," the woman said in a Welsh lilt slightly less tuneful than Uncle Emlyn's.

"Oh, dear," September said wondering what to do next.

"There's nothing there now, just a pub, The Moon and Stars, and it's on the steep mountain road. No buses go that way."

"Oh," September said again. How stupid of her. Uncle Emlyn said the place was in the mountains and deserted. Why did she expect there to be a frequent bus service?

"Do you need somewhere to stay, cariad?"

"Erm, yes, I suppose so." September had hardly thought about the time but it was gone nine o'clock now and if she wasn't going to get to Llelluched tonight then she would need somewhere to sleep. Autumn seemed to have come earlier here than at home and there was a chill in the air. Sleeping rough didn't seem a pleasant idea. "Is there a Youth Hostel?" she added as an afterthought.

"Well, no, not in the town, but there are other places. There's a hostel which walkers and cyclists use. Just follow the road up to the clock and turn left. Go past the museum and you'll see it on your left."

"Thank you," September said adjusting the rucksack on her shoulders.

"That's alright, cariad. Nos da."

September set off up the road. It wasn't far to the clock tower in the centre of the town. She followed the directions she had been given and walked down the deserted main street until she came to a large old house with a board outside that announced itself to be the hostel. She rang the doorbell.

It was a minute or two before the door was opened by a short, round man with a bald head.

"Hello?" he said looking her up and down.

"Is there a bed I can have for tonight, please?" September asked trying to sound confident and experienced. The man shrugged.

"It's a bit late but yes, we've got plenty of room tonight. You know we're a hostel don't you; you have a bunk in a shared room. Except that there's no-one else in tonight. It's getting close to the end of the season, see."

He opened the door wide allowing September into a broad hallway. He said his name was Rhodri and quickly took down her name and address – she gave Poppy's details – and he relieved her of another eighteen pounds of her precious cash. She looked forlornly into her purse realising she'd already spent half of what she started with.

"I see you've got a sleeping bag so you won't need a duvet," Rhodri went on. "You can take your pick of the beds in the rooms upstairs. The use of the shower is free and you can help yourself to breakfast in there in the morning." He pointed to a room off the hallway. "There's cereal with milk or toast and spreads."

"Thank you," September said lifting her rucksack.

"What brings you to Machynlleth?" Rhodri asked.

"I'm on my way to Llelluched," September answered wondering if it was the right thing to say. If there was nothing there perhaps there was no reason why anyone would choose it as a destination.

"Ah, you're following the Llywelyn Trail," Rhodri said nodding his head approvingly.

"That's right," September said, agreeing despite not knowing what he was talking about.

"It's quite a step to Llelluched. Fifteen miles and a fair climb."

September nodded in agreement. Fifteen miles! I'll die walking that far.

"It's quite a rough path," Rhodri went on and looking down at her trainers added, "Are you planning on wearing those shoes?"

"Yes. They'll be fine. They're very comfortable." She set off up the stairs before Rhodri could offer any more advice. At the top of the stairs she chose left and opened the door into a room which had four bunk beds in it. There wasn't a lot of space but as there was no one else in residence it didn't seem to be a problem. She picked the bunk furthest from the door and window, set her rucksack on the floor beside the bed and sat down.

She started to shake. What was she doing here, all alone, in a place she didn't know? Wasn't it just silly to think she could find the answer to her problems in the middle of nowhere? Problems, what problems? Just another person in her head that wanted to make her do dreadful things. She'd shut out the memory of what had happened in the biology lab while she made her escape but now it came back in a rush. Reliving that scene reminded her why she needed to get away and why she was here. Llelluched was the only lead she had to finding a way of dealing with Malice.

Despite the novelty of being away on her own in a large empty hostel she slept well. She awoke to a clock chiming seven feeling refreshed and determined to carry out her plan. She hurried to the bathroom and had a pleasant shower, relieved that she didn't have to compete with other guests. She dressed in her jeans and T-shirt and stuffed her purse in a pocket.

The hallway was empty when she headed downstairs for breakfast but before she went into the dining room she noticed maps on the reception desk. The cover of one showed a sketch map with Machynlleth and LLelluched marked. She picked it up.

"Do you need a map?" Rhodri asked. September wondered where he had appeared from.

"Um, yes, I seem to have lost mine." Her lie didn't sound very convincing.

"That one's seven-ninety-nine," Rhodri said.

"Oh, thank you. I'll take it." She sorted the amount from her purse and handed it over. Rhodri gave her the penny change. She picked up the map and went into the dining room, relieved that Rhodri didn't follow her.

Once she had made a plate of toast, buttered it and taken a generous portion of jam she opened up the map and began to eat. Map reading was not a skill she had learned; she had always left that task to Father and Gus when she had been dragged off on family walks. Walking had never appealed to her when exercise was not high on her priority list. She soon found Machynlleth on the map though, and a short while later the much smaller print showing the location of Llelluched. She wasn't sure what all the lines on the map meant but beside one was written Llywelyn Way. She followed the dotted line with her finger. It snaked from Machynlleth past Lleluched and down off the map. When she looked closely the path seemed to miss Llelluched itself but a yellow line went closer. She followed the yellow line back to Machynlleth and decided that must be the road. Perhaps if she followed the road rather than the path she might not have to walk the whole way.

She ate up her toast and returned to the bedroom to roll up her sleeping bag and complete packing her rucksack. She looked out of the window and saw it was dull and drizzling. Sighing, she put her anorak on and hoisted the rucksack onto her back.

As she got to the bottom of the stairs Rhodri appeared again as if from a secret door.

"Have a good walk," he said.

"Thanks," she replied and hurried out before he could offer any more advice. She marched up the road away from the centre of the town wondering if she had interpreted the map correctly. A signpost pointing up a side road suggested she had. It said 'Llelluched 15 miles'. She groaned and set off up the road. How long could it take to walk fifteen miles?

She was on the edge of the town before a car came up behind her. She stuck her arm out and waved her thumb. She'd never hitched a lift before and guessed that Mother would be horrified at the thought of her endangering herself but she was prepared to take the risk to get out of the long walk uphill. The car went by without slowing. September shrugged, thought a few uncharitable thoughts and continued walking. Over the next hour she stuck her thumb out at four other cars and small vans without success. She had begun to realise that Rhodri was correct in being suspicious of her shoes – her feet were already starting to get sore. There was nothing much to see as the clouds were almost down to the ground and she was getting thoroughly wetted by the misty rain. She plodded on miserably.

She heard a noise, louder and deeper than a car, coming up behind her. It was a lorry. She raised her thumb and was delighted to see it slow down and stop beside her. The side of the lorry advertised a variety of beers and lagers. She reached up to open the passenger door.

"Where you going, darling?" the middle-aged man in the driving seat called.

"Llelluched," she replied.

"So am I. Hop in."

She took off her rucksack and hauled it and herself up into the passenger seat. She pulled the door closed and the lorry started before she got the seatbelt round her.

"Why you going there?" the driver asked in the customary Welsh accent.

"I want to have a look around," September replied.

"Not much there," he said shaking his head, "just the pub."

"The Moon and Stars?"

"Yes, I'm making a delivery there."

"That's good. Thanks."

"Pleasure. Place is a bit of a wasteland actually. Waste tips from the mines that closed decades ago."

"I want to have a look around where the miners lived."

"Not much left of actual buildings love. Are you one of

them industrial archaeologists? You seem a bit young for it, if you don't mind me saying."

"School project," September said hoping he'd accept the excuse.

"Oh, aye, I see. Not the nicest of mornings to be out," he said nodding at the windscreen where the wipers swished back and forth.

"No. I'm very glad I don't have to walk through it anymore."

"Well, it may brighten up later when you're pottering round the ruins."

The lorry climbed the country road with ease but September became more and more thankful that she was sitting in a comfortable seat rather than trudging along the road or, indeed, the path. Soon they completed the climb and the road crossed the marshy summit in generous curves. As they started to descend the drizzle eased off. They crossed a ridge into a broad U-shaped valley and September began to see signs of the mining activity. There were heaps of grey stone fragments beside the road and places where the land had been levelled but with no sign of a building.

"Here we are," the driver said turning off the road and onto a narrow lane leading up to a white painted building. A sign announced that the Moon and Stars Inn was open for drinks and food throughout the year. The lorry pulled up outside.

"A bit before opening time," the driver continued, glancing at his watch, "but I'm sure Doli will give you something before you start your work. You won't be wanting anything alcoholic will you," he winked at her. He's guessed I'm not eighteen, she thought. She opened the door and leapt down to the ground. An elderly lady emerged from the front door of the inn.

"Hey, Doli, I've brought a customer for you."

"That's good of you, Gareth, every one's welcome. Come on in, love."

September followed the grey-haired, slightly stooping woman into the pub, followed shortly by Gareth carrying a crate of bottles.

"What would you like love. A hot drink? It's not the weather for a cold lemonade is it?"

"A coffee would be lovely, thank you."

"Take a seat, love and I'll get it for you."

September was in a bar with a dozen rectangular wooden tables and old wooden chairs. There was no one else there of course so she took a chair by the window and looked out. She watched Gareth moving in and out with full and empty beer barrels and crates of bottles. He didn't make many journeys before making one final unburdened entry.

"That's it Doli. I'm off to Llani," he called out from the hallway then turned to peer round the door at September. "Enjoy yourself here, darling."

"Thanks for the lift," she called back but he'd already gone and moments later the lorry drove off. A few minutes later Doli appeared with a thick mug of coffee and a small jug of milk.

"There you are dear. That'll be one pound and sixty pence." September got the money out of her purse and handed it over. "Now dear, what brings you here all on your own?"

"I want to have a look round where the miners and their families lived and worked."

"And why are you interested?" The old lady examined her over her spectacles.

"My family came from here," September replied, "they were miners I think."

"That would be a long time ago," Doli smiled, "the mines closed in 1884 and although they tried to re-open one or other of them a few times, nothing came of it. Eventually everyone left, except me."

"There was more than one mine then?"

"Oh yes. There are shafts all over this valley. In its day it was very busy. Over a thousand people lived here at one time – miners, their wives who worked in the dressing sheds and their children. They worked too."

"What did they mine?"

"Metals, all sorts. Mainly lead but some copper and tin, even a little silver."

"No gold or iron or mercury?"

"No love, but I think they found some of those not far from here. The veins of metal run through the rocks all over here.

Now what was the name of your ancestors? Perhaps I know some tales about them."

"Evans."

"Ah, there were quite a few of that name that worked the mines."

September took a gamble.

"I think one of my great grandmothers was called Rhiainwen."

The lady stroked her hairy chin and nodded.

"Now that name does ring bells. Rhiainwen Evans. And seeing you with your gorgeous hair is making me think. Ah yes, Rhiainwen. She was buried up at the Methodist Chapel; died young, only eighteen, in childbirth and she the seventh child of her mother."

"Really?" September was astounded that Doli should know something about her ancestor over one hundred and fifty years later.

"Yes. The reason I remember is that there were lots of tales told in Lleluched that have been passed down from one generation to another."

"Tales?"

"Yes, stories about white-haired women."

"There were more of them?" September couldn't help looking astonished.

"Oh, not many. I don't know how many there were all together but the stories go back centuries."

"What were the stories about?"

"Well, I suppose the one about Rhiainwen is the most recent. Apparently when she was in labour, and it was a long one, she described visions she had seen."

"Visions?"

"Yes, she told of being attacked by giant birds and horses made of water and wicked fairies; and of bright flashing lights."

"Oh. What did people think? Was she mad?"

"Well, I think they thought her dreams had been of the old folk tales they told to children. Like the Tylwyth teg, the Welsh fairies. And this place does have more than its share of thunder and lightning, sometimes with no sign of clouds or rain."

"That's it I suppose. It was just dreams."

"Yes, I'm sure that's what it was, but you see Rhiainwen's stories were similar to those told about the other white-haired women. They each became known as something like witches. Their stories tell of fighting mythical creatures and they warn about the coming of evil. Of course when people moved away from here the stories were forgotten. I expect I'm the only one who remembers them now."

"You've lived here for a long time?" September asked although she was so excited by Doli's stories that she really wanted to know more.

"Four generations have run this pub, although not for much longer. I'm selling up and having a rest."

"But these stories of the white ladies have been passed down from one generation to another?"

"Yes. Many generations lived here."

"Do you believe them?"

Doli looked surprised.

"Believe them? What is there to believe? They were just stories told to pass the time. It wasn't always as easy to get here as it is now, love. People were cut off and had to entertain themselves."

"But the witches with the white hair. They existed?"

"I'm sure they did, love, but I don't know if they were really witches. They were all just mining families. I'm sure the rest of the people here saw them as something special because of how they looked. Don't you get attention because of your hair?"

"Well, yes, I do." September did not need reminding of all the catcalls she got because of her distinctiveness.

"Well there you are, and Rhiainwen, well, she was remembered because she died so young, when she was still a beauty, after such a dreadful labour. Her daughter survived though."

"And that's why I'm here."

"Why, love?"

"Because the daughter survived and had children herself and then there was me."

"Of course."

"Where did Rhiainwen live?"

"Oh, I couldn't tell you that, love. Some of the miners lived further up the lane here and others had homes scattered all over the workings. They're mainly on the other side of the road. You'll see a track that leaves the road and runs on along the bottom of the valley." September looked out of the window to where Doli was pointing. Gareth had been right about the weather. The cloud was breaking up and the Sun was shining through, brightening up the scene of desolation.

September drank up her coffee and hoisted her rucksack on to her shoulders. She promised Doli that she would be back later for something to eat, and another chat. Doli didn't seem to be expecting much business.

She went out of the pub into bright sunlight. Although the ground was still damp the air was now warm and dry. September went down the lane to the road, crossed and walking along the verge found a gate blocking a track. The track opened up into a level area bare of any grass or other green life. There was a culvert which emerged from under the road through which water gurgled and rushed.

The gate only opened to give a narrow gap but September pushed herself through and closed it behind her. She stood and looked around. Ahead there was a steep grassy slope which rose several metres then levelled off before rising steadily up to a ridge about a kilometre away. In front of her was what must be the remains of the mine workings but other than a few scattered pieces of rubble and iron and heaps of rock fragments there was no trace of buildings or any hint of how people lived and worked.

The shallow stream curved off to the right accompanied by a track which September began to follow. Other narrow, rough paths went off to left and right climbing and running along the banks on both sides. After walking a hundred metres or so she noticed some more substantial remains of a building up on her right. There was a chimney of stone and some remains of walls but she had no idea what the building was. Perhaps it was a house or a workshop. Further along, the track divided. One branch veered off almost at a right angle heading straight for the bank where she saw a roughly circular black hole surrounded by brambles and ferns.

September decided to have a closer look.

Before she got to the tunnel entrance she came to another hole in the ground on her left. It had a wooden post topped by a rusty iron rod sticking out of it. She approached but stopped a metre from the edge where the rough ground started to slope inwards. The hole was over a metre across and she could not see to the bottom. A mine shaft she guessed.

She walked on towards the first hole she had seen. This was wider and almost high enough for a person to enter standing up. The track started to descend into the mine. September was tempted to enter but the path looked very rough and she was worried that loose rock could fall on her head. She thought about the men and boys who had gone into the mine day after day, year after year, to dig out the ore. What must it have been like to live that life?

September returned to the original track and continued along the valley. There were other signs of mine workings, other holes in the bank and ground, other ancient pieces of iron including a huge bucket made from riveted rust-covered iron sheets. Gradually the valley narrowed and the vegetation, grass and gorse and wild flowers covered the bare rocky ground. The stream and the narrow path that accompanied it followed a twisting course so that when she had been walking for several minutes all sign of the mine behind her had disappeared.

She rounded a bend and stopped in astonishment. After all the desolate, industrial ruins and wasteland she had not anticipated such beauty. The valley opened into a circular grotto. Its steep sides were covered with purple-brown gorse and grasses in all shades of green. Ahead there was a waterfall that descended from a height of fifty metres or so in three leaps. The lowest fall emptied into a heart-shaped pool surrounded by soft grass flecked with the blues and yellows of small flowers. There was the constant sound of pouring water and buzzing insects and the odour of verdant vegetation. She stared, taking in the magnificent sight.

"Hello, September."

She flinched, surprised by the voice, and turned to see a young man sitting on a rock at the side of the grotto. He almost blended into the background because he was curiously dressed. He didn't appear to be older than his twenties and had thick brown hair and deep brown eyes but he was clothed as if from an earlier age. He wore a green tweed jacket over a rough check cotton shirt and brown trousers that seemed almost fluffy. Was that what they called moleskin? September found herself wondering. His shoes were brown brogues, still polished and shiny despite the damp, dusty path that he must have used to get here. A smile accompanied his greeting.

"You know who I am," September said wondering if she had imagined him say her name.

"I've been expecting you, September. It is why I am here. Come and join me." He indicated a convenient grass-covered hump beside him. September took the few steps to approach him and released her rucksack from her back. Having lowered it to the ground she took off her anorak as she was feeling warm. She placed it over the rock and sat down then looked closely at the young man. He looked relaxed and confident and he exuded a feeling of well-being.

"Why did you know I was coming?" September asked.

"There are things you want to know," he answered.

"Who are you?"

"I think you know," he said, smiling cheekily. Of course, she did know. Who else could possibly have understood why she had run away from home to escape the person who was in her head, and made her way here of all places, simply because a distant ancestor may have lived here.

"You're a Cemegwr."

He frowned slightly.

"That is the name used in Gwlad, as you know. Here, well, I am given various titles – ghost, apparition, god."

"Because you appear unexpectedly but don't really exist."

"You could say that. I am a manifestation."

September shivered when she heard that word, thinking of the manifestations of the Malevolence that had besieged the communities of Gwlad. There was no aura of evil around the young man and she recalled that the Cemegwr had referred to being manifestations themselves."

"You mean that you're not really you?"

"What you see and hear is part of a vastly greater, more

powerful being that exists beyond this universe."

"Beyond?" Was this silly or wasn't it? She was chatting with a man she'd never met in as remote a spot as she could find about the existence of other-worldly beings. Yet she knew that he was what he said he was and that she was on the verge of finding out what was happening to her.

"You know, September, since your time in Gwlad, that this universe that you see and feel around you isn't the only one."

"Yes, but…"

"Even some of your scientists now talk about the multiverse. Many, many universes similar to this one are forming every moment when an electron moves to the left instead of the right."

"Um, yes." September had heard Gus going on about universes where there was just a subtle difference to the one that was known or places where anything was possible.

"Well, that is only part of the story. In the Omniverse every sort of universe can exist, every sort of anything can exist – and does."

"And you are from this, erm, Omniverse?"

"We are creations of the Omniverse, chance formations of thinking beings, brains if you like, with powers and intellects greater than anything you can think of or know."

"Really." September didn't understand what he meant but coming from the slightly nerdy young man it sounded like a brash boast. "So why are you interested in me?"

"We have interests in many things and many universes, some of which we have thought into existence ourselves."

"Such as Gwlad."

"Yes. I believe the Cemegwr told you that miniature universe grew out of an interest in the quaint ideas some of your ancestors had."

"It was a toy that you made as a hobby." September remembered the dismissive attitude of the Cemegwr.

"That would be a good way of putting it. But it was a toy that has become something special."

"What is special about it?"

"The Malevolence."

"I was told the Malevolence is everywhere."

"It is. It too is an entity of the Omniverse and pervades

every universe that exists. It draws on the remnants of spirits that exist in many universes and grows in hatred and the urge to destroy. If the Malevolence had purpose in its destruction it would rid the Omniverse of order and intelligence. We have taken on ourselves the task to oppose it and to encourage the development of interesting universes."

"But something has happened."

"Yes."

"Something to do with me."

"Yes. Your twin has a unique ability to guide and shape the Malevolence. It's a matter of probability. It was going to happen sometime and now it has."

"Couldn't you have foreseen it?"

"We are powerful but not omniscient. We are part of the Omniverse not its whole."

"The Cemegwr gave me an elixir. They called it the Alkahest and said it would help me drive the Malevolence from Daear by drawing Malice into me. They said we would become one."

"That's correct."

"It didn't work though."

"No."

"She joined me inside my head but wants to take me over."

"Yes."

September realised that she didn't have to describe all that had happened since she returned home from Gwlad. The young man knew.

"Can you help me?"

"That is why I am here, September." He reached out his hands. September placed her hands in his. He closed them together. He felt warm and strong. "What would you like to do?"

September was surprised by his question. What did she want? She had a list.

"I'd like to go back to Gwlad to see if I really did help them survive. The Cemegwr didn't seem too bothered whether Gwlad carried on existing or not. And I must get Malice under control, to stop her trying to take me over. And I'd like to be slim and fit and smart."

He chortled quietly.

"You are smart, September, and it is within your power to be whatever person you want to be. I'm glad you want to return to Gwlad. The elixir you were given harnessed the energies and forces of that universe which are not the same as this. The Cemegwr intended that you and Malice be united fully but it proved to be more difficult than we anticipated. Her attachment to the Malevolence is powerful. And that isn't wholly bad."

"It isn't?"

"No. Through the link between you and Malice we have been given a connection with the Malevolence that could help us reduce its depredations elsewhere in the Omniverse."

"I can be of use to you?"

"Yes, September. Don't be surprised. Remember that in the Omniverse anything is possible but nothing is certain."

"Oh." September recalled how she had felt when she had been summoned to the Land for the first time. She had been confused, had no idea what was expected of her and had no idea of the powers that would be hers to command. "Will I be in danger?"

"Of course. There are always dangers, but we will help you." He released her hands. "Malice is a great danger to you and to this universe. You are evenly matched though she is more driven by her hate. If we can complete the union between you then you will have unique powers."

"Unique?"

"Perhaps it is the wrong word to use in an Omniverse where anything can happen at any time but for now there are only the two of you that form a bridge between the Brains and the Malevolence."

"Why me, us?"

He stood up and gazed up at the rim of the grotto.

"I suppose it started here."

"Here? What is special about here?"

He looked at her, mildly amused.

"One of those chances that happen in any universe. This place just happens to be a point of contact with beyond. Like a ball sitting on a table. Every point on the sphere is the same but only one point touches the flat surface."

"So what is it? A doorway?"

"That, and a power connection and many other things."

"Has it always been here?"

"Yes. Leakage of the energies drew the metal ores into the pattern of veins in the rocks. The first people to come here, the Celts, felt the power and made their home up on the ridge. The Romans followed, mined the metals and built their own fort. Since then other people have come, dug up the rocks, lived and died."

"There's no one here now, except Doli in the pub."

"That is true, but you have other ways of connecting with the spot now. There's a radio aerial on the ridge. You are still connected through the genes of your ancestors."

"So I can get to Gwlad from here. I don't need the starstone."

"That's right, but not yet."

"When?"

"Tonight when this point on the Earth is turned away from the Sun. Meet me on the ridge at the Roman fort. The aerial is beside it."

He walked towards the pond and stepped onto the water. He didn't sink or even seem to get his shoes wet.

"Wait!" September called. He turned to face her, standing quite calmly on the water. "Do you have a name, something I can call you?"

"I have many names," he replied. "Names are unimportant, but if you wish you may call me Cyfaill." He turned away and stepped across the pond causing no disturbance of its gently rippling surface. He entered the waterfall. Light sparkled but the falling water didn't break its pattern. He had gone. September sat staring at the gently pouring water for minutes. She could barely believe what she had heard. Her dreams had been answered. She would see Gwlad again and the Cemegwr would help her control Malice, but what did the 'Brains' expect of her in return?

Clouds had covered the Sun again and it had got cooler. She felt spots of rain on her face and head. She got up and pulled on her anorak. How much time had passed? She felt hungry; it must be past lunchtime.

13

She was confused and torn. How could her sister love her while the Malevolence filled her with hate? If September had compassion, why did she keep her trapped in this subatomic prison while the Malevolence gave her freedom to be wherever she wanted? She wanted to be free to destroy and hate, but... her sister's love gave her feelings that she had never experienced before, doubts that she had never had before.

Enough! She must regain her power and find the answer to these unsought-after questions.

Malice stretched out to the full size of her atom, extended along the bonds that held the atom in its molecule. She met the beams of light that confined her. She was darkness. Darkness absorbed light. The rays fell on her body, flickered and faded. She was free. She explored carefully the other molecules that surrounded her. September's creations, the molecules that slowed down the metabolism of the cell, freezing her in time, remained. Just a few of them.

She projected a beam of energy and blasted the molecules out of existence. The cell was hers. She filled its cytoplasm, reaching out through the membrane. September's third line of defence was there defending the synapses, stopping her from leaping from one nerve cell to the next. These molecules were designed to absorb energies. Her power was ineffective. She would have to think of another way of re-establishing her dominion over the body's senses and muscles. She would wait, but her chance would come.

14

The plate of pie and chips was a temptation that September couldn't resist, particularly as Doli was so insistent. She did have guilty feelings about neglecting the diet she had been following for, what was it – days now. She reasoned that she had been exercising so needed the carbohydrate.

Doli had been delighted to see her when she returned from the mines. The pub was still empty but Doli seemed prepared for hordes of tourists who hadn't turned up or ever looked like doing so. September had ordered a glass of water and Doli had provided it with a copy of the menu. Everything seemed to come with chips. September had tried to tell Doli that she was working on a tight budget but Doli wouldn't have it and promised a special price for pie and chips. They were good.

The shower she had been caught in on the walk back had passed and now she sat in the window seat watching the clouds scud across the sky and the shadows move across the opposite side of the valley. Her anorak was drying out on the back of a chair.

"So, dear. Did you see all that you wanted on your walk?" Doli asked emerging from behind the bar.

"Yes, thank you. I think I will just have a look in the graveyards before I move on."

"Where are you heading next, love?"

Where would she be later? Amaethaderyn or Mwyngloddiau Dwfn or somewhere else in Gwlad? But she couldn't tell Doli that. Where could she say she was going on to? Where was the next place on the path? Where did the delivery driver say he was going? Llani? Of course.

"Llanidloes," she said.

"That's a long walk my love. You'll have to climb up to Penybryngolau to join the path."

"I hope I can get a lift, but what did you say? Pen…"

"Penybryngolau. The top of the hill of lights."

"That's a strange name?"

Doli pondered and replied, "I suppose it is. I've always known it called that so I never thought of it as strange before."

"Why does it have that name?"

"The old tales say that sometimes lights were seen at the highest point on the ridge. That's where the old Celtic and Roman forts are. I've never heard an explanation for the lights."

September had to hold her excitement in. That was where the young man had told her to meet him.

"Have you seen the lights up there?"

Doli shook her head. "Can't say I have, love. The lightning plays around the hilltops when we have a storm but that's all. I wonder if that was what the tales meant."

"I wonder? Well, I'd better set off," September said rising to her feet.

"That's right love, while the weather's nice. I think they're forecasting rain for tonight."

Oh, dear, September thought, when I'm supposed be on the top of a mountain.

"Are you sure you've had enough to eat, love?"

"Yes, thank you." September pulled her anorak on and heaved her rucksack on to her back. She headed towards the entrance. Doli disappeared but then called out.

"Here you are love, before you go. Take this for your journey." She thrust a cling-film wrapped roll into September's hand.

"Thank you. You've been very kind, Doli."

"Well, it's always nice to see some young people up here enjoying the mountains. Take care, love."

September dropped the roll into her anorak pocket and strode out of the door. She turned left rather than down to the road and headed up the track to a patch of shrubs and nettles that marked the remains of a building, the ruined Methodist chapel.

It was only mid-afternoon and she had a long time to wait before her meeting with Cyfaill, the Brain, on the hilltop but she hadn't wanted to hang around the pub with Doli asking questions and wondering where she was going to stay for the night. It was something September was also considering. On her previous visits to Gwlad no time seemed to have passed when she returned so perhaps later on tonight she would find herself back on the hilltop in the dark and in the rain, if Doli's forecast was correct. It wasn't something that she was looking forward to but she couldn't see any alternative.

The nettles around the old chapel and its small graveyard were thick but she found a spot where she could push through. The interior was almost overrun with brambles and nettles but the humps that marked the graves were just visible and easily felt under foot – she stumbled a few times finding her way across. As Emlyn had informed her, there were a number of gravestones, some still standing erect and others at crazy angles. They were weathered and covered with lichen making the wording very difficult to read. September managed to interpret a few of the marks as dates and names, even though she couldn't manage to translate the epitaphs which were either illegible or in Welsh. The dates ran from around 1800 to the 1880s and there were a variety of surnames including Evans.

She had been searching for nearly an hour before she found the one she was looking for – Rhiainwen Evans, died 1842. It was as Emlyn had said. She imagined the young woman, with the likeness of herself and her mother, in agony as she gave birth to the girl who would continue the line of Cludydd o Maengolauseren, although she wouldn't be one herself. She felt tears in her eyes at the thought of the death of her ancestor. She had no idea if any of the other graves belonged to Rhiainwen's parents or grandparents but feeling a close bond to the disused chapel she departed.

It wasn't a long walk to the ridge where her meeting would take place but now it was autumn it would be getting dark about seven. She didn't fancy fumbling around in the darkness trying to find the correct spot. She walked back down the track to the road and crossed. She could see the path snaking down from the ridge and the point where it joined the road a few metres along to her left. She opened the gate, went through and began the climb.

Halfway up she had a view of Llelluched laid out before

her. There was the Moon and Stars pub on the opposite side of the valley, looking lonely as it was the only building in sight. There were a few patches of vegetation betraying the remains of houses or other buildings and many flat, cleared areas where there must once have been mine buildings. Between and around all of these were the tips of discarded stone, the waste from the diggings. The grey heaps formed something like a lunar landscape. Recalling the scene at Mwyngloddiau Dwfn, the mountain mining town on Gwlad, September tried to imagine a thousand people living and working here, the noise of the machinery and smoke from forges and steam engines. Now though there was silence but for the wind in her ears.

She turned and continued her trudge to the ridge. Nearing the top, the path levelled off and her view of the valley disappeared. Now all around her were the peaks and ridges of the surrounding mountains. She arrived at a T-junction with a wooden signpost announcing the Llewelyn trail. To her right she could see an aerial tower pointing to the sky. That must be it. She set off towards it.

The path inclined upwards almost imperceptibly so that when she arrived at the aerial she found she was at the highest point, a few metres above the rest of the ridge. The tower was a simple steel pole with what looked like TV aerials attached. There was a rusty barbed wire fence around it. She had the feeling the aerial was not in use now.

A few metres away was a low grassy bank, about thirty metres long. She walked to it and saw that it was part of a rough rectangular earthwork. Was this where the Romans camped? It seemed so quiet, peaceful. Why would an army need to camp here? What were they guarding? The mines in the valley below, or something else?

September stood on the highest part of the bank trying to imagine a more imposing rampart with perhaps a wooden stockade at the top. From here the defenders would be able to see any attackers approaching from across the neighbouring hills although the valley bottoms on either side of the ridge were hidden. There was also a wonderful view of the sky, or there would have been but for the clouds. There was not much of the clear blue that had been there on her climb. The clouds were growing, apparently merging from all sides and forming a grey dome over her. There was no wind but the air temperature had dropped. She felt a few drops of rain fall on her bare head.

She did up her anorak and pulled the hood over her head. She glanced around wondering where she could shelter from the rain. There was no shelter. The only structure was the aerial. She retreated to it and lowered her rucksack to the ground then sat with her back against the chain-link fence facing the camp. The rain began to fall as a steady drizzle.

A glance at her watch told her that there was still an hour or so of daylight. There was nothing to do but wait. For what? She had no idea how she would be transported to the Land without the starstone in her hand. The young man, the Cemegwr or the Brain, would show her the way she hoped. He called himself Cyfaill and she wondered what that meant. He had said her transport would happen when the Sun had gone down and the stars were visible, but with this cloud there would be no stars to see at all. She sat and fretted. What would happen to Malice when she transported? Would she emerge from wherever she was hidden in her head? Would Malice try to take over her body or would she be restored to the existence she had before they had left Gwlad? September didn't have answers to her questions but they worried her. She sat in the rain feeling miserable.

Time passed and she grew more bored. She remembered the bread roll that Doli had given her. It hadn't been long since her late lunch. That wouldn't have mattered to her before she went on her diet, before she had discovered what it was like to be fit, powerful and responsible. Perhaps she should keep the roll for when she returned. If she returned here. Or since time didn't seem to pass when she was away then eating it now would make little difference.

The lack of things to do persuaded her. She took the roll from her pocket and undid the cling film. She bit into the soft bread and chewed. At one time food had been her friend, her company, her reassurance, but she had changed. She just didn't feel hungry. She wrapped the cling film around the roll again and returned it to her pocket.

She looked up. The cloud overhead was thinner and the

rain was easing. She watched as a patch of clear sky appeared directly overhead. It was still quite bright so no stars were visible. Slowly the clouds moved apart and the area of blue sky grew. The wisps of cloud poured over the ridge filling the valleys. The Sun appeared as an orange globe hanging above the peaks in the west. September stood up and faced it, joyfully soaking up the rays although on this early October evening there was little heat in the sunlight. The mist flowed up the hillside towards her, rising to obscure the near and distant mountains.

Now she was standing on a green hilltop surrounded by a sea of fluffy mist with a hemisphere of clear sky above her. To the east the sky was already dark enough for a few stars to show. She turned back to the west and saw the Sun touch the mist and begin to sink into it. The mist glowed yellow, then orange. There was a flash of green and then the Sun sank out of sight.

"Good evening, September."

September jumped and turned to see the young man, Cyfaill, approaching her along the path.

"Hello. I didn't see you coming," she said surprised at his sudden appearance.

"You wouldn't," he said with a smile on his smooth face.

"Is this the time?" September asked.

"Not just yet," he replied. "When the sky is filled with stars will be the time."

"How can I go to the Land, without the Maengolauseren?"

"The starstone is within you, September. At least, its powers are. Once you were the bearer, the Cludydd as the people of the Land called you. But you learned its secrets. Now you are the Maengolauseren itself."

"So I can just go where I like?"

"Almost. There are channels of energy from this universe to others. This spot and the starstone, that is, you, are connected to similar points on Daear. Sometimes they change but it will be a place that is familiar to you."

"And that's it. When it's dark and the stars are out I'll go."

"It sounds simple and for someone with your powers it is, although the action will appear dramatic."

"What do you mean?"

"Wait and see," he grinned as if he was enjoying teasing her.

"What will happen to Malice? Will she come too?"

"Ah, now that is uncertain." Cyfaill frowned and stroked his chin. "Malice is the anomaly, the unexpected. There is no precedent for her existence. You are the seventh Cludydd that the Cemegwr planned to be the saviours of their little universe, but they didn't plan for your twin becoming a tool of the Malevolence."

"You, the Brains, the Cemegwr, whatever you are, have the power to create whole universes so why can't you just get rid of Malice somehow?" September asked.

"Perhaps we could, in this universe, but elsewhere and elsewhen in the Omniverse she would still exist." The young man answered with a kindly smile. "We do have powers, miraculous to inhabitants of universes like this one, such as yourself, but we are not the gods that some of your religions worship. We have knowledge but are not omniscient, power but we are not omnipotent. Neither is the Malevolence, but it pervades the Omniverse, striving everywhere to destroy all that exists."

September struggled to understand all that Cyfaill said. Mother believed in God, or at least she had done up until their joint visit to Gwlad. She trusted in her faith and believed that her God had all the answers. September was more prepared to accept the existence of fallible super-beings.

"So you don't know what will happen to me or Malice?" she said.

"No, but we do think that you and she are and can be an instrument to help us in our endless battle with the Malevolence."

"Me? A fat, dumb girl. You think I can help you?"

"Yes." It was a simple answer, without any explanation, but Cyfaill said it with such empathy and feeling that September believed him.

"What do I do when I get to Gwlad?"

"The Cemegwr who gave you the Alkahest to unite you with Malice will help you to complete the process within the constraints of their universe. What else you do I cannot say or know. Like your twin you are unpredictable. We hope that when you are combined you will help us fight the Malevolence elsewhere, but that is up to you."

September felt uncertain. What would become of her when the Cemegwr completed her union with Malice? What dangers would she face if she joined the Brains in their war with the Malevolence? It all sounded rather unpleasant and difficult. Being plain, simple September seemed much more comfortable and preferable, but she knew she couldn't go back to being the plump, silly teenager. Memories of helping her friends battle the manifestations of the Malevolence returned to reinforce her wish to see what had happened in Gwlad. And there was Malice. She was there inside her now, lurking somewhere in her mind awaiting a chance to emerge again, to take over her body and carry out whatever ghastly deeds she felt necessary through her hate. She had no choice but to take whatever solution the Cemegwr had for her.

"Will you come too, Cyfaill?"

"This manifestation is bound to this universe, September," the geeky young man said. "The Cemegwr are manifestations of, if you like, my brothers and sisters. I will be there with them in some form. Now I think the time is nearly here."

September looked up. Night had covered the sky as they talked. Darkness broken by a myriad points of light – stars and galaxies, and one or two planets. September could not recall ever seeing so many. She had never stood at night on a dark hilltop, miles from any major habitation – not on this world anyway. The Moon was just rising in the east, full or almost full. Its radiance banished the light of the stars near it. "What do I do?" she asked. "The other times I looked through the starstone at the Moon or the stars and the light flooded through and took me."

"Just look up and think about where you want to go," Cyfaill said from a few paces away.

She stood, her arms hanging by her side, her head bent back to face the heavens, her vision filled with the hemisphere of stars. She felt dizzy.

The stars above her seemed to move, swirling into a whirlpool. Surely the stars couldn't be moving. Perhaps something was bending the light or maybe it was just in her head. More stars were drawn into the maelstrom rotating over her. Although the hillside seemed fixed, the whole sky above her was turning, twisting, as if falling into a tornado of light that was reaching down to her.

She shivered with fright but her feet would not move. There was no shelter on this hilltop, no place to hide from this descending cone of light. She couldn't take her eyes off it.

"Think of your destination," Cyfaill shouted. Wind blew around her from all directions and the great rotating corkscrew of light came lower. She thought of her three previous journeys to Gwlad, and the ridge, similar to this one, where she had arrived. The light touched her.

She was surrounded by light, innumerable points of light of all colours. Cyfaill, the hilltop of Penybryngolau, the aerials; all were obscured by the spinning sparks. What would Doli be seeing down in the valley, she wondered; would she understand now how the ridge got its name? Faster, the lights turned, enveloping her in a column of incandescence.

The ground was no longer pressing on her feet. She cried out and fell.

15

The defences still held her within the single nerve cell. Time had passed, she had no sense of how much, as she tested September's barrier. While she tried over and over again to leap to the neighbouring neurones she considered her twin's thoughts and memories. She lived again September's childhood, experienced the love, in all its forms, of her mother, father, sisters and brother. She enjoyed the companionship of friends and the fear of the loathing of her enemies. She grew with September to become the young woman that she now was and felt the desires, the urges, the needs and the pressures that September felt. She took part in September's war with the Malevolence on Gwlad, her battles against manifestations and against herself. The fears and gratitude of the cludyddau and the people overwhelmed her and she witnessed, though failed to understand, September's control of the emotions of power – compassion, anger, sorrow, joy, hope, love, surprise and fear.

Malice was confused. How could one person, September, contain within her all these memories and emotions? Her own thoughts were dominated by hate, her only desire was destruction of all around her, and her only companions had been the mindless, hateful spirits of the Malevolence. Exploring September's memories so enthralled her that she had given little thought to alternative ways of escaping her captivity.

The light was a surprise, its source unknown. It was all around and within her, spinning, wrenching, tearing her from her prison. She felt exulted. Something was happening that was releasing her from her bondage. She would be free again. She spread herself, throwing back the light. But freedom wasn't hers. Not all the bonds were broken. Something held her to her twin. Like the two poles of a magnet, they could not be separated.

Malice raged in her frustration.

16

September knelt with her hands and knees on the dew-damp grass. She knew this wasn't the hilltop of Penybryngolau, this was the ridge above Amaethaderyn, the village on the bank of the Afon Deheuol; the destination she had visualised. She breathed in, keeping her eyes closed. On her first two arrivals the grass had smelt fresh and verdant and there had been other smells of meadow flowers. The last time, after the Malevolence had descended from above the stars, there had been the stink of decay and the grass had been burned. Now the odours were faint, but pleasant and clean.

She opened her eyes. The sky was dark and filled with stars like at home but different stars September thought. In the east there was a glow on the horizon. Dawn. The light silhouetted the top of the ridge where the Cysegr, the refuge of the villagers, was. She stood up to get a better look but there wasn't much to see. Instead of the proud stand of trees she had seen on her first visit there was a mound. In the dim light she couldn't tell whether it was a dense collection of shrubs or simply a heap of decaying tree trunks.

She looked at herself. Her body was encased in a radiant violet glow, as it had been previously when she was the Cludydd o Maengolauseren. She shook her head and her long white hair floated up like the froth of milk on a cup of cappuccino. Her head felt clear. Perhaps her head was all her own again. What had become of Malice? Was she gone? Was she free to inflict her hate on this world again?

There was no time for delay. If Malice had escaped then she needed to find people and the Cemegwr. First she would see what had become of Amaethaderyn. She summoned the essence of arianbyw. She sang a few notes of 'Twinkle, twinkle little star,' surprising herself with unpredictability and soared into the air as an eagle with vibrant blue feathers. She gained height then swooped down the hillside towards the river. The water flowed lazily but clear. It had lost the putrid, polluted appearance of her last visit. Just beyond was the lake, refilled with water and between it and the river was the village. It was easy to spot in the growing morning light as a clearing amongst trees but she was surprised. There were many fewer of the round thatched houses than she had seen when the village was busy and filled with people.

She circled low over the rooftops. People ran from doorways, looking up, pointing. Their shouts came to her, some of fear but others of joy and recognition. She descended into the space between the buildings changing back to her human form as her feet touched the ground. Immediately a circle of people formed around her keeping a respectful distance. September examined them. They wore the familiar simple clothes in white and grey and shades of brown, the women in ankle length gowns and the men in knee-length tunics or loose trousers. There were many older men and women and some who were middle-aged but she saw no children.

A chubby grey-haired man stepped towards her, his arms reaching out.

"Cludydd? Is it really you?"

"Berddig?" September said. "Yes, it's me, September."

Berddig ran towards her and embraced her.

"This is a day I never expected to happen," Berddig said, "I dreamed of it, but never dared hope we would see you again."

September felt other hands touching her tenderly. She looked up. A tall, upright woman was at her side. Her black hair was flecked with white, but her skin was smooth and had a silvery sheen.

"Eluned?" September asked. The woman nodded and grinned.

Berddig and Eluned released her and issued instructions. Some people hurried off in various directions while the remainder gathered around as September's two old friends guided her towards a building consisting of a reed roof supported on wooden poles but with the sides open. There were low benches arranged in a circle under the shade. Berddig urged September to sit and then he and Eluned sat beside her. Other people joined the circle with those unable to find space, standing. The scene resembled her first visit to Amaethaderyn although some things were different.

"Berddig, you look old," September blurted out before she could choose her words with more tact. Berddig grinned.

"Well, I am. We are," he said and Eluned nodded in agreement.

"It's been over fifty years since the Conjunction," Eluned said.

"Fifty?" September said, "but only two weeks have passed at home. I know time passes more quickly here, but not that fast."

Berddig shrugged and then frowned.

"It has been a lifetime for us, although it feels but yesterday that you were among us fighting the Adwyth."

"It's still fresh in my mind," September agreed.

"But how are you here now?" Eluned asked. "There will be no Conjunction for hundreds of years and we are not beset by evil manifestations."

"It is unknown for the Cludydd o Maengolauseren to reappear," Berddig added.

"I know but things were a bit different last time. I wanted to find out what had happened to you after I failed to stop the Malevolence coming down."

"But you succeeded when you returned with the sixth Cludydd," Berddig said.

"The darkness lifted from us and the evil spirits disappeared from the world," Eluned said.

"My mother helped me do it," September said deciding not to mention the Cemegwr just yet. "I'm so pleased to find you here, peaceful and well."

Berddig frowned.

"Well, there are some difficulties that we face," he said.

More people arrived carrying jugs, trays of food and wooden goblets and bowls. Space was made for them to enter the circle and distribute the drinks. September held out the cup to be filled. She recalled the stimulating drink she had found so refreshing on her earlier visits. She lifted it to the lips, sipped and was disappointed. The taste was insipid. It would do to slake a thirst but it did not fill her body with vitality as it had done before. She wondered whether her memory had played tricks and exaggerated the wonderful properties of the drink.

She was given a bowl containing fruit and a hunk of bread. She bit into each in turn anticipating glorious and exciting flavours that did more than merely satisfy hunger. The fruit flavours were bland and almost indistinguishable from each other and the bread almost tasteless and stodgy. She ate wondering how her memory could have misled her so badly.

"When I left you, you were sheltering in the forest. What happened?" September asked between mouthfuls.

Berddig looked thoughtful. "It is so long ago but seems so fresh in our memories." Eluned nodded in agreement. "We knew the moment that you succeeded in defeating the Malevolence because the spirits rose and left us, the darkness was banished and we felt alive again."

"But the village was destroyed," September said.

"Yes," Eluned said, "but we had hope again. The Adwyth was gone and we knew we would not be attacked by manifestations. We set to rebuilding with joy and anticipation."

"Anticipation?" September asked.

"We thought we could look forward to long, fruitful lives with the assistance of the powers of the cludyddau." There was a sadness in Eluned's voice that confused September.

"You succeeded. The village is rebuilt, the lake is full, you have food," she said and waved her arms to encompass all that there was around her.

"Yes, but things didn't turn out quite as we expected," Berddig said, his usual joyfulness replaced with a gloom that surprised September.

"What's wrong?" September asked.

"The Land is dying," Berddig said.

"Dying?" September looked around at the people and beyond at the trees that ringed the village and, in front of the meeting hut, the reeds at the edge of the lake.

"Yes, that is how we must describe what is happening to us," Berddig said.

"It was a few years before we noticed," Eluned said. "A few children were born immediately after the Cysylltiad but their numbers fell. No children have been born in Amaethaderyn for twenty years now. It is the same across the Land."

"And our crops and animals are the same. They are less productive. We work just as hard to produce our food but each year there is less. If our numbers weren't dropping, we would be starving."

"That's awful," September said. "What are the cludyddau doing about it?"

"That is another of our problems," Berddig said grimly. "Our powers are failing."

"Failing!" September was astonished.

"The mines in the Mynydd Tywyll are worked out. They are not producing metals for us to work with. The number of cludyddau is falling and our skills are weakening."

"I struggle to transform, these days," Eluned said and September felt the depth of her sadness. "It is not simply that I am old, the energy in my dwindling stock of arianbyw is less."

"And my alcam fails to strengthen the other metals," Berddig added.

"Are there no other cludyddau here?" September asked, horrified and saddened by what she had learned. She knew that Arianwen and Iorwerth, the silver and iron bearers had been killed in the battles against the Malevolence and that Padarn, the lead bearer had been close to death. "What happened to Padarn and Catrin?"

"Padarn died soon after," Berddig replied. "He couldn't recover from the exertion of protecting us all. Catrin recovered her power of efyddyn when the Malevolence left but she died a few years ago."

"So you have no contact with other places?"

"That is true. We have no contact with the network of copper bearers," Eluned said. "We rely on the few river travellers to bring news from across the Land."

"And what about Aurddolen?" September asked of the gold bearer and Mordeyrn, the leader of all the People.

Berddig shook his head. "He never recovered from the death of his daughter and he never returned to us. He passed on his position as Prifcludydd o aur to Heulfryn and slowly drifted into death."

September remembered Heulfryn as a blonde youth full of hope. "So Heulfryn is the Mordeyrn?"

"He was the last time we heard any news, but his powers are slight compared to those that Aurddolen once wielded."

This was not what September had expected to hear on her return. She had anticipated a welcome from the happy, hard-working people to a land free from the perils of the manifestations of evil. She had wanted to find a solution to her own problem – Malice – but hadn't expected to be faced by the Land experiencing its own problems.

"Do you know why these things are happening?" she asked. Berddig, Eluned and the village people who had sat quietly listening to the conversation all shook their heads in unison.

"It is a mystery," Eluned said.

"There is nothing like this recorded in the tales," Berddig added. "It is as if the whole universe is dying, fading away. Even the Sun is less bright."

The Sun had now cleared the treetops and sunlight was streaming into the shelter. It was a pale globe in a clear sky. September had little to compare its brightness with but she found she could look at the Sun without hurting her eyes. Surely that was a sign in itself. Could Berddig be right and the universe of the Cemegwr was fading away with time passing ever faster? She now had two questions to put to the Cemegwr if she succeeded in finding them again.

September stood up, feeling determined.

"You have suffered enough," she said, "I will try to find out what is happening here. I feel it's my duty."

There were mutterings of agreement but no rapturous applause as she had received on her previous visits. She noticed Eluned looking at her strangely.

"Cludydd. Why do you have two shadows?"

September looked at her and then saw that everyone was looking at her feet. She looked down. The Sun was directly in front of her and cast an indistinct but definite shadow behind her but, slightly to the side there was another shadow, darker, blacker than coal, with arms and legs and head just like the other. There was no source of light to cast such a shadow. As September stared, frozen, the dark shadow moved shaking its arms and straining to pull its feet away from hers without success.

"The darker shadow seems to have an existence all its own but it is bound to you, Cludydd," Berddig said.

Then September understood. Malice had been expelled from her head but they were still united as one because what could separate a shadow from its owner?

"It's Malice," she said. "When I defeated her she became part of me. One reason for coming back was to find out how I can stop her taking over my body."

The people scrambled to get away from her. Even Eluned and Berddig edged along the bench.

"You returned knowing you contained part of the Adwyth," Berddig said.

September was upset. She had wanted to meet her friends again, not to worry them that she had brought danger with her.

"I wanted to come but I couldn't without help. He urged me to come."

"Who did?" Eluned asked.

"Cyfaill. He's a Brain or something, like the Cemegwr."

Berddig shook his head. "I don't understand. We thought the Cemegwr were just beings from children's stories until it was reported that you found them and they had helped you defeat the Malevolence, but I don't know what you mean by 'Brains'."

"Cyfaill means 'friend'," Eluned said. "That's a good sign, surely."

"Perhaps it is, but a friend of whom? I don't know what is happening anymore." Berddig trembled and wept. September had never seen him so upset. Even when the onslaught of the Malevolence was at its greatest he had retained his joy at the slightest sign of hope.

"I think you had better search out your Cemegwr again," Eluned said. "Perhaps they will provide the answers to the questions you have."

"Yes," September said stepping away. The welcome she had received was replaced by suspicion. Her longed for meeting with her friends had turned sour. "I will find an answer," she promised. She walked into the dusty clearing between the roundhouses, conscious now that she was dragging the dark shadow at her feet. It seemed to struggle and resist but had no power to stop her. She leapt into the sky changing into the eagle. At least her powers of transformation had not diminished. She circled over the village then turned to the north towards Coedwig Fawr.

17

It was familiar – the land, the sky, the stench of life. She was disgusted that it existed, still. She wanted to destroy it all. No longer trapped in her prison within her twin she sensed the world around but still she was bound to her sister. She twisted and struggled but could not break free. She should have freedom as this was her realm; the place where she had led the forces of the Malevolence to a victory, short-lived though it was. The stars and the planets along with the plants and animals and people still existed. She raged with frustration.

She reached out. Where were the spirits who had been her companions of hate? They had filled this land when she had defeated her sister but now they were gone. She could sense them nowhere in the universe. Without them she had no power. She was still a captive of her sister, forced to follow wherever she went. But she would have her revenge. She knew her sister now, her memories and her emotions, though she still did not comprehend them. Once she had broken the bonds her victory would be assured. She would hate and destroy and the Malevolence would have domination.

<h1 style="text-align:center">18</h1>

September flew across the green canopy that filled valleys and covered hilltops. There was barely a break in the leaves and branches except for the rivers and streams and the great waterway of the Afon Gogleddol, the northern river. She gloried in the pleasure of flying, swooping low to examine the treetops and soaring into the clouds. The feeling of the air rippling her feathers thrilled her but she was also aware of her shadow hanging from the tips of her talons. The shadow had not transformed as she had done. It still had arms, legs, head and the body of a woman – her sister. As black as a starless night she seemed like a hole in the daylight. Unceasingly the shadow wriggled and stretched, its efforts to separate itself from her to no avail. Despite all the shadow's efforts, September felt nothing. It had no weight, did not impede her progress and, thankfully, had no connection to her mind. Nevertheless, its presence worried her. The shadow was Malice. It showed that she was still attached to her twin sister and that Malice still had an existence of a sort. While she seemed to have no power at the moment, September was sure that Malice would still be spewing her hate. She must find the Cemegwr and learn how to free herself of Malice or at least tame her spite.

She circled over an area of the forest much the same as any other, though her memory told her that this was where she had met the Cemegwr on her previous visit. She landed on a sturdy branch at the top of a tall oak tree, transformed into the indigo cobra and slid down the trunk dragging Malice behind her attached by dark feet to her tail. She reached the leaf-litter strewn ground, bare of plants. She returned to her human self. Her unnatural shadow was almost invisible in the dim light of the sub-canopy.

September listened carefully. There was silence here at the base of the trees; no rustling of creatures, not even wind in the branches. She took a few steps. The leaves beneath her feet crumbled to dust. She rested a hand against a tree and pieces of bark flaked off. Just like at Amaethaderyn, the forest was decaying, not through pests or disease but just, well, what? Time? A fading of universal energy? A lack of will? September was convinced that the Cemegwr had the answer because this universe was their creation. They had planned it, constructed it. They had even prepared for the attacks by the Malevolence by drawing her and her predecessors from the other universe. But where were they?

The first time she had met the Cemegwr they had seemed prepared for her, had even drawn her to them. Here there was no sign that they existed, no hint of where they could be found. If they didn't want her to find them then she had no idea where to look but Cyfaill had said the Cemegwr would solve her problems. Were they testing her? Perhaps they were waiting for her to do something to draw them to her.

September sat down in a patch of open ground between the thick trunks of the trees. The leaves and branches interlocked overhead so there was no view of the sky but the space felt large, like a cathedral. She crossed her legs and straightened her back – that wasn't something she could do at home where her flab prevented such a posture. She enjoyed using her body here in ways she couldn't at home and it reinforced her desire to get fit when she returned to her own world. She closed her eyes and thought.

The Cemegwr knew where she was. They knew, if not everything, then pretty well most of what happened, so they must be waiting for her to do something. They wanted her to assist them, so Cyfaill had said, so perhaps they wanted proof that she was still in control, that Malice had not come through the transport in charge, proof that she still had her powers as Cludydd o Maengolauseren. They had probably observed her arrival, her meeting at Amaethaderyn, her flight here to Coedwig Fawr. What more did they want? A demonstration?

She had come expecting to be met by the Cemegwr with the Land a peaceful, prosperous place full of contented people. It wasn't like that at all and probably it was a deliberate plan by the Cemegwr. They had suggested that they weren't bothered about the future of the Land and the universe it was part of but they had given her the means to defeat the Malevolence. Perhaps they were passing the responsibility to her to revitalise the Land. Was that their test?

September felt a surge of excitement. That was it. The Cemegwr wanted her to bring the Land back to health and fruitfulness – she was sure of it. But how? No-one presently living in the Land would know but there were others who might – the spirits of the cludyddau past and present who resided on the planets. She must meet them. She jumped to her feet confident that she knew what she had to do. Previously, she had floated up to the Moon and beyond but she knew how to move faster now. She closed her eyes, clenched her fists and stiffened herself. She saw herself on the Moon, not the Moon of the astronauts but the silver Moon of the alchemists.

She felt, rather than saw, the column of violet light that surrounded her and carried her upwards. The ground beneath her feet changed from soft, rough, leaf litter to something hard and smooth. She opened her eyes and was delighted to discover she had arrived. She was on a silvery white plain with darkness overhead, studded with stars. The Sun and the Earth, or rather Daear, the People's name for their planet, were the largest objects in the sky. But even here there were signs of the universe failing. The silvery lustre was, if not tarnished, then dulled. Around her, as she expected, were assembling a throng of silvery wraiths, the cludyddau o arian, more transparent and ethereal than on her previous visit and their faces were etched with fatigue. Most of the female faces were unknown to September but she recognised Arianrhod, a very elderly woman and Arianell who was also much older looking than she recalled. She searched the faces for another known face.

"Hello," she said. The crowd of white haired, silver clothed women bowed their heads. "I don't see Arianwen among you." She was the first silver bearer that September met and she had appreciated Arianwen's kindness.

Arianrhod replied, "Sadly, Cludydd, Arianwen is not with us. She was taken by the Malevolence. Her spirit was torn from us and merged with the evil above the stars."

"No!" September cried. She could not imagine the spirit of the kind and compassionate Arianwen being lost and becoming filled with hate like the other spirits of the Malevolence.

"We're sorry but that is what has befallen her," Arianell said. "We recall all the people, cludyddau and others, who were lost to the Adwyth, and the agony of their hate. It is something we all dreaded when we were beset by the manifestations of evil but thanks to you that danger has passed."

"We see that you carry with you a remnant of the Adwyth," Arianrhod said. September looked down at the shadow of Malice writhing at her feet. She seemed to be a hole into the depth of the moon, as black as the space above her head.

"It is Malice, my twin sister. She is joined to me."

"So long as the Malevolence is banished from the world she is powerless but take care, Cludydd. Evil always finds a way back."

September didn't need the silver bearers' warnings as she was worried enough by her hateful twin dangling at her feet. But there was another matter she must talk to the silver ladies about.

"The Malevolence may have gone but you must know that the Land is dying. It's decaying and fading away," September said as she felt heat rising in her. She made herself remain calm.

"Yes, we have witnessed the changes in the universe," Arianrhod agreed.

"Can't you do something about it?" September said with a degree of impatience.

"How can we influence the workings of the world?" Arianell said.

"Aren't you the cludyddau who have the power of silver?" September said looking out at the throng of hundreds of women. "Surely together you can do something?"

The ghostly women talked amongst themselves apparently intrigued by September's urgings. After what seemed like many minutes of conversation, Arianrhod once again faced September.

"There is something in what you say, Cludydd. We think you should visit Haul and speak to the cludyddau o aur. Gold is the chief among metals and its power the greatest of all in giving hope. They will be able to guide you and perhaps you can indeed find a way for the cludyddau of all seven metals to save the world."

"That's what I'll do," September said. She would travel directly to the Sun missing out Mercury and Venus which lay between the Moon and her destination. "I will return with a plan." She composed herself for symudiad and visualised the surface of the Sun.

A flash of blue light transferred her instantly from the silver surface of the Moon to the golden Sun, which though bright was nevertheless not as dazzling or brilliant as she recalled. Golden-skinned, blonde-haired men surrounded her immediately with the familiar figure of Aurddolen at the front. He seemed to have regained some of the powerful stature and imposing presence that he had had when September first met him, the leader of the People, but even so he seemed faded and careworn. She had to remind herself that this was just his spirit and that he no longer existed with the living in Gwlad.

"Cludydd, what a pleasure it is to greet you and welcome you to the company of cludyddau o aur," he said.

"I'm pleased to see you again too."

"Nevertheless, we had not expected you once you had defeated the Malevolence at the Conjunction and left Gwlad."

"I'm here for two reasons. One is to deal with Malice." September gestured to her feet where her shadow had the appearance of a black pit in the surface of the glowing Sun.

"Ah, yes. You defeated her by making her part of yourself."

"Yes, but it didn't completely work. She tried to take over my body. Now she is part of me but outside of my mind. I need to find what I can do to control her forever."

"I do not know how we can do that. Malice is beyond my knowledge as a cludydd. The Toddfa Penbaladr that the Cemegwr gave you is not something that I or any cludydd can understand."

"I know. I have another request."

"What is that?" The gold bearer looked confused.

"I want you to save the world from fading away."

"Ah, I see." Aurddolen's manner changed and he became mournful. "Sadly all things come to an end and it seems the world is reaching the end of its existence."

"But it doesn't have to," September insisted. "You can't just give up. You showed me that there must always be hope. You can do amazing things with your gold and there are lots of you. You and the bearers of the other metals could tap into the energies of this universe and give it a kickstart, get it going again and bring new life to the Land." She truly felt as though it was possible although she didn't really understand where the energy came from. Perhaps she was wrong and the Cemegwr held all the power. Perhaps these cludyddau were just part of the problem, using up the energy available rather than tapping into new sources.

Aurddolen's blonde eyebrows were raised. "I do not understand what you mean by 'energy' September. Is it some term you use in your own world?"

"Well, yes it is," September said, "I don't understand it really but energy is what makes the planets move, the rivers flow and things grow."

"The planets move around Daear because they have the potential to do so, September. Rivers flow down to the sea because the water is seeking its natural place, and living things grow because they have the potential for growth."

Aurddolen's explanations were nonsense to September. It sounded as though he was quoting ideas that had disappeared long ago, before this universe had been built by the Cemegwr.

"But what power do you draw on when you use your gold? I saw you destroy manifestations and you have gold powered machines like the boat I travelled in."

"Ah, then, Cludydd, we draw on the essence of the planets linked to metals in Daear by the specific emotion that we employ. You know that because you learned it on your previous visit to us here in the heavens."

How she could invoke the power of the metals by just choosing the right mood still mystified September, although she could do it at will.

"OK. Well, why not use that power to give this universe a boost. Re-boot it. Rewind the clock or whatever is needed."

Auddolen scratched his smooth, golden chin and the other gold bearers muttered to each other.

"Perhaps it is possible but I think it will require more than the power of the seven metals. Perhaps your friends, the Cemegwr, can help."

"I'm not sure they're my friends. They're too powerful to have friends who are just humans. But I think they will help, except that I can't find them."

"What do you mean, Cludydd?"

"I was sent back here to meet them, but they're not where I met them before. They haven't contacted me since I arrived. I think they are waiting for me to give them a sign."

"A sign of what?"

"That I still have all the powers of the Maengolauseren."

"Ah, that may be so."

"I thought that if you could think of a way that we could bump start the universe then that would be a demonstration of what I can do."

"Hmm, let us discuss this." Aurddolen went into a huddle with the other cludyddau while September stood surrounded by the golden vapours of the Sun. After a few minutes she grew bored and impatient and stared up at the dark sky trying to pick out the points of light that were the planets, that like the Moon and the sphere of stars, moved in circular orbits around Daear. The planets were worlds while the stars merely lanterns in the sky but she could not spot the different objects from the Sun. Eventually Aurddolen separated from the cluster of spirits with another gold bearer. He too was old but September thought she recognised him.

"Heulfryn has an idea," Aurddolen said. Now September recognised the features of the young gold bearer of the mining town.

"A symptom of the malaise afflicting Gwlad is the failure of the mines of Mwyngloddiau Dwfn," Heulfryn said.

"Berddig said you had run out of metals."

"Yes, the veins that carry the metals from the centre of Daear have not been replenished, but perhaps we can restore them at least for a short time."

"What can we do?" September was interested again and eager to find out.

"It will take all the effort of all the spirits of the cludyddau who have ever lived in all the planets, but they will not be sufficient without you Cludydd. You control the egwyddorpum."

"That's the stuff the Maengolauseren and the stars are made from."

"That's right, Cludydd," Aurddolen said. "The quintessence together with the four elements that make up the seven metals, form the matter of our universe. You will be needed as the focus of the power of the cludyddau to regenerate the heart of the world."

"That sounds as though it would impress the Cemegwr," September said. "What do I have to do?"

"You must be at the very centre of Daear, the centre of the universe," Aurddolen said.

"Isn't that solid or liquid and very hot?" September asked. The centre of the Earth was molten iron wasn't it? September reasoned to herself. But of course, this wasn't the Earth they were talking about but Daear, the Cemegwrs' version of an Earth modelled on ideas from before modern science.

"It is egwyddorpum, Cludydd, the material from which you get your power. You will be part of it."

"Oh, OK."

"We will contact the other cludyddau on the other planets to tell them what is required. When you are prepared we will focus our powers on you. You will channel our emotions through the egwyddorpum into the four elements that surround the core of Daear and the metals will grow again in the veins of rock and Gwlad will be rejuvenated." Aurddolen was full of hope now and broadcasting the plan to all the other cludyddau as well as to September.

"Right. I'll go then. I just have to imagine being in the centre of universe?"

"Yes, September. Thank you for coming to us again and bringing with you your enthusiasm as well as your hope for our well-being. I hope you find your Cemegwr."

"So do I." September composed herself for symudiad just

thinking of the glowing white material of which the stars were made and the centre of Daear. She had one final glimpse of the golden inhabitants of the Sun as the shaft of blue light engulfed her.

Part 6

~

Union

19

She was floating in a dense, white cloud. No, not floating; she was the cloud. She could not see or feel any part of her body and there was nothing in front of her eyes but whiteness. Where did the light come from if she was at the centre of the planet? The stuff itself, the egwyddorpum, must be glowing. There was just one exception to the brightness. It wasn't a spot in her eye; it was her shadow. Malice was still with her, a wriggling puppet of blackness amongst all the white. Were they still attached? Much as she wanted rid of Malice she feared what may happen if when she was cast off she became free. She hoped that when she had carried out the regeneration that Aurddolen had devised she would return to the surface, regain her body and then with Malice still bound to her, she would seek out the Cemegwr again. Now though she had to make contact with each of the planets and their cludyddau.

She thought of closing her eyes but it made no difference to what she saw as it didn't feel as if she had eyes. Panic gripped her for a moment. What if she couldn't get out of here and she was stuck in this white nothingness forever? The momentary nausea passed. Of course she could get out. She was the Cludydd which all the spirits of the planets were looking towards. She reached out with love, using the power of efyddyn, copper, to communicate. Her sphere of awareness grew out beyond the core of Daear. She heard the muttering thoughts of the people who lived on the surface and the clear beacons that were the living cludyddau o efyddyn. The few that she could sense dismayed her as it revealed the diminished numbers of cludyddau that inhabited the Land. She did not have time to dwell on the situation on Daear because the sphere continued to grow. It reached the Moon and she felt the presence of the silver bearers, then Mercury, Venus, the Sun, Mars, Jupiter and finally Saturn.

There was a clamour of thoughts from the multitude of past and present cludyddau.

She declared herself and they all responded and began to compose their characteristic emotions. She felt the first ripples of compassion, anger, joy, sadness, wonder, love and hope. There were spots of colour amongst the white – silver, gold, blue-grey, red, more silver. The colours danced and span around her weaving spirals. More and more spots of colour appeared until they coalesced into a great swirling ball. The emotions mixed in her, a confusing melange that made her happy, melancholy, excited all at once but in their confusion made it difficult to think clearly. The struggling spectre of darkness that was Malice shrank as the colours pressed in around it. Or was Malice receding from her? The waves of emotion grew stronger, overpowering her own thoughts. She was just a conduit for a torrent of sensation that passed through her and spread out into the egwyddorpum and the other four elements around her. She was losing touch with herself, her identity dissolving.

"Stop!"

The contact broke. The voices of all the cludyddau disappeared and the ocean of emotion and colour drained away. September found herself again, breathless and exhausted. She was still floating in the whiteness but no longer alone. In her vision appeared a figure, one that she recognised. It was the ageless female Cemegwr she had first met in Coedwig Fawr. There her hair had been brown and she wore a brown dress. Here though, she was white on white so that her features could barely be made out. September sensed rather than saw who it was.

"Why did you stop me?" September said or thought; she wasn't sure how she was communicating with the Cemegwr. "We were bringing the Land back to life."

"You may have succeeded, for a short period." The voice was resonant despite the dense solid, liquid or gas they were immersed in.

"I want to save the people, help them live," September cried. "The spirits of the cludydds on the planets were helping me." The memory of the confusion of emotions left September disorientated and upset. "Do you want them all to die?"

"What you were doing was laudable, September, but pointless. The cludyddau don't have the power to maintain this universe but what you were doing was going to destroy yourself and free Malice."

"What?"

"You are great and powerful here, September, but even you cannot hold the emotions of all the cludyddau across the universe. Your identity would have been overwhelmed as you restored energy to Daear, and Malice would have been freed to re-join the Malevolence and resume her campaign of hate and destruction."

Fear gripped her. Was what the Cemegwr said, true? Had she allowed her pride at being the Cludydd to overcome her common sense? What would happen to her if Malice was freed from her bonds? *I'm still the stupid, fat teenager*, she thought. But nevertheless she saw in her memory her friends, much older and greyer, fading away.

"But how can I save Berddig and Eluned and the rest of the People?"

"That is not your responsibility, September. You performed your role at the Conjunction as the Cludydd o Maengolauseren. You banished the Malevolence."

"At the second try, with the help of my mother and your liquid. What did you call it? The Alkahest."

"Yes. The 'Toddfa Penbaladr' in the People's tongue. You know September, that Malice was an unexpected development. We had not prepared for her and had to, how shall we say it – improvise. You needed our help to prevent the Malevolence from gaining intelligence. This universe is a construct designed to draw the Malevolence and distract it. It has done all we planned for it so now it has reached the end of its usefulness."

"You told me that before and you promised you would restore it once the Malevolence had gone."

"We did. The People survived and live."

"But they are not having children. The planet is fading away."

"It is decaying as universes do. It is shedding energy into the Omniverse and is shrinking."

"Shrinking?"

"Yes. The planets and stars spin faster and time speeds up."

"Is that why fifty years passed while I spent just a couple of weeks back home?"

"That's right. Soon it will shrink to a singularity and dissipate."

"What will happen to the people?" September cried.

"They will barely notice any change. Their lives will pass at the same pace in their perception until they die naturally."

"Can't you reverse it?"

"Of course we could. Almost anything is within our power, but why? This universe has achieved its purpose but generated new problems – Malice. It is best to let it fade away."

"But you said before that the Alkahest would stop Malice."

"Not stop her. The Alkahest is a universal solvent. It mixed the powers of all the five elements to enable you to push the Malevolence back. It also bound Malice to you. We expected you and Malice to dissolve into one being but it turned out that your identities were so opposed that you couldn't mix thoroughly. You are like oil and water separating out after mixing."

"Is that all? At home, Malice tried to take over my body. I barely held on to being me. Here she is my shadow."

"A shadow that threatens to cut itself from you and resume her dark existence administering hate."

"So she is still dangerous?"

"Of course."

"Can you help me?"

"You are important to us, September."

"Us?"

"The Cemegwr, the Brains, the entities that occupy the Omniverse."

"Cyfaill said you had a task for me."

"That is correct. You have acquired unique powers, unusual in the Omniverse where anything can exist. Through your twin you have a connection with the Malevolence which we can use to expel it from other universes. But first we must stabilise your relationship with Malice, put her under your control and complete the process that the Alkahest only began."

"You have a way?" She wasn't sure she was ready to be a slave to the Cemegwr's plans but she wanted the threat from her twin to be extinguished.

"Yes, but it is difficult."

September had felt that coming. Everything she had been asked to do had been demanding, exhausting and tested her skills and ingenuity to her limit. Nevertheless, she had to go on as the thought of Malice taking her over and unleashing her hate was a bigger worry than what the Cemegwr might have prepared for her.

"What is it?"

"It requires what the People would call the Gwlyb Hoedl Gwyrthiol."

"The what?"

"The Miracle Liquid of Life or the Elixir of life."

"Oh. I've heard of that. It's supposed to make you look young and make you immortal." She thought of some of the creams Mother rubbed into her face. Didn't they promise something similar?

"It will seem to have that effect but its power is somewhat different. You will appear unchanged throughout time."

"Isn't that the same thing?"

"No. The Gwlyb Hoedl Gwyrthiol will give you the power to move through time in the same way that symudiad enables you to travel through space."

"Time travel?"

"That is correct."

"But why? How will hopping through time help me control Malice?"

The Cemegwr frowned, the wrinkles on her face forming faint shadows in the whiteness.

"We have determined that the key to unifying the persons of you and your twin lies with your predecessors as Cludydd o Maengolauseren."

"Mother and my great grandmothers?"

"Yes. You are all inhabitants of the two universes. In this world you share the core of egwyddorpum in your hearts. In your home universe you each have the genes that made you the Cludydd."

"The white hair!"

"That is an obvious expression of some of the genes."

"We share some genes. That's not surprising."

"Not some, many, and we planted epigenetic markers so that the genes of the Cludydd are expressed in the seventh child.

September was confused now, her school biology stretched to the limit.

"But we've all had different fathers?"

"The Cludydd genes are on the chromosomes inherited from the female line. We have just ensured that they all have been passed on together."

No wonder she and Mother resembled each other so much.

"OK, so what has this got to do with me and Malice joining together?" As she said it September wasn't sure that was something she wanted to do.

"Malice is your identical twin so she also has the full set of genes. She could have the powers of the Cludydd. Your mother should have had non-identical twins but instead of there being two embryos there was only one and it divided to form the two of you."

"You mean you weren't able to make everything happen as you wished." September felt that the Cemegwr fell short of being all-powerful beings.

The Cemegwr responded haughtily, "In a universe as complex as yours there are many possibilities and some impossibilities. It is unlikely that we could ever control every outcome. The error occurred and two identical embryos developed."

September realised that the Cemegwr must have been aware that two potential Cludydds were developing in her mother's womb.

"You killed Mairwen," she cried.

"We had to choose one embryo to be the Cludydd and ensure it was the seventh born," the Cemegwr said. "That was you."

"You let my twin grow inside my mother and then made her die."

"It was unfortunate."

"You gave her to the Malevolence."

"That is the fate of all spirits that fail to achieve life," the Cemegwr said calmly.

September laughed. "You thought you'd disposed of her but she came back to threaten your plans for your model universe."

"We had not expected her to retain her identity."

"But she was special, like me and Mother and the others. You had made us different so we could be Cludydds."

"As I said, we don't control everything in the Omniverse, the Malevolence in particular." The Cemegwr waved her indistinct hand dismissively. "The Alkahest drew Malice from the Malevolence and planted her in you but it was unable to merge you into one spirit. We have given much thought to this and think that if you joined with your six predecessors then the Alkahest that is within you would be able to dissolve the darkness into the greater light."

September had listened to the Cemegwr's statement with a growing sense of bitterness. "You're saying I've got to round up the other bearers of the starstone and merge myself with them."

"Yes, at the moment that they achieved their power over the Malevolence."

"At each of the Conjunctions."

"That's right."

The Cemegwr was asking her to submit to a process which might dissolve her personality into a soup of her predecessors' characters along with Mairwen's. The same Cemegwr who had cast away Mairwen's spirit like a piece of rubbish.

"And if I don't do this?"

"Malice will break free and lead the Malevolence on a trail of destruction throughout the Omniverse. This universe, your own and many others will be destroyed and the spirits of the inhabitants turned to evil."

"Oh." The Cemegwr's words took a few moments to have meaning. "You mean your little mistake of throwing Mairwen out into the darkness threatens to destroy everybody I know."

"That is unfortunately the situation." At least the Cemegwr sounded a little contrite. "But it is also a great opportunity. If you succeed then Malice's link with the Malevolence will give us power over it."

"You said, give 'us' power."

"Will give you power," the Cemegwr conceded.

Her dilemma was made clear. She had to follow the Cemegwr's instructions, whatever it meant for her, in order to save her family, friends, the people of two universes and possibly even more. Fear made her invisible body tremble. Would she survive as a person? What about Mother, Eirawen and Rhiainwen and the others for whom she had no names? Would they all become one person? She couldn't imagine what it would be like to lose her self-awareness but the thought of all the people of Earth becoming creatures of the Malevolence, turned to evil and hate, well, she didn't feel heroic but she had to do whatever was asked of her, even if she didn't fully trust the Cemegwr.

"OK. What do I have to do? Let me have this Gwlyb stuff."

"Not here, September. There is only egwyddorpum here. You need the four other elements and their qualities to make the Gwlyb Hoedl Gwyrthiol. You must go to LLosgfynedd yn'r Cwmwl."

"LLos… where?"

"It is where all the elements and their qualities exist together. The Mordeyrn will guide you. I will meet you there to help you. Go now. This universe does not have much of its timespan left."

"I'll do it." September felt bolder now she knew what she had to do. "But only if you restore the Land to how it should be."

"I told you it had passed its usefulness."

"I know and I don't care. Come on, you are as powerful as superheroes or gods. You can do it if you want to, and you owe me something for all the mistakes you've made."

"Our power is not unlimited, September, as you now know, but if it is what you want, I promise it shall be done."

"Thank you. Now, if I need the Mordeyrn you must mean Heulfryn. I guess he's still at Mwyngloddiau Dwfn." She closed her eyes shutting out the uniform whiteness and composed herself. An image of snow-covered mountains and the dark grey buildings of the mining town filled her mind.

20

She was almost free just then; almost able to break away from this twin of hers who professed to love her but kept her bound and powerless. The storm of emotion had been agony, each drop of compassion or love or joy like acid burning her, but while the hurricane of colours and feelings whirled about her, her connection to her sister had faltered. She had drawn herself away, stretching towards the spirits who were her real kin. Their hate, faint though it was, beckoned her with its familiarity. How she longed once again for unity with the Malevolence.

Then it was gone, the colours, the emotions, the rain of metals. There was just the whiteness and the unseen binding that kept her in the vicinity of her twin. The feel of the quintessence on her was an agony. She had squirmed and struggled to avoid its touch but there was no escape – yet. But now her hate had purpose. She knew that the Malevolence was not far away, the cries of the spirits, distant though they were, lingered just in the range of her senses. They gave her strength. The bonds with her captor must have weakened. Surely a chance would arise when she could free herself and wreak her revenge. Yet, those shared memories of her sister's life lingered. The images and words of love and pleasure gave a comfort that she had never experienced. She found herself almost reluctant to relinquish them.

21

The squat towers of the miners' homes were all around her. She felt the cold through the insubstantial blue glow that surrounded her although it did not bother her. She was back in Mwyngloddiau Dwfn. There was silence, no noise of clanking machines, no smoke from chimneys. The thick covering of snow and ice in the alleyways was undisturbed by passing feet. Overhead the sky was grey, threatening more snow although as the air was so icy, September wondered if it was too cold for a snowfall. She looked around her feet. Her shadow was still there, writhing and stretching. It seemed more elongated than before, extending several metres from her feet. Seeing Malice struggling to get free spurred September to get on with her task.

She called out, "Is anyone there? Heulfryn, where are you?" and reached out with the power of efyddyn to contact Heulfryn or any living soul.

"I am here," came the faint reply. September walked between the cold, dark buildings following the trace of the voice. She came to a familiar small square and recognised what had been Aurddolen's house. The door opened a few inches and a blonde head looked out.

"Cludydd?"

"Yes, Heulfryn."

He pushed the door open wide and stood in the opening. His wrinkled face revealed that he was elderly but he still stood upright. Nevertheless, he was very different to the youth that September recalled.

"Can it really be that you have returned after all this length of time?"

"It is, but we've already spoken to each other on the Sun."

"Ah. You have visited my spirit. You forget, Cludydd, that while we live we have no conscious contact with our spirits in the heavens."

September had forgotten that fact. She changed the subject.

"Where is everyone? You are the only person I can detect in the whole town."

Heulfryn shivered and pulled his robe tight around him.

"I am the only one, but come in quickly. It is so cold I will perish."

September hurried to join him in the house and he closed the door behind her. The ground floor room was little changed to when Aurddolen had occupied it fifty years before. There were low stone tables and cushions scattered across the carpeted floor. The walls also were hung with brightly covered tapestries that made it feel warmer than the outside, though not a lot.

"Follow me," Heulfryn said, leading her up the stone stairs to the first floor and into a room that she did not recognise. It was small and furnished simply with a single stone ledge with a mattress and a floor cushion beside another low stone table. There was a fireplace in which logs burned giving out just sufficient warmth to raise the temperature above freezing. Heulfryn rubbed his arms to warm himself and sat on the bed. He pointed to the cushion.

"Please sit, Cludydd."

"You need to burn wood to keep warm?" September asked as she lowered herself into a cross-legged sitting position. "Can't you use your gold powers to heat yourself?"

"Sadly, Cludydd, I cannot," Heulfryn said with a glum face, "though I was taught well by Aurddolen I am unable to summon a great deal of power from the little gold I possess." He held up his hand bearing a single gold ring."

"What has happened?" September asked though she suspected the answer.

"The powers of all the metals have faded over time and we have been unable to find new metal lodes in the mines. That is why there is no one here. The miners and their families have left, some to seek other sources in the mountains elsewhere and others to find a new living in the forests."

"I understand. The Land is decaying."

Heulfryn nodded.

"But I'm going to change everything, get it going again," September continued. "Have hope."

Heulfryn gave a thin smile and his ring produced a faint yellow glow.

"Thank you, Cludydd. It is a miracle that you are with us again and if you can help us regain our powers then we will be eternally grateful."

I'm not sure about eternity, she thought, but perhaps the Cemegwr will keep their promise and give the Land a new future.

"Thank you," she said, "but I need your help."

"Anything you ask, Cludydd. I can see that you carry the darkness with you." He nodded at her writhing shadow. He appeared concerned but not as scared as the people of Amaethaderyn.

"It is my twin. We are bound together."

"I see. She is separated from the Adwyth?"

"Yes, but I do not control her. The Cemegwr say she is still a danger."

"Ah, the Cemegwr. They helped you defeat the Malevolence."

"That's right. Now the Cemegwr says I need to get to LLosgfynedd yn'r Cwmwl, wherever that is."

She saw a look of fear fill Heulfryn's face and he shook.

"That is a place no person wishes to visit," he said.

"Why not? What does the name mean?"

"The Fiery Mountain in the Cloud," Heulfryn said. "It is so high no-one has ever climbed it."

"No mercury bearer has ever flown there?"

"None that is known of, Cludydd. If they have tried they have not returned. Why do you wish to go to such a place?"

"The Cemegwr says that is where I will find the elements to make the Glib Hoy something or other."

Heulfryn was thoughtful.

"Do you mean the Gwlyb Hoedl Gwyrthiol?"

"That's it. That's what she called it."

"She? You mean the Cemegwr?"

"Yes."

Heulfryn shook his head.

"When I was a child the Cemegwr were the fabled creators of the world. You have shown us that they are real and they helped you in the fight against the Malevolence. Now you say they'll give you the Elixir of Life."

"That's what it is. Do you know the recipe?"

Heulfryn's eyes opened in wonder.

"No, Cludydd. The existence of the Elixir is as mythical as the Cemegwr once were. No cludydd has even come close to the formulation of it."

"Apparently I need all the elements and their qualities."

"Ah, that would explain why we have to reach the top of LLosgfynedd yn'r Cwmwl."

"I thought no one had ever been there."

"That is true, but even from its lower slopes we can see the fire that spurts from the earth at the peak. There is frozen water there and the air that is all around us."

September saw an image of a mountain belching fire.

"Oh, it's a volcano."

"Yes, Cludydd, and the highest mountain in Gwlad where the Mynedd Tywyll and Bryn am Seren meet."

"Right, let's go there then."

September leapt to her feet and reached forward to hold Heulfryn. She prepared for symudiad. Heulfryn wrenched himself away from her.

"Wait, Cludydd. Are you sure you should do what the Cemegwr suggest?"

"Why?" September looked at Heulfryn wondering what he meant.

"You know that Aurddolen was suspicious of the Cemegwr."

"He said they didn't exist."

"Well, most of us agreed with him on that until you proved him wrong, but more than that, Aurddolen confided in me after your victory over the Malevolence."

"He did?"

"Yes. He wondered why the Cemegwr should reveal themselves at just the moment when we were faced with destruction by the Malevolence in the hands of your twin sister."

September wasn't sure how much she should relate about the Cemegwr. Should she tell Heulfryn that Malice's existence was their fault or that this whole universe and all the lives of the People was a lure to draw the Malevolence into a battle with the Brains, with her and the previous Cludyddau o Maengolauseren as their weapon?

"Perhaps Aurddolen was right. We should be wary," she said, thinking that was enough, but Heulfryn hadn't finished.

"And the Gwlyb Hoedl Gwyrthiol is very powerful and dangerous, Cludydd."

"You said you didn't know anything about it."

"I don't *know* Cludydd, but there are stories. I said no-one had ever succeeded in making it but some have tried and there are tales handed down from generation to generation describing what the effects of such an elixir might be. They're not all beneficial."

"Like what?"

"The Gwlyb Hoedl Gwyrthiol bestows on its owner eternal life, but there is no guarantee that that life will be one of contentment or free of pain. Some stories suggest that the consumer of the elixir will suffer eternal torment."

"The stories may be true, but I don't have a choice, Heulfryn," September said. She pointed to her elongated writhing shadow. "If Malice breaks free from me she will be able to lead the Malevolence again and I may not be able to beat her a second time. I don't trust the Cemegwr either but doing what they told me to do seems to be the only choice I've got."

Heulfryn looked at her sadly and said, "You are too young to carry all this responsibility."

"I don't think my age matters," September replied, "I just don't seem to have any choice."

Heulfryn gave her a smile that reminded her of Aurddolen. "You are truly worthy of the title Cludydd o Maengolauseren. I will give you whatever assistance you need. But first I must prepare myself." He went to the end of the bed where there was a pile of furs. He sorted through the assorted coats and boots and selected items that turned him into the form of a very stout bear.

"It will be colder even than the white wastes beyond the mountains," he said finally.

September recalled her trek across the ice cap to the meeting with the Malevolence. It had been extremely cold although the starstone had kept her comfortable.

"I get it," she said. She began to enfold him in her arms. "Give me an image so we can transport there." Nothing came into her head.

"I can't Cludydd. I do not know the appearance of the top of the mountain. No one does."

"Oh!" How were they to get there if not by instant transportation? There was only one other way.

"In that case we must fly. Come on." September bounded from the room, down the stairs and out onto the snow covered square. Heulfryn followed more slowly, wary of tripping over in his thick, fur boots.

September thought of wonders she had seen in Gwlad, the surprising properties of the metals demonstrated by the cludyddau, and changed to the form of the iridescent blue eagle.

"Climb onto my neck," she said. Heulfryn approached her warily and when she lowered her head clambered onto her. "Hold tight," she cried and leapt into the sky. She circled once over the deserted town then headed westwards to where the two mountain ranges of Gwlad met.

The further west they flew the higher were the peaks. Nowhere did bare rock show through the covering of white and overhead the clouds formed an impenetrable grey blanket. September flew as instinct told her, hoping she was maintaining a line. Heulfryn clung on immovably and she worried that he had frozen to death. Her shadow dangled from her talons, apparently growing longer as time passed but she felt no presence in her head. At last a smudge appeared on the horizon and Heulfryn stirred.

"There," he shouted through the wind that whistled passed them. "The smoking mountain."

The mountain was surrounded by peaks but stood out as it towered over them, its summit hidden in dark clouds. It grew rapidly with the speed of September's flight and she found she had to climb higher and higher into the atmosphere. The cloud remained above them but the snow-covered sides of the mountain kept on rising. They entered the cloud and they were surrounded by grey mist which cut off their sight of the peaks. September circled, afraid that she might collide with the mountainside. The air was thinning and she had to beat her wings harder to maintain lift. For the first time of all the occasions she had spent as an eagle in flight she began to feel fatigue and struggled to draw enough breath. The cloud thinned and at last they emerged into clear air. Above, the sky was dark but the sunshine reflected off the billowy white clouds below them. The summit of LLosgfynedd yn'r Cwmwl was there in front of her but still above them. Its steep sides were bare of snow and ice so she could see that the peak was a truncated cone. She beat her wings harder in the thin air striving for the height necessary to pass over the ridge surrounding the volcano's crater.

With her lungs about to burst she cleared the guardian rim of bare rock and saw the almost perfect circle of the volcano. The inner walls of dark grey rock sloped steeply down to a lake of bubbling molten lava that glowed bright orange. Flames burst from the surface, almost rising to the height of the rim and smoke billowed into the sky. Approaching the lava lake September felt the heat of the fire and could smell the sulphurous smoke. She turned away and headed back to the ridge. The sides were steep. If they had been able to transport directly here from Heulfryn's home they would have tumbled down into the molten lava.

Now she needed to find somewhere to land before tiredness caused her to drop like a stone. Her eagle eyes searched the inhospitable walls of the volcano for somewhere to plant her feet. At last she saw it; a narrow ledge just inside the rim which was almost level. She headed for it, folding her wings just before she landed to give her room to stand.

Here the air was warm, heated by the lake of molten rock at the bottom of the crater. Looking down September could see small pools of water in cracks in the rocks that glinted in the sunlight.

Heulfryn slid from her back and groaned as he stood up, wary of the edge of the ledge.

"That is not the most comfortable means of travel, Cludydd," he said taking a deep breath and coughing.

"I'm sorry," September said returning to her human form, "but it was the only way. This is amazing. I've never seen a real volcano before."

"Nor I. This is the only fire-belching mountain in Gwlad."

Heufryn wheezed. "It is said it is where the first Cludydd o Maengolauseren defeated the Malevolence."

September grinned at that revelation. So that was why the Cemegwr had brought her here. It wasn't just to pick up samples of the four elements.

"The Cemegwr said I would find the four elements and their qualities here. I know the elements are fire, air, water and earth but what are their qualities?"

Heulfryn sank to the ground panting.

"What's the matter, Heulfryn?" She knelt beside him.

"Can't breathe," he whispered.

Of course, how could she be so uncaring? They were very high so the air was thin and the sulfur fumes made the air poisonous. Being the Cludydd she wasn't troubled, but Heulfryn was suffering. What could she do? A shelter would help. She had summoned a defensive dome before so perhaps she could make one that was more substantial. She stood over Heulfryn and thought about something joyful, her birthday party perhaps, and something sad such as missing her friends. She felt the power of tin and lead well up inside her. She raised her right arm and span around weaving a cone of alloy that began the size of a thimble, became an ice cream cornet and grew till it touched the ground and covered them both like a metal tepee.

Now with compassion she could use the power of silver to provide what was needed to heal Heulfryn. She blew on him. A gentle breeze sprang from nowhere forming a vortex around them. It was cool, clean, thick air, just what was needed to soothe his aching chest. Heulfryn coughed once and sat up.

"Thank you, Cludydd. The sphere of air is thin. This high up I was short of air to breathe."

"The sphere of air?" September asked.

"Yes. It lies above the sphere of water which forms the oceans, and that lies above the sphere of earth, the rocks. At the centre of Daear is the sphere of quintessence, egwyddorpum."

"Yes. I have been there," September said trying to understand Heulfryn's description. "You've mentioned the other elements. Is there a sphere of fire?"

"It is above the sphere of Air. That is why flames rise. The blue sky above us is the base of the sphere of fire. It extends out to the spheres of the planets." He started to pull off his furs. "We are close to it. That is why it is warm here."

This didn't seem to agree with what September had learned about the structure of the Earth but she knew now that things were different here.

"But the rocks poke through the water to make the land, and here there is fire in the rocks."

"Sadly Daear has lost its perfection. The spheres are broken and the elements mixed up. It is our presence that has brought imperfection."

"That's what you think is it?"

"It is what is taught."

"Well, it's just as well that the spheres are broken so that here we can collect samples of earth, air, fire and water."

"And the qualities too are here – heat and cold, dry and wet."

"Oh, that's what qualities mean is it; but how do I find them?"

"Each element represents two of the qualities. The earth is cold and dry, water cold and wet, air hot and wet and fire hot and dry."

"I see. I had better go and collect them. I don't know when, or even if, the Cemegwr will appear."

Heulfryn lay on the floor of their conical hut.

"I look forward to meeting a Cemegwr," he said.

September stepped through the metal sheet onto the bare rock of the volcano. Her dark shadow stretched down towards the glowing lake. It was longer than ever. It worried September and she hurried to start her task. She picked up a loose piece of grey rock. It was indeed cold and dry. That was simple but how do I hold water, fire and air? I need containers. They had brought no bottles or jars with them. What could she do? She stood and considered. She was the Cludydd with the powers of all seven metals at her disposal, but there were no metals here just the raw, unmixed elements – earth in the form of rock, water, air and fire. She had seen Aurddolen and Iorwerth shaping metal; perhaps she could shape rock. The molten lava would have to be her material.

First she had to reach the fiery lake. The side of the volcano shelved steeply down only just starting to level out at the glowing surface of the lake of molten lava. The best way down would be to scramble – or slither. Transforming into a cobra with glistening blue scales, she slid swiftly down, over and around the rocks, until she reached the edge of the lava lake, then changed back to human form on her knees. Aurddolen had shaped molten gold with his own hands so perhaps she could do the same with the liquid rock. The immense heat wouldn't hurt her although she could sense it. She trusted that her Cludydd's body could not be harmed by the natural elements of Daear and reached down to the surface. Her hand sank into the liquid and she felt the great heat but not as pain. She scooped a handful of the glowing gloopy mass and lifted it up. It was an amazing sight to be holding a heap of red-hot, molten rock in her bare hand.

Skill was needed to shape the rock. Summoning the anger of iron and the hope of gold she set to moulding the rock between her hands. A simple squat bowl took shape. When it was complete she set it down on the hard rock beside her. Its glow slowly faded until it resembled a dark brown glass. September took out another scoop of lava and shaped a bottle and then another. Finally, she fashioned a stopper to insert in the neck of her bottles.

Now she just needed her samples. She took a bottle and waved it in the air before jamming the stopper in. That was the air sample. Next she watched the surface of the lake. Huge bubbles were constantly forming and bursting to release flames of blue and red and yellow which rose up towards the sky. September changed into the eagle and gripping a bottle in her talons soared into the air over a lake. She flapped her great wings, hovering until she saw a large bubble grow and burst. As the flame rose she flew past it scooping the flame into the bottle. Quickly she returned to the ground, changed back and stoppered the bottle. Only water was left and that was simple. Holding the bottles and bowl in her arms she began to climb up the side of the volcano towards their campsite. When she was quite close she came across a small pool of water trapped by the rocks. She placed the bowl in the pool and scooped up the water.

Then balancing the bowl and bottles carefully in her arms she resumed her climb.

September reached the ledge where the silver-grey metal tent stood. She picked up a piece of rock to add to the bowl of water and the bottles of air and fire and ducked, ready to enter the shelter.

"You have the samples of the elements?"

September straightened and turned to see the Cemegwr standing behind her. She was gleaming white as she had been at the centre of the earth.

'Yes and Heulfryn, the Mordeyrn, is inside."

"Good, bring him out."

"He has trouble breathing in the air here. That's why I made the shelter."

"He will have no difficulty breathing in my presence."

"Oh. Why did he have to come?"

"He guided you here did he not?"

"Yes, but from his description of this volcano I could have come here on my own. I could hardly miss the tallest mountain, especially as it smokes."

"He has another task. We must get on. Your shadow lengthens and Malice may free herself."

September looked at her shadow. The black slash now stretched down the mountain almost to the bubbling, fiery lake. It was so elongated it was difficult to recognise as the silhouette of a person. September ducked into the shelter. Heulfryn stirred at her arrival.

"You have the samples," he nodded at the bowl and bottles and piece of rock in her arms.

"Yes, and the Cemegwr is here. She wants you outside."

Heulfryn's face lit up with anticipation, then clouded.

"But I cannot breathe outside."

"Don't worry, she says you'll feel OK. Come with me."

September waved her hands and the metal of the shelter began to fade away. Heulfryn stood. When he saw the glowing figure of the Cemegwr he let out an involuntary cry. September almost expected him to fall to his knees but he just stared in wonder. He seemed to have forgotten his difficulty with the air.

"Now we can begin," the Cemegwr said. "Hold out your

hands together," she commanded Heulfryn. He did as he was told raising his cupped hands to the glowing woman.

"September. Place the earth in his hands then pour on the other elements."

Juggling the bowl and bottles, September placed the rock in Heulfryn's cupped palms. Then she took the bowl of water and tipped it up. The water ran over the rock but miraculously, it didn't spill or run through his fingers. It remained in the container formed by his hands. Next she took the bottle of air, took out the stopper and held the bottle above Heulfryn's hands. Nothing appeared to come out but the surface of the water rippled as if blown by a breeze. Finally she took the bottle of fire, pulled out the glass stopper and held the rim of the bottle against Heulfryn's hands. Flame licked out of the bottle across the surface of the elements already in his hands.

"Now, Mordeyrn, Cludydd o Aur, recite your ritual of mixing," the Cemegwr said.

Heulfryn looked at her uncertainly, then nodded. He began to speak in the old language. September knew it was some form of Celtic or Welsh but she couldn't make out all the words. She heard 'cymysgwch' and 'toddwch' at which the mixture in his hands began to bubble and stir. The lump of rock crumbled and sank into the fluid and the flames died. Heulfryn was left holding a clear liquid.

"Is that it, the, um, Goo…?" September asked.

"The Gwlyb Hoedl Gwyrthiol," the Cemegwr said. "Not yet. It needs the egwyddorpum, the fifth element."

"But I don't have any," September said. "There's none here. It was at the centre of Daear where we met."

The Cemegwr smiled, "You forget September, that you are the bearer of the egwyddorpum. It is part of you."

"Oh." September was bewildered. What was expected of her?

"Drink from the Mordeyrn's hands and the Elixir will be formed within you. Only you can gain the power of immortality because only you possess the Maengolauseren."

There was a roaring noise and a rush of wind. September looked down into the bowl of the volcano. Her shadow had reached into the fiery pool and a column not of light, but of absolute darkness was rising from it.

"Be quick, September," the Cemegwr cried. "Malice is almost free."

"What?" September froze unable to think or act. The birth mark on her hip began to itch, the itch becoming a burn. She knew what it meant. Evil was approaching.

"Now, September," the Cemegwr urged. "Drink. The Elixir will form in you and you will have the power to move in time. Find your predecessors."

A towering, dark cloud appeared overhead growing as she looked. In it September could see shapes forming.

"Manifestations!" Heulfryn cried out, trembling but still holding his palms together. "The Malevolence comes."

From the cloud descended Adarllwchgwin, the giant birds with devil-like riders. Cwn annwn, the fiery dogs, leapt through the smoke and cloud towards September. Great winged horses dripping water, the Ceffyl dwr, galloped across the surface of the fiery lake and the snarling fairies, the Tylwyth teg, scrambled up the slope.

"The Adwyth has spawned manifestations of each element," Heulfryn shouted turning his head away from the approaching swarm.

"They come to answer the appeals of their mistress, Malice," the Cemegwr explained.

September stared at the approaching manifestations, her limbs frozen, her hip on fire. *No, it can't be happening again, I sent you back!*

A gale roared in her ears as the Adarllwchgwin circled chaotically around the crater searching for Malice. The Cwn annwn leapt across the lake, their flames mixing with the fires rising from the molten lava. Ceffyl dwr pawed at the rocks on the crater sides, dislodging lumps of rock and spilling the trapped pools of water while the Tywyth teg crawled up towards the ridge grabbing at loose pieces of rock and tossing them into the lava lake. The actions of the manifestations were undirected as they awaited their mistress' orders. Above the molten lava the dark column was taking on the form of a woman – head, shoulders, arms, breasts, abdomen. Malice was regaining her three-dimensional shape but still her dark elongated legs and feet stretched up the sides of the volcano to September.

"Drink, September," the Cemegwr urged. Her command penetrated September's fear-befuddled brain. She dipped her head to Heulfryn's hands. Her lips touched the clear liquid. It was neither cold nor hot, but tepid. She sucked, drawing the liquid into her mouth. It didn't taste like pure water, more like an oil with an earthy flavour and a fiery kick like chilli. It slipped down her throat and the rest of the liquid drained from Heulfryn's hands into her mouth. She swallowed. She felt the liquid run down her gullet to her stomach. For a moment she felt it there, warm, heavy, burning in her core. Then the Elixir began to spread through her, a tingling reaching into her limbs.

Below, the shadow's blackness was being replaced by the colour of flesh and the white of Malice's hair. The manifestations had given up their aimless wanderings and now were approaching September, Heulfryn and the Cemegwr. They flew, crawled, clambered up the rocky volcano sides. They were almost on them, spreading around to encircle them on the edge of the volcano's rim. The devils on the backs of the Adarllwchgwin drawing back their arms to throw their tridents, the bounding Cwn annwn spouting fire, the Ceffyl dwr rearing up to fall on them dripping water and the Tylwyth teg spitting acid that dissolved the rocks.

"Go, now," the Cemegwr shouted, "before Malice breaks away."

Go where? Transport to somewhere? But the Elixir gave her the power of time travel so she'd been told. When should she go? Heulfryn had said the first Cludydd had defeated the Malevolence here, back at the beginning of time, of this universe at least. Then, that was it, the time she must go to. The Gwylyb Hoedl Gwyrthiol filled her. Her skin burned, her fingertips and toes felt like irons in a blacksmith's fire and her head as if her hair had turned to flame. September screamed.

22

Freedom was close and her fellow spirits had been drawn to her to obey her commands. She had stretched and pulled herself to free herself from her captor. She had dragged herself across earth and water, pushed through the air. Now she had reached fire. She felt the heat and the cold, the wetness and the dryness of each of the elements through her insubstantial form and she felt the power of evil returning to her across the darkness of space.

Yes! This was her moment to break free; to regain her position of supremacy; to be enabled to destroy and spread her hate. The spirits aided her by transforming as in times past into the manifestations of the Malevolence. They would be hers to direct as she pronounced her vengeance on all life. There would be more to do her bidding, Pwca, Cyrhyraeth, Gwyllian, Llamhigwyn y dwr, Draig tân. Nothing would stop her. Not this time.

But yet, she was still joined to her twin. A slender thread it was true, but still there was that link to the memories of love and happiness, of play and pleasure. She strained to break free but still September held on to her.

A fire seeped into her, a different fire to the raw element that surrounded her. This was something flowing from her twin, a powerful energy. She felt a tug. The force was pulling her back to her captivity. She screamed and struggled but the force was too great. The darkness withdrew from her. She called to her spirits, the manifestations that circled looking for her, but her voice was weak. Her appeals went unheard and then they were receding from her.

Then she felt a greater wrench. Not only was her freedom being denied to her but she was being drawn out of the present into another time. She struggled more but to no avail. Her twin had power over her.

23

Little seemed to have changed. She was still standing on the side of the volcano with darkness around her and a roaring wind that deafened her but the Cemegwr, Heulfryn and her metal shelter had gone. In her head was the repetitive chant of 'Hate' from innumerable spirits of the Malevolence. As the dizziness of the transition cleared from her head she felt that there was something in her hand – another hand. She looked to her side and saw herself, at least in the features – white hair, pale complexion – but clothed in black not blue.

"Malice!"

"Let me go," her twin cried and tried to pull her hand from hers.

"No!" September grabbed Malice's arm and pulled her to her. She wrapped her arms around her sister holding her still. Malice fought but couldn't free herself.

As September struggled to maintain her grip on her twin she managed a glance down into the volcano searching for the source of the noise and the darkness and saw herself again. A figure just like her stood in the middle of the lava lake stretching her arms up into the cone of darkness and swirling hordes of evil spirits descending from the sky. In her hand was a white stone. It was glowing brightly and becoming brighter with every passing moment.

"It's her," September said. "The first Cludydd. We must join her."

She stumbled down the slope, dragging Malice with her. Her feet slid on loose rocks and more than once she nearly lost her balance but she didn't fall. As they descended, the roar of the gale that swept towards them increased but the figure on the lake held still and the glow of her starstone became a beacon that shone so brightly it was impossible to look at. It alone opposed the darkness.

They reached the edge of the glowing lake. A great heat

came off it and flames leapt up to be swallowed by the darkness. September put a foot forward. She didn't sink into the molten rock and neither was she burned. She stepped onto the churning surface and pulled the struggling Malice with her towards the shining blue figure.

The sphere of radiance of the Maengolauseren in the girl's hand grew, forcing back the dark as September and Malice approached her. The girl was screaming at the heavens but what words she was using September could not tell. They reached her side. September released one arm that had embraced Malice and extended her hand. Her fingers touched the blue light that clothed the girl's body as she shouted one word.

"Ymadaelwch!"

Light exploded all around them. The darkness was lost in the outpouring of light. The molten lava and the rock of the surrounding volcano disappeared from sight and the cries of the spirits ceased. A tornado swept all three of them up and span them round so swiftly that September lost all sense of where she was. She closed her eyes.

There was hard ground beneath her. She was lying awkwardly, one leg under the other. The air was cool and her skin had stopped burning. She opened her eyes. It was dark above but not complete darkness; there were stars. Some of the patterns were familiar. There was Orion. Did it mean that she was home?

September sat up and looked around. She was indeed on the ground, fine gravel over hard packed earth. There was a building just a few metres to her left. In the dim light it looked like a shed built from rough planks of wood and trunks or thick branches of trees bent into a house shape.

She pushed herself to her feet, feeling sore all over, and looked around. There was a black ridge to one side and another on the other. She was at the bottom of a valley. Ahead of her a full Moon was sinking towards the dark horizon. The wooden hut seemed to be the only sizeable building close to her but there were other shadowy structures and a cart with solid wooden wheels nearby along with a heap of long-handled tools. She looked at herself. She was wearing a coarse, woven dress that rubbed against her skin telling her that she wore nothing else. This wasn't like the clothes she wore on Gwlad or at home. Where was she?

The door to the hut opened and a figure looked out. In the dim light the woman seemed to be dressed similarly to her except that she had on a white bonnet.

"Gwenda?" the woman called softly. "What are you doing out here? Come to your bed."

September glanced around. There was no one else who the woman could be addressing. She must be talking to her. Who was Gwenda? Nevertheless, she did as she was told and followed the woman into the hut. The room was pitch black because there were no windows and no light. It stank of wood smoke and sweat. September heard the woman clambering onto a bed which seemed to be inside a cupboard because the wood panels creaked.

Carefully she put one foot in front of another until one caught against something and she stumbled. She put out an arm to stop her fall and felt a rough material which gave with a rustling sound. A mattress filled with straw? She put another hand down and felt warm flesh.

"Oi, Gwenda. Watch what you're grabbing," scolded a sleepy boy's voice.

"Shut up and go to sleep," bellowed a deep, gruff voice from across the room sounding as if it came from another chamber. September felt with her hands, finding a space on the mattress not taken up by the boy's body. She carefully laid herself flat and froze, not wanting to disturb the inhabitants of this house whoever or however many they were.

What had happened since she had grabbed the other Cludydd with Malice in her arms? She closed her eyes.

They were there, in her head. She opened her eyes again in alarm. The room was still in darkness and there were the snores and snuffles of others sleeping around her. There did not seem to be any danger. She closed her eyes again, looking into herself.

Malice was moaning, complaining and threatening dire consequences but she didn't seem to have any power over her body. There was another presence, gentler, confused, fearful. September saw echoes of memories from this character, some of which resembled her own – battles with manifestations of the Malevolence, a journey to the planets that orbited Daear, accompanied by a white robed figure of a Cemegwr. Then there were other memories not of the Land. She saw the hut she now occupied and people – an older man and woman, an even older man, two young men and four other young women. It was as if they were her own memories but she saw them as if in a dream. She knew who she was, where she was, even, when she was. There were other memories too – Malice's. Memories of loneliness and darkness and hate and destruction but also of power and of controlling the spirits of the Malevolence. The three personalities seemed to overlap so that she wasn't sure which memory was hers and which belonged to Malice or Gwenda. Gwenda – her ancestor, the first Cludydd o Maengolauseren.

<Gwenda?> she thought, <Can you hear me?>

Increased terror and wonder.

<Who are you? What are you doing in my head? Are you a spirit of good or evil?>

<I'm September, a Cludydd o Maengolauseren like you. You have just been to the Land and defeated the Malevolence.>

September felt the fear of her companion which she tried to calm. Puzzlement remained.

<That is the title I was given by the white woman and the name of the evil I fought. I thought I was in a dream. Then I thought it was a vision sent by God but as the days went by it came to feel real. The Cemegwr guided me to learn miraculous powers and then I fought the manifestations of evil. At the Cysylltiad I was to fight the might of the Malevolence and drive it from the Land. I remember the volcano, the darkness descending, the hate of all the spirits. I did what I was told to do and called on the power of the Maengolauseren. Did I succeed in my task?>

<Yes, Gwenda. The people of Gwlad who came after you lived their lives peacefully until the next conjunction and the arrival of the next Cludydd.>

<That is all as I was told, but what has happened to me? I

seem to be in my bed in my home with mother and father and Pedr, my brother, and my sisters but they do not seem surprised by my return. Many days and nights have passed. Why did they not notice my absence?>

<It's difficult to understand I know, but for them no time has passed. To them you have not been away.>

<So it is still the night of the full moon when I looked through the stone I had found?>

<That's right.>

<I do not understand. Is it a madness that causes to me to talk with myself? And there is something else in my mind. A part of the evil I fought against. Will it make me hate as it made others do? What is happening to me?>

September struggled to soothe Gwenda's worries.

<You are not mad, Gwenda, and I don't understand what has happened either. But there are three of us here. Three individuals in one body – yours I suppose. Like you I was called to the Land to fight the Malevolence but at a different time. The other person you can feel is Mairwen, my twin sister. She became a servant of the Malevolence calling herself Malice. I have fought her many times. We share each other's memories but you, Gwenda, and I must subdue Mairwen.>

There was more fear in Gwenda and her body trembled.

<If a part of the Evil is inside me and has come back to my home, we must destroy it.>

<No. The Cemegwr want me to use Mairwen to fight the Malevolence.>

<This is indeed madness. I will become like the demented who roam the wilderness excluded from the places of normal folk.>

<No Gwenda. We can stop Mairwen taking over. Together you and I and the other Cludydds can learn how to control her and cancel out her hate. Sleep now. We must work out what to do next.>

How could they sleep when three minds occupied one body, especially when one opposed the other two? Nevertheless, the fatigue that suffused Gwenda's body began to take effect on them. Gwenda calmed as did Malice and at last they both slept. September too felt tiredness creeping over her and she fell into sleep.

"Come on Gwenda, get moving."

There was bright light on the other side of her eyelids. She opened them. Sunlight through the open door and a window which had its shutters flung wide dazzled her. From somewhere came the repeated crash of machinery. A young man, the brother, was looking down at her. He had a rough leather jerkin on over loose woollen trousers.

"I'm off to the mine with Tad. Mam wants you to work. What are you lying there for?"

"Go away Pedr. I'm coming," September said using the name she recalled. It seemed to work because the boy went away grumbling about lazy girls. She rolled on to her front and pushed herself up onto her feet.

<Gwenda, are you awake? I don't know what to do.>

<I'm here. Give me my body back.>

What if she let go and allowed Gwenda to have control? Could she ever get her own body back? But she didn't know what to do here or how to react to the mother and father, brothers and sisters. This was the time when the first Cludydd lived, centuries before her own lifetime. She made a decision.

<OK, but we mustn't let Mairwen take over.>

<Of course not. I will not allow evil to rule me.>

What do I do? She stood still, closed her eyes, tried to relax. She felt Gwenda pushing to the front, elbowing her into the background. She felt numb. Her limbs were no longer hers to move, but she still heard the noises that had awakened her; she felt the warmth of the sun on her skin, and the hard floor on the soles of her feet. Her eyes opened and her body moved towards the door and outside. It was a little like sitting in a cinema and watching the scene move as if the camera was the eyes of the actor. It was unsettling but she stopped herself from mentally reaching out and wrenching control back from Gwenda. This must have been how Mairwen had felt when she had been a passenger in her body.

Now that it was daylight and Gwenda's memories were available to her she knew where she was – at Llelluched, of course, in the narrow valley she had walked yesterday. Then it had been quiet and grassy, now it was a noisy, dusty scene of industry.

Gwenda walked across the open yard, strewn with heaps of rock, towards an open sided shack. It felt weird feeling her body move under someone else's volition. She was a passenger in her own flesh, like the rear rider on a tandem that does not have any say about where the bicycle goes.

The thump of hammers was louder now. September saw a thin, sad donkey trudging along in what looked like a giant wooden hamster wheel. The wheel turned a thick timber axle which disappeared into the shack. Gwenda entered the building and the noise became louder, almost unbearably so. She wanted to cover her ears but Gwenda seemed untroubled. The three huge hammers were rising and falling onto a stone floor. The iron shod feet pounded pieces of stone thrown into their path from a shovel wielded by a young man, Gwenda's other brother, Iolo. After each crash of the hammer an older man, her grandfather, shovelled up the fragments into a wheelbarrow. "Come on girl. Get this to your mother," Grandfather shouted as the hammers continued to crash. He straightened his back after adding another shovel of rock to the barrow. September realised that the words she was hearing were being spoken in Welsh, as indeed all the speech had been since she had arrived. She marvelled that she understood the conversations through her sharing of Gwenda's knowledge and experiences. What could she do with Malice/Mairwen's knowledge?

Gwenda bent to grasp the handles of the barrow, lifted the heavy load and pushed it to the other end of the shed. Gwenda's mother and two of her older sisters, Bechan and Nona, were working there. September knew from Gwenda's memory that they were sorting the black shiny bits of lead ore from the waste rock by shaking the crushed ore in sieves with water from the stream that ran through the works.

"It's about time you appeared, girl," her mother said, looking up from her task. "After you've taken that back to Tadcu, take Megan's place in the sorting shed."

"Yes, Mam." Gwenda tipped up the barrow beside her mother, adding the heap of stones to the pile. The barrow was returned to the elderly man and then she walked a few paces across the yard to another, smaller shed. Megan sat at a table which had a high sided tray on it. She sifted through the larger lumps of rock, sometimes bashing a piece with a heavy mallet.

"Mam says it is my turn to sort, Meg."

The girl stood up and stretched. "About time too. I've been doing this for hours. What have you been doing all this time, Gwen? Sleeping?"

"My rest was disturbed," Gwenda said.

"You been having them dreams again?"

"Yes."

"Well, at least you're here now. I'll bring you some milk."

"Thank you, Meg." Gwenda took Megan's place on the stool and began to pick up bits of rock. Black shiny pieces were placed in one bucket and the lighter-coloured waste rock in another. Larger lumps she hit with the mallet to separate the ore from the waste. Soon September realised that Gwenda was working without having to think about her task.

<All your family work the mine?> September said although she knew the answer was yes.

<Yes. Tad and Pedr are in the adit and sister Tegan is with them to collect the rock that they dig out.>

<It is a lot of work for one family.>

<Tad would like to employ more and enlarge the mine. He says we should dig a channel for the stream from beyond the waterfall to feed a waterwheel.> September recalled the waterfall, the place where she had met Cyfaill for the first time.

<Why doesn't he?>

<We cannot afford it and times are uncertain. Since the abbey was closed and the monks dispersed, the mine belongs to King Henry. Tad is afraid to approach the King's steward for help. Perhaps now that the King has married again, for the sixth time, life will become settled and the price of lead will rise.>

Megan returned carrying a leather cup. Gwenda took it and drank thirstily. September shared the taste of the honeyed milk. It was sweet and thick but gave her energy. Gwenda was left alone to get on with her task. The heap of stones to sort hardly seemed to diminish but the buckets slowly filled. The repetitive actions coupled with the incessant rhythmic banging from the hammers lulled September's active mind. Since transporting to the Land she seemed to have been thrown into one new experience after another with little pause to think and analyse what had happened or even to worry about her own existence. Now though she reflected on what she had learned.

She knew where she was, but when? From what Gwenda said the time was during the reign of King Henry VIII. Now when was that? Sometime in the sixteenth century wasn't it? How could she return to her own time? How could she regain control of her own body? How could she follow the Cemegwr's instructions and meet the other five Cludyddau? Did she want to? The Cemegwr had killed her twin resulting in her becoming Malice so did she trust the Cemegwr? The questions went round and round in her mind. She retreated into her own thoughts, abandoning Gwenda – and Malice.

24

She had been restricted, forced into a corner by her two opponents, both the Cludydd; denied the freedom to move at will or access to senses. She struggled but was imprisoned in the depths of the brain. Nevertheless, she shared the memories of the two women, the one her former adversary, September, and the second, Gwenda, an opponent from the past conflict between the Malevolence and the Cludydd o Maengolauseren. She observed their varied lives before they were summoned to the Land, their experiences as the Cludydd, their battles with the Malevolence. She felt, but still failed to comprehend, their love for their families, friends and their homes, but she understood now that her death at the whim of the Cemegwr and her banishment to the dark of the evil above the stars was what had driven her to hate. She was confused by the other emotions that she felt through her two captors but her hate still burned the most strongly. She would be free.

The pressure on her decreased. The bonds holding her melted away. Gwenda was distracted by her task and September was self-absorbed. Malice took her chance. She bounded out of her confinement, pushing Gwenda from her position of control. She took over the body.

Malice leapt to her feet sending the stool rolling. She had the mallet in her hand and she swung it, scattering bits of rock from the tray. Freedom! She had it! Freedom to move, to destroy, to kill.

She strode from the shed and looked around the yard. It was bright and hot in the August sunshine. Too bright, too hot. She wanted the dark and cold she was familiar with; somewhere to hide and think; a place to plan her new reign as the servant of the Malevolence. Gwenda's memories told her where to go.

"Hey, Gwenda. Where are you going? There's work to do,"

Tadcu called. Malice ignored him and lurched up the track towards the mine. The track lead directly towards the steep side of the narrow valley. All vegetation had been cleared revealing the blue-grey rock. As she approached the small, dark entrance to the mine, Tegan appeared from the shadows, pushing a heavily laden barrow of rock. Malice continued to stride onwards. Tegan only looked up at the sound of Malice's shoes on the gravel.

"Gwenda! What are you doing?"

Malice swung her arm holding the mallet and stepped towards Tegan. Tegan's head turned to watch the head of the mallet swinging towards her; she ducked but not quickly enough. The weight of the heavy tool hit the back of her head and she fell sideways to the ground. Malice marched on without any pause.

She reached the mine entrance and went in. The path continued level but now with the rough-hewn rock pressing in on both sides and from above. Malice had to lower her head to avoid bashing it against the ceiling of the tunnel. Just metres from the mouth of the mine she was in darkness. Further in the air became cooler and water dripped from the roof. There was a sound of metal hitting rock. It sounded nearby but Malice knew from Gwenda's memories that the sound was deceptive and was transmitted from deep in the mine. Malice pressed on, feeling her way forward with her spare hand while the mallet dangled from her side in the other.

The adit went straight into the hillside along the course of the vein of lead-bearing ore that filled a fault between masses of worthless rock. Over many years Gwenda's family and her ancestors had carved out the tunnel pursuing the mineral that earned them their living. Now Tad and Pedr were hammering at the face deep under the ridge. As Malice ventured deeper into the darkness, the sound of their hammering grew louder and reverberated down the tunnel towards her. At last, in the distance ahead, appeared the tiny, yellow light of their single tallow torch. She went on, treading carefully on the wet rock floor. This would be her refuge. She would reach out to link with the evil that filled the universe.

The hammering stopped.

"Tegan? Is that you? You were quick." Tad's voice reached Malice. She raised the mallet feeling confident and determined. These men were unimportant, despite the love that Gwenda felt for them. They would not be expecting her attack, but she would have the darkness to herself. She strode forward towards the lighted candle and the voices.

25

September was jogged out of her daydreams by the change in movement but she couldn't see or hear. Panic gripped her. What had happened to her? Why was she imprisoned in her own head, cut off from all but the simplest of senses? The answer arrived very quickly. Malice. She had allowed her hold on Mairwen to weaken while Gwenda took charge. Mairwen must have taken the opportunity to escape the bonds by which she had been held and Gwenda wasn't prepared because she was unfamiliar with Malice. Now Malice was in control.

She must fight back, must not allow Malice to wield her hate. But how? She must unite with Gwenda. Together they could overpower Mairwen/Malice. She imagined reaching out into the dark. She saw herself stumbling in the vacant, lightless space, stretching her arms, hoping to grasp something. Her fingers touched another hand. They entwined.

<Gwenda?>

<Yes. What has happened to us?>

<It's Mairwen. She's taken over and trapped us in a corner of her brain.>

<I want my body back!>

<I know, Gwenda. I'm sure if we act together we can defeat her. The two of us must be stronger than her.>

<But what can we do? I cannot feel anything.>

<You're the Cludydd, Gwenda. Think about the powers you learned. Mairwen doesn't know how we can use our emotions to fight the evil.>

<Well, I feel angry.>

<That's a start. Use your anger to push against her.>

September felt the heat of Gwenda's anger wash over her. A spot of light appeared in the darkness which grew into a picture that appeared as if on an old fashioned TV. It was indistinct and black and white but she could see Gwenda hammering at a wall with an iron hammer. The wall was the barrier that Malice had built to imprison them. The wall was not marked by Gwenda's furious assault. Malice's hate withstood it.

<We need to try something less obvious,> September thought. <Something that Mairwen won't expect.>

<What do you mean?>

<Something like this.> September thought of Mother and Father, how they had loved her as a child. That love would have been for Mairwen too if she had lived. September dwelled on the loving feeling, broadcasting the comfort and joy it gave her. The appearance of the wall began to change from hard stone to something that looked more like chocolate. Its surface took on a glaze as if the chocolate was melting. Bits fell from the top turning into liquid as they fell and splashing thickly as they hit the virtual ground around them.

<Come on, Gwenda. Surely your family loves you. Think some loving thoughts and include Mairwen.>

<But she only thinks of hate and destroying us all.>

<That is all she has known but she was my sister. She could have been me. Imagine her as one of your sisters. You love them don't you?>

<Yes, of course.>

It was a small nugget of warmth at first that September felt alongside her but it grew and joined with her own feeling of love. She imagined being at home with Mairwen, sharing her life with her, enjoying each other's company. The melting of the wall accelerated as the heat of September's and Gwenda's love increased. The syrupy liquid flowed from the surface and the wall slumped. Holes appeared that grew until they were large enough to leap through. They were free. The fuzzy picture dissolved revealing Mairwen/Malice in her black-gowned authority. September leapt on her, wrapping her virtual arms around her.

<No. I won't let you back!> Malice cried, silently. September felt their shared body stagger as they fought for control. She maintained her grip on her twin allowing Gwenda to slip back into control of her limbs. September

shared her senses again, but still she couldn't see. The darkness was all around her but this was a different darkness. It was outside rather than within. Where were they? September thought. Gwenda reached out. She knew. The cold, wet rock was close and she skinned her knuckles on the sharp stone. She turned and there was a faint, small light. There were people close.

"Tegan? No. Gwenda. What are you doing here?" Tad said.

"Where's Tegan?" Pedr asked.

"I don't know," Gwenda said, "I don't know how I got here."

"Have you been having one of your 'turns' again, daughter?" Tad said with a hint of exasperation but also tenderness. "Let's get you out of here."

Her father took Gwenda in his arms and gave her a hug. There was barely room for two people side by side in the tunnel, but Tad squeezed around Gwenda without releasing her hand and tugged her towards the exit. Pedr followed along behind carrying the tools and the candle.

As she stumbled along, September held Mairwen in her imagined arms. Mairwen struggled.

<Don't push me away! I don't want to be alone again!>

<You're not alone. But we can't let you get control and do whatever you were going to do.>

They reached the entrance to the mine. Gwenda closed her eyes as the bright sunlight blinded her. Tad released her hand and ran forward.

"Tegan! What is wrong?"

Gwenda squinted through partly closed eyelids. Pedr pushed passed and ran to join his father. Tad knelt by the girl who lay on the ground beside the barrow. He turned to Gwenda, his face dark and forehead furrowed.

"Did you do this?"

"No. I don't know," Gwenda raised a hand to her mouth in horror.

<What did you do, Mairwen?> September asked.

<She was in my way.>

<You hit her?> Gwenda dropped the mallet from her hand. She ran to stand beside her father and sister. September tied mental bonds around Mairwen to keep her prisoner.

"Get water, and a cloth," Tad said to Pedr. The young man ran off. "I don't understand," Tad said to Gwenda. 'Why would you hit your sister? She loves you and you love her."

"I know." Gwenda had tears running down her cheeks. "If it was me that did this thing I didn't mean to. I must have been in a trance."

"Trance! Huh." Tad lifted Tegan up, cradling her bloody head in his hand. She moaned. "It's alright my love, your Tad's here." He lifted her hair to examine her skull. "I think it looks worse than it is. Pray that she will fine. It's alright my dear we're looking after you."

Pedr ran up with a bucket from which water sloshed. He put the bucket down and drew a grubby but sopping cloth from the water and handed it to his father. He held the cloth gently against Tegan's bleeding head. She moaned again, stronger this time.

"Help me carry her, Pedr. Gwenda too," Tad said. "We must lay her in her bed out of the sunlight." Together they carried Tegan back along the track to the works. Mam saw them return and left her post to fuss over her daughter. They took her into the shack and laid her down on the matting. Mam rested Tegan's head on a pillow and examined her.

"How did this happen? Did she fall or was she attacked?" Mam said. Tad and Pedr looked at Gwenda. She shrugged.

"I don't know."

"What were you doing at the mine, Gwenda? You should not have left your task," Mam said, looking at her with a mixture of confusion and anger. "Go. Take my place at the buddle. We'll talk of this later." She turned back to give her attention to Tegan. Gwenda's eyes filled with tears and she ran from the hut.

<Gwenda! Stop running. Calm down.> September thought.

<What did Mairwen do to Tegan? Why did she do it?>

<She was in my way. She is of no importance.> Malice said from her confinement.

<She is my sister.> Gwenda cried silently. <I love her as I love myself and all my family. How can I carry on if I am responsible for the hurt she has suffered?>

<It wasn't you, Gwenda,> September insisted.

<Mam and Tad don't know that.>

<They will forgive you if you say that you didn't mean to hurt Tegan, that you were unwell.>

<You mean say that I am possessed by a devil.>

<No, not that. Just that you were sick and did not know what you were doing. Now do as Mam said and get to your work.>

<But what if she breaks out again? Mairwen must not hurt my family.>

<She won't.>

<Do not be so confident, twin sister. The spirits of the Malevolence await me.> Malice broke her silence.

<Not here they don't.> September said, but she knew they couldn't remain in Gwenda's sixteenth century home. They had to complete their quest. <But we can't stay here, Gwenda. We've got to meet up with the other Cludydds and take Mairwen's power from her.>

<But that means returning to Gwlad.>

September understood Gwenda's uncertainty. Gwenda no longer had the starstone but September had learned more about the powers the Cemegwr had given her.

<Yes. Again. But I know how it is done now and with the power of the Elixir we can move to the times of each of the Conjunctions.>

<When? How?>

<Tonight. We must climb to Penybryngolau.>

<Mam, Tad, will be watching me after what has happened. They won't let me wander away.>

<When they are asleep, that's when we'll leave.>

<Alright, but keep Mairwen out of my mind. She scares me.>

<Me too but don't worry. I have her now.>

Malice growled her disagreement but could do nothing as September kept her enveloped in folds of compassion. Gwenda walked to the shed where Nona and Bechan still worked at separating the lead ore from the waste. They looked up as Gwenda joined them, but said nothing. Gwenda settled to her task.

September felt Gwenda's fatigue when at last work finished for the day. A number of buckets of ore had been collected and washed ready for sale to the smelter. When a few more were ready Tadcu and one of the girls would load up the cart, hitch the donkey and set off to Machynlleth to make the trade. This evening though, all except for Tegan sat down together outside the shack that was their home and ate supper. Gwenda sat a little apart from her sisters and concentrated on spooning the food from her bowl into her mouth. September tasted parsnip, cabbage, beans and small strips of a tough meat which she suspected was mutton. No potatoes of course, this was Tudor times. Nothing was said about the incident as Tegan still had not regained consciousness. Mam had given her a herbal potion to make her sleep and pressed other herbs on her injury to ease the swelling. She was satisfied that Tegan was now resting normally.

By the time the meal was over the Sun had sunk below the western horizon and the family were ready to retire. Mam and Tad climbed into the enclosed bed at one end of the single room and Tadcu lay on his wooden framed bed with a wool-filled mattress resting on leather straps. The seven children each settled onto the thin reed mattresses laid on the earth floor. Gwenda positioned herself nearest the door, curled up and acted as if she was quickly drifting into sleep. Soon she was surrounded by softly snoring bodies.

September listened to the sounds for some time before she urged Gwenda to move.

<Now. Let's go but be quiet. We don't want to wake anyone.>

Gwenda yawned and complained that she needed rest. Malice stirred but could not escape from September's grasp. Gwenda rolled onto her knees, stood up and took slow, careful steps to the door. When she pulled it open there was a creak which September thought was loud enough to wake anyone, but no-one stirred. Gwenda slipped through the gap and hurried across the yard. It was very dark as the Moon had not yet risen but Gwenda knew her way. She followed the stream along the valley for a few hundred metres. She slowed down, examining the ground carefully. In the starlight the path she was looking for appeared as a light grey strip against the darker grass of the hillside. Gwenda turned onto the path and soon she was climbing up the incline towards the ridge. September thought it was the same track as she had taken to Penybryngolau almost five hundred years in the future.

Gwenda reached the ridge as the almost full Moon appeared on the eastern horizon.

<Where do I go now?> she asked.

<Go up to the highest point where the Roman camp was. Do you know it?>

<The ancient fort? Yes, of course.> She set off along what looked to be a well-used track. September searched Gwenda's memory and found the knowledge that this was the main route between Machynlleth and Llanidloes. The road she had travelled in the brewery van did not exist.

The brow of the hill seemed very much as September remembered it except there was no aerial pointing to the sky. Gwenda stopped beside the straight bank of the fort. It was no higher than it appeared in September's own time.

<What do we do now?> Gwenda asked.

<I just have to think about where I want to go – and when. The power of the Maengolauseren is in me – us – to take us to Gwlad and the Elixir the Cemegwr gave me will take us to the time.> But where and when? She didn't know where on Daear the other Conjunctions had taken place or when. All she knew was that at the Conjunction the seven wanderers of the heavens lined up. None of them had been on Gwlad at the Second Conjunction but the Malevolence was there and Mairwen carried within her all the knowledge of the Evil, submerged though it was in the hate. The Malevolence waited beyond the sphere of stars for the Sun and Moon and planets to move into position. It was an event that took place regularly in the clock-work like cosmology at the centre of which sat the immobile Daear.

<Mairwen. You know when the Conjunctions happen.>

<I do?>

<Yes. Gwenda was at the first, at the start of the universe. Think about the time of the second.>

<How?>

<It's there in your mind. Your connection to the Malevolence.>

<Ahh.> Malice thought, beginning to recall memories she

never knew that she had. They spilled into September's consciousness. They were horrifyingly familiar. Swarms of evil spirits embodied as manifestations destroying villages, people, farms, livestock, forest, grassland, lakes, rivers. Overhead the planets and the stars moved in their orbits. Darkness was descending from above the stars. And then the figure of a young woman in radiant blue appeared, holding the glowing starstone above her head. An explosion of light erupted from the stone but froze as if a film had been paused.

<There, that's it. One of them anyway.> September signalled to Mairwen. <Hold onto that memory. That's when we're going.>

"Gwenda? What are you doing climbing up here at night?" The boy's voice carried in the cool night-time air.

<It's Pedr. What is he doing?> Gwenda thought.

<He must have heard us leave and followed us.> September reasoned.

<He'll stop us from leaving.>

<There is still time. He is still some distance away.>

<What will happen to him?>

<I don't know. Perhaps he will see the lights the hill is named after.>

<What do I do?> Gwenda asked.

<Stand still. Close your eyes. I have to visualise the Conjunction,> September said. Her view of the stars disappeared, replaced in her imagination by planets revolving in order around Daear. Moon, Mercury, Venus, Sun, Mars, Jupiter, Saturn. She saw each move into position forming a straight line. She felt the exhilaration from Mairwen as she shared the memory of the black cloud of the Malevolence streaming through the sphere of stars towards Daear on the opposite side to the assembled planets.

Gwenda was buffeted by a gust of wind. A tornado span her around lifting her onto tiptoe. She opened her eyes and saw the stars above her spiralling down to her. The swirling starlight reached down to the Earth and snatched her up.

"Gwenda! What's happening?" Pedr's cry was almost lost in the roar of the hurricane.

Gwenda, September and Mairwen turned around and around each other in a cone of rainbow light. September felt nothing but dizziness, her feet and hands and body were free of contact with anything. Still though she kept her mind fixed on that recurring union of the planets and Mairwen's recollection of the Cludydd o Maengolauseren.

26

"I am coming," Mairwen shouted as she fell through the deluge of light. "I will be with you again."

She saw the torrent of spirits of the Malevolence wailing and screaming hate as they poured from beyond the stars. Together they would dominate and destroy Gwlad and all that lived in it. She would see men and women torn apart by the talons of Adarllwchgwin and Coblynau; burned by the flames of Draig tân and Cwn annwn and the acid of Tylwyth teg; crushed by Ceffyl dwr and Pwca; poisoned by Llamhigwyn y dwr and Cyhyraeth and turned to dust by Gwyllian. Once again she would have power.

Yet, she knew she was not free. She was still held by Gwenda and September and they would not let her go. Her manifestations would rid her of those bonds and she would be Malice once again. But, that would mean losing the memories and feelings of the Cludydds.

Mairwen felt a strange fondness for the thoughts she had experienced first with September and then with Gwenda too. Their love and compassion had revealed a pleasure that had been denied her. Death and destruction never gave such lasting satisfaction and she had always needed more to assuage her hunger. Could it be that the Malevolence could not provide all that she required?

<h1 style="text-align:center">27</h1>

Her feet slipped on uneven rock. She opened her eyes and it occurred to her that she was in charge of her own body again. She stumbled, regained her balance, looked around. Once again she was clothed in blue light. Beside her were the figures of Gwenda and Malice looking as disorientated as her. It was dusk, almost night and the three of them were standing on a rocky promontory. Below them, in the fading light she could just make out jagged rocks and beyond, the pale foam of waves. The sound of the crashing breakers came to her from three sides. To her right there was a faint and diminishing orange glow on the horizon. A few wispy cirrus clouds reflected the red light of the setting Sun. Ahead and to her left, the east, the sky was dark. Above there was some cloud but a largely clear sky through which a myriad stars shone.

"Where are we?" Gwenda asked.

The air felt very hot, even the soft breeze off the sea was warm. September thought she could guess their location.

"I think we must be at the southern tip of Gwlad, beyond the desert. The ocean is on all sides."

"Where is the Cludydd?" Gwenda asked again. "If this is where the Malevolence is descending then surely she should be here."

"Perhaps we're early. The Sun has only just gone down." September imagined the Moon slipping into line with the Sun and the other five planets causing an eclipse. With all seven heavenly bodies lined up on the other side of the world, the Land was exposed to the evil from above the stars. She felt the start of an irritation in her hip. She wasn't surprised. She looked up. "It is starting. Look!"

Directly overhead there was a patch of dark ringed by the light of stars that had been pushed apart. The dark was growing perceptibly.

"My servants are coming," Malice shouted and pointed out to sea. In the growing darkness all September could make out was what seemed to be a huge wave stretching from east to west. It was a little paler than the surrounding ocean but above it was a dark cloud that moved towards the coast at the same pace as the wave. September stood for what felt like minutes watching the wave and cloud approach until it was close enough to make out what it really was.

The wave was made up of hundreds, thousands perhaps, of giant winged horses and the cloud, a similar horde of gigantic birds.

"Ceffyl dwr and Adarllwchgwin," Gwenda cried.

"They come to me!" Malice stretched out her arms in welcome.

"No!" September leapt on Malice pulling down her arms and folding her own around her. Her hip burned the warning of impending evil. Malice screamed and wriggled.

"What are you doing?" Gwenda shouted.

"We must not let Malice make contact with the Malevolence."

"What can we do?"

September struggled to hold Malice tight while she thought. They needed to shield Malice from the spirits and manifestations of the Evil. Shielding. That was one of the purposes of lead, plwm, here on Gwlad. "Think sadness," she said, distracted by the pain in her hip that was spreading up her back.

"What?"

"We must bind Malice in lead to shield her."

"Oh, yes."

"I'm sorry we have to do this Mairwen. I'm really sad about it."

Thick ropes of grey metal coiled around Malice from her feet to her head until she was wrapped like a mummy. Malice's cries were muffled and she struggled but the metal bonds meant that there was no movement from her. September laid her gently on the ground.

"It's getting close," Gwenda said pointing up into the sky. The circle of blackness had grown to cover a quarter of the sky and a twisted cone of dark was reaching down through the air.

"Where is she?" Gwenda asked again.

"I don't know, but we must do something about them," September cried, pointing to the approaching army of water horses and giant eagles now only a few hundred metres off-shore. Her body burned. A deep, deafening roar came from behind them. September turned her head to see a giant lumbering towards them across the isthmus. Its bearded head was thirty metres above the ground on a stooping hairy body. In its right hand it brandished a tree trunk roughly carved into a club and on every other huge step it let out its cry.

"What is it?" Gwenda asked.

"It must be a Pwca," September said recalling the many forms the shape-shifting water manifestations could adopt. "And look, there are more." She pointed to the cliff face below them where Coblynau were emerging from caves they had dug. The dwarf like creatures started to climb towards them, grasping at rocks and flinging them into the sea.

"Do we still have the power of the starstone?" Gwenda said looking from one set of attackers to another with fear in her eyes.

"Yes. It's in us." September raised her right arm. Gwenda joined her and took September's hand in hers.

In unison they shouted, "Be gone! Ymadaelwch!" From their joined hands emerged a double cone of brilliant violet light. It spread out to the south over the ocean until it reached the advancing line of horses and birds. The first creatures it touched exploded in a fountain of water or vapour. The destruction spread along the line both east and west as each Ceffyl dwr and Adarlwchgwin were reduced to their base elements.   The second cone of light spread northwards blasting a hole in the giant Pwca's chest. It imploded in a deluge of green water with a final cry that became the roar of a tumbling torrent that poured over the sides of the headland. The edges of the cones of light caught the climbing Coblynau. They crumbled into dust. Thunder rolled across the sea and land to September and Gwenda.

In moments the attackers were gone but still above them the circle of dark grew.

"Look!" Gwenda pointed into the sky a little behind where

they stood. A solitary seagull was approaching, circling, as if deciding where to land. It swooped down towards them. They could see that it was no ordinary seabird. It was much larger than a normal gull and even in the dim light its plumage glowed violet. For a moment it hovered beside them, then its feet touched the rock and it folded its wings. The bird transformed. A white haired, violet clothed young woman stood before them, a likeness of September and Gwenda.

"Who are you?" the arrival asked. Her face showed confusion.

"We are here to help you," September said, "but you have a task to carry out. The Malevolence is approaching." She pointed to the sky where darkness, blacker than any black stretched across half the sky and reached down towards them like a huge dark tornado.

"What do I do?" the terrified young woman said.

"You know what to do. You are the Cludydd o Maengolauseren." September surprised herself in speaking with an authority she had not felt before. "You have learned the skills of the cludydds and you have the starstone in your hand. It will do what it does."

"Yes, that is what I have been told, but I wasn't expecting others to be here that looked like me."

"We can explain later. What is your name? The name you are known by in your home."

"It's Dilwen."

"Well, Dilwen, the moment has come when you must do the task you were brought here for. We'll support you."

Dilwen looked uncertainly from September to Gwenda and the bound figure of Malice lying on the ground. September stooped and hauled Malice upright. She put her right arm around the immobile body and took Gwenda's hand in her left. Gwenda grasped Dilwen's left hand.

"Go on. Do it. It's time," Gwenda urged.

Dilwen raised her right hand holding the Maengolauseren and looked up into the darkness descending upon them. The screaming of the millions of spirits coming down out of the charcoal blackness filled September's head. Dilwen shook and began to shout at the spirits of evil. A blue glow formed in the stone which brightened until it was like a beacon.

Dilwen's screams grew louder and her body stiffened as she poured out her fear of the Malevolence. The violet beam spread out from the stone in a vertical column that reached up to the ebony cloud that fell towards them.

September stared but the light was so bright it hurt her eyes. Her whole body hurt. She felt Gwenda's grip on her hand tighten. The column of light stretched upwards and expanded. The cacophony of the spirits grew louder.

Light and dark met. The sky and the land shuddered and then an explosion of illumination engulfed September and her companions. She held on to Malice and grasped Gwenda's hand more tightly still as she and they were spun in a whirlwind of violet light. *Where next?* she thought as the dizziness became nausea. *The next conjunction?*

She couldn't breathe. There was a weight on top of her. It shifted, rolled off, groaned. It was another Cludydd, Gwenda or Dilwen, she couldn't tell which. September realised she was lying on the bound form of Malice. She scrambled to her feet. It was still dark but the air was cool and fresh. The burning in her skin had reduced to a faint irritation in her birthmark. There was soft grass beneath her feet and tall trees formed a palisade around a clearing about fifty metres across with the stars shining overhead. Another Cludydd was getting up from the ground. September couldn't tell one from the other as they looked identical and just like her.

"Where are we?" the one who had rolled off September asked.

"Gwenda?"

"Yes."

"I think we may be in Coedwig Fawr."

"What happened? Why are we here?" The third Cludydd, Dilwen, looked around with a lost expression on her face lit up by her glowing clothing.

"You defeated the Malevolence. You must have as this wouldn't exist if you hadn't," September said, waving a hand at the surrounding forest. "If you are the second Cludydd, Dilwen, this should be the time of the third conjunction. Look." She pointed to the patch of sky visible above the trees. A circle of stars was being pushed aside.

"The Evil is coming again," Gwenda said.

There was a rustling and crashing amongst the trees. Something was approaching, a large creature. It burst into the clearing, a large bear with fur a shimmering violet-black.

"What is it? A Pwca?" Dilwen raised her hand to fire a bolt from the Maengolauseren but then discovered it wasn't in her hand.

"No!" September cried to prevent Dilwen from attacking the creature. "It's the third Cludydd." As she spoke the bear transformed into yet another image of herself and her companions.

"Who are you?" The new arrival looked to each of them in turn with a perplexed expression.

"We are like you, bearers of the starstone, or we were," September explained as she stepped forward to greet the third Cludydd. "What is your name?"

"It is Wenhaf. But I don't understand. I thought I would be alone in opposing the Malevolence."

"You are right. It is your task to push it back above the stars, and the time is nearly upon us. There." September pointed upwards to the growing darkness and the descending chorus of black spirits.

"Why are you here then?"

"To help you and join with you."

Barking and baying of hounds interrupted the conversation. All four Cludydds turned to see flaming Cwn annwn emerging from the forest.

"We'll deal with them." September raised her hand. "You get ready for your task." She fired off a bolt of violet light at one of the fiery dogs, dissipating it in a ball of fire. Gwenda and Dilwen joined her. The fiery dogs erupted in flame in all directions. For a moment the clearing was as dark as before then from between the trees came the hissing of Tylwyth teg. The thin, grey fairies crept towards them spitting acid. Again the three Cludyddau fired their violet lightning and the creatures disintegrated into dust.

Wenhaf had reached the centre of the clearing where there was a low mound. She stood on it and raised up her hand bearing the stone which was already gleaming. September gathered up Malice and dragged her to join Wenhaf. Gwenda and Dilwen took each other's hands, linked with September and held Wenhaf's spare hand.

The darkness was already descending below the top of the trees and Wenhaf was screaming at the evil spirits as the familiar column of light grew from the starstone. September prepared herself for the coming disorientation and fall. Where would they go next?

The explosion of light came with unexpected swiftness and all five of them were scooped off their feet.

Water lapped against her body and she felt soft, shifting sand beneath her. She sat up. In the starlit night she could see that she was on a beach. She stood up. The beach was a small sandy island. All around was water flowing passed similar sandbars as far as could be seen in the starlight. Malice lay in the shallow water and the other three Cludydds were hauling themselves to their feet.

"Are we at the fourth one now?" one Cludydd that must have been Gwenda said.

"This looks like where one of the great rivers reaches the eastern ocean," another said.

"What happened?" said the last, who September guessed was Wenhaf.

"Look!" September stuck out her finger. The others looked where she pointed. From the flow of water around them she was looking landward. Towards them, coming across the water were shadowy shapes. Green glowing eyes in frog-like heads with batwings and scorpion tails.

"Llamhigwyn y dwr." A Cludydd identified the dozen or so creatures.

"Yes," September called, "and do you see? Ahead of them, in the water. They're chasing something."

"It looks like a whale," another said. The whale swam over the surface with its violet-black fin cutting through the water.

"It's the Cludydd," September cried. "We must defend her. The creatures are almost on her."

She raised her hand and sent a beam of violet light to the first manifestation. It exploded in a torrent. The others joined her and flash after flash of light transformed the creatures into fountains of dark water. The whale reached the shallows and transformed into a radiant young woman, the fourth Cludydd. She strode towards them.

"I don't understand. You look like me and you destroy manifestations of the Malevolence, but who are you?"

"There's no time to explain." September offered her hand to the Cludydd to pull her on to the dry sand. "What is your name?"

"It is Rhiainwen."

The name gave September a start. Of course, the fourth Cludydd was the first of which she had already found the name, the forbear whose grave she had visited at Llelluched. There was so much she wanted to ask Rhiainwen and her earlier ancestors, but there was no chance to pause for conversation.

"It is time for you to perform your task," she said.

"Yes, tonight it is the time of the Cysylltiad and I am to defend Gwlad from the Adwyth."

"It's coming." One of the others pointed to the sky. Already a quarter of the night sky had been engulfed in darkness, the stars pushed to the edge of a circle of black. Rhiainwen hurried to the highest point on the tiny sandy island, stood erect and raised her right hand with the shining stars-stone. The others formed a line hand-in hand, with September at the end clutching the motionless, lead-bound form of Malice. She watched Rhiainwen repeat what Gwenda, Dilwen and Wenhaf had done before but which she had failed to do on her first attempt. The descending horde of the evil spirits met the rising tower of light given off by the Maengolauseren. September thought she would be ready this time for the explosion but she wasn't. She found herself flung off her feet, spinning around and falling.

Falling, hitting ground, rolling, striking something hard – rock; stopping at last. September opened her eyes, stunned and sore. She was on a mountainside with clumps of spiny grass amongst rocks. She sat up. It was dark. Of course it was. This would be the next Conjunction, the fifth. The others were scattered over the peak each slowly picking themselves up and rubbing various parts of their bodies. Only Malice, bundled in her grey rope, lay immobile. September lifted Malice up and hauled her, limping, to the summit. The others joined her.

"Where are we?" was said by more than one. The place seemed familiar to September. They were on a mountain peak and although there was a cold wind blowing into her face there was no snow. There were other peaks around them but none higher. Not the Mynydd Tywyll, she thought, more like the Bryn am Seren where the Arsyllfa had been located. Except that mountain had a flat summit on which the observatory-cum-fortress was built. Of course, it came clear to her; Heulyn, the Mordeyrn at the Sixth Conjunction, must have chosen the location of the previous victory over the Malevolence for his place to prepare for the seventh.

Above them the clear sky revealed a hemisphere of stars, but September easily picked out the spot from which the Malevolence would enter the universe. Already a small patch of sky had become a black hole. Nearby was another noticeable spot, this one bright. As she stared it became a disc developing a tail.

"Draig tân!" someone called before September had a chance. The fiery comet grew and roared through the atmosphere towards the mountain top.

Where was the fifth Cludydd? The answer popped into September's mind from the depths of her memory. She knew who the fifth Cludydd was. She recalled the conversations with Gran and Uncle Emlyn. They seemed so long ago now and literally in a different time and universe. The fifth bearer of the stone was her great-grandmother, Eirawen, born in Swansea.

"She's coming. The Cludydd's coming," someone called. September looked around and saw one of her companions pointing to the sky. A great dark bird with iridescent violet plumage was approaching, but so was the Draig tân. A Cludydd, September did not recognise who it was, raised her hand and a cone of violet shot out spreading to engulf the descending comet. It exploded into a fireball with a deafening clap of thunder and then was gone.

The bird swooped towards them and as its talons grabbed at an outcrop it changed into a figure that resembled the others. Here we go again, thought September, no time to explain but at least I can greet her.

"Hello Eirawen."

The woman stepped back in surprise.

"You know my name. Do I know you? You look like me." She looked at the four young women standing together. "You all look the same."

"We are all the Cludydd as you are, Eirawen," September said. "The others are your ancestors from Llelluched."

"I know that place. My mother moved from there before I was born when the mines failed."

"That's right."

"But who are you? You look like the others."

"I am your great-grand-daughter, the seventh Cludydd."

Amazement passed across Eirawen's face, "My great-grandchild?"

"The Evil comes!" The cry came from September's side. She glanced up and saw that the darkness had spread across half the sky and the spirits were descending in a screaming mass.

"We cannot talk now," September cried and pushed Eirawen to the summit. "You must complete your task."

"Yes, yes!" Eirawen looked up into the sky and raised her right hand. The stone was there burning brightly. One of the others took her left hand and the rest linked hands. Once again September hauled Malice to her side and grasped the hand of the Cludydd next to her. As they waited for the expected outpouring of light, a memory came to September. The next destination would be the desert where she had finally defeated the Malevolence and where Mother, the sixth Cludydd, had achieved her success. But it wasn't the image of Breuddwyd, as the young Cludydd that filled her mind but a memory of Mother at home with her family, looking after her, listening to her worries. Homesickness and desire for that old humdrum existence filled her. The explosion of light surprised her but the nausea from falling was becoming familiar.

28

The bonds of lead burned her as if they were made of fire. They were. The elements of this universe, earth, air, water and fire, of which, in certain proportions, all materials were made, were inimical to her, a creature of the darkness and an aspect of the Evil. She struggled and screamed to no effect. Her twin had bound her too efficiently.

As through a thick wall she heard the spirits of the Malevolence descending but her cries failed to pass through her binding to the spirits. They did not know she even existed. They came to wreak their individual vengeance on those who had life but could not respond to her unifying and directing powers. She was cut-off, alone with her hatred.

There was a dislocation, a falling, a thud of a landing which the lead ropes at least protected her from; more screeching spirits and another moment of disruption. The same events repeated twice more, and then…

The bindings were gone but her freedom was not restored. Again she found herself in the recesses of another's mind without sense of the environment in which she existed but this time she was not alone. She was surrounded, merged with, absorbed by, six other identities. She knew them all from their memories which she shared.

Gwenda, Dilwen, Wenhaf, Rhiainwen, Eirawen and September. Their thoughts and feelings bombarded her. She re-lived their experiences. The struggle for a living as a mining family. The knowledge of rocks, of ores, of processes for separating the two. These ideas ran through the core of four of the personalities. All had experienced love and rivalry as the youngest of seven siblings, the care of parents and grandparents. These were all unknown concepts to Mairwen but they intrigued her, drew her. Yet still hate infused her. Domination and destruction were her right.

29

Moist, thick grass cushioned her. Her shoulder rested against something hard, straight and vertical. A cold, damp breeze made her shiver. This wasn't the great desert, not even at night. Her head seemed full of confusion. She had trouble thinking, concentrating, being herself.

September opened her eyes. There was no-one else with her and she lay on the ground at the top of a hill on a dark night with clouds scudding across the stars. The steel supports of a fence pressed into her back. She was clothed not in glowing blue but in her dull jeans and anorak which were getting wetter by the moment. Now she knew where and when she was – Penybryngolau in her own time. What had gone wrong? Why weren't they all in the desert waiting for Breuddwyd to dispatch the Malevolence for the sixth time? That was the event she had been thinking of – wasn't it?

For a moment the absence of the sounds of battle gave her some rest. There was just the murmur of the wind in her ears. She was exhausted by the sequence of battles against manifestations, the stand of each successive Cludydd against the Malevolence and the jump to one Conjunction after another. Her heart thudded in her chest as the excitement of the five encounters drained from her.

What was she doing? In leaping from one encounter to another, meeting her ancestors, she had forgotten her purpose. Oh, yes, that was it – she was gathering the other Cludyddau so that Mairwen/Malice could be subdued once and for all and her skills, whatever they were, added to her own. Why would she want to adopt Malice's hate and her control of the spirits of evil? Because the Cemegwr wanted her to do it, the same Cemegwr who had killed Mairwen and exiled her to the Malevolence in the first place. Why should she obey their wishes? Because she couldn't think of any other way to stop Malice taking over her mind and body and continuing on her crusade of destruction. September sighed. She had no choice but to go on and complete the assembly of all the Cludyddau while Malice was bound in ropes of sorrow.

Where was Malice? Where were the other Cludyddau, all five of them? She looked around her. Even in the dark she could see that she was alone. Had Malice escaped? Her heart thumped in her chest. Surely Malice wasn't free to carry out her promise to destroy everything?

She remembered. This was her own universe, not that of Daear, Gwlad and the power of the seven metals. There was no place here for those Cludyddau who had lived and died in the past. Not one of them, Malice included, existed as an individual in this time and place. Then she realised that the moaning in her ears wasn't just the air blowing over the hilltop, rustling the grass and vibrating the mast behind her head; it was a chattering of silent voices speaking unintelligibly all at once. The chattering was in her head. Not only Mairwen and Gwenda but now the other four occupied her too. Each was dismayed and disorientated to find themselves thrown together in one body. She felt dizzy.

"September? Is that you?" Mother's voice. Not in her head but a real shout through the night air. Mother! That was who she had been thinking of when the transport occurred, not Breuddwyd the sixth Cludydd at her desert meeting with the Malevolence, but her own homely, mother. Subconsciously she had brought herself here in her own time to meet her rather than at the sixth Conjunction. She hauled herself to her feet, unsteady as the others struggled to take control in her head. Out of the darkness Breuddwyd approached along the path from Llelluched waving a dim torch in front of her.

"Yes, I'm here." September waved and stumbled to meet her. She fell into her mother's outstretched arms. They hugged. "What are you doing here?"

"I came to ask you the same thing!" Breuddwyd extricated herself from September's embrace and cast the torchlight up and down her, checking her for injury.

Though her mind was filled with the questions and arguments of the other six individuals in her head, September was driven to explain herself.

"I had to come here to find a way of controlling Mairwen and discover how it all started. The other Cludydds, the starstone, everything. To see if I could get back and find out if the Land survived."

Mother nodded. She spoke soothingly, "I thought that was the reason why you left. We spent last night searching for you at home but then I thought about why you would have gone away. I spoke to Emlyn and he mentioned this place. I know it's where we come from. Have you found anything?"

"Yes, but there isn't time to explain." September took her mother's hand in hers and tried to drag her the few metres to the top of the ridge.

Breuddwyd resisted, refusing to move. She shone the torch in September's face. "What do you mean 'no time'? Are you alright, Em? You must be wet through. Are you cold?"

"I'm okay. We've got to go." September tugged on Breudwyd's hand and they stumbled a few paces towards the summit.

"I saw lights as I climbed the hill. Was it lightning?"

"You know what it was." September was impatient and Mother wasn't helping. "I need you. We need you."

"We?" Breuddwyd refused to move another step.

September didn't answer but wrapped both arms around her mother. Where should she go to now that all seven Cludydds were together? There was no longer any need to go to Breuddwyd's meeting with the Malevolence, but she knew the answer. Back to where this quest began, the centre of Daear, of course. Keeping a firm grip on Breuddwyd she raised her right hand to the sky. Ribbons of light of all colours of the spectrum wrapped around them. The hillside was obscured. Mother screamed.

They formed a seven-membered ring, each hand in a neighbour's. All of them clothed in luminescent blue with long white hair, identical in features. She could not tell the identity of the owners of the hands she held, could not decide which of the circle was Mother or Gwenda or each of the other Cludydds. The ring enclosed Malice, clothed in black that defied the light, but otherwise with the same appearance.

She crouched, her face showing confusion, fear, trepidation. The circle danced in the white space that September had experienced before, the core of Daear, the centre of the universe.

"Your task is nearly complete." The voice of the Cemegwr was familiar but the woman did not appear. The words came from the whiteness that surrounded them.

"We're all here. All the Cludydds and Mairwen." As September spoke she felt her fellow Cludydds thinking the same thought.

"So I see. Eight personalities, one line."

"Yes, but we're still all separate even though we look the same."

"You are on the verge of dissolution, in a metastable state, all but ready to tip over. The Toddfa Penbaladr needs one final push, an initiator, a catalyst of change."

"What do you mean? What is it? Where is it?"

"Do not fear. You do not have another quest. I am it. The Dechreuwr."

"You will join with us?"

"No, I will be unchanged. It is you that will be transformed."

September was apprehensive. "What will happen to us?"

"The eight will become one. One mind, one identity, one destiny."

September was confused. "How can we become one? Each of the seven of us had separate lives in our own times. We're all descended from each other, from Gwenda at LLelluched."

"Each individual will live on in their own time and place. The fabric of your universe will not be disturbed."

"You mean we'll just carry on our lives as if none of this happened?"

"All the Cludydds' powers and those of Malice will be channelled into the One."

She didn't comprehend. Would she be plain old September, plodding along at school, coping with puberty, upset by her flab, ridiculed by the bullies, or would she retain the confidence, the assurance, the control and all the skills she had learned as Cludydd?

"All will be understood. Now begin." The Cemegwr's

voice came from all around, inside, through her. Her circle began to move. Stirred by a subconscious desire to dance, her feet skipped as though they had no contact with a floor. All seven responded to the same hidden urge to rotate while Malice remained frozen at the centre, fear etched into her face. With their hands linked, the seven moved faster and faster. Her fellow dancers flickered in front of her eyes like the pictures in one of those rotating cylinders that produced moving images. Faster still they turned till each was a blur of blue with the fixed black of Malice at the centre. As she revolved she and the others began to tumble head over heels, arms and legs entwining, mingling; she did not know which limbs were hers and which belonged to her fellow Cludyddau. They were beginning to mix.

Lights exploded in the uniform whiteness, red and blue, orange and green, yellow. She heard noises, explosions, snatches of music, drum beats. There were smells, flowery perfumes, rancid odours, fruits and on her tongue, sweetness, salt, bitterness. Then there was heat, and cold, the absence of heat, all temperatures from Siberian frost to Saharan scorching, wetness, dryness, roughness, smoothness, pressure. Her skin tingled.

All the sensations filled her and swirled around her. Was she still in her circle? Did she still have a body? She couldn't answer. Memories flickered through her mind. Childhood, growing up, Mother, Father, April, May, June, Julie, Gus, Gran, aunts, uncles, friends, bullies. Schooldays, holidays, birthdays, special occasions and everyday routines. Then other memories not previously her own but now possessed by her. Gwenda's Tad and Mam and Tadcu and brothers and sisters working at the mine, hauling and sorting the rock; King Henry's men collecting ore. Dilwen and her family working in a similar fashion, Royalist and Roundhead armies sweeping through the valley. A waterwheel turning, Wenhaf labouring with more people around her and the heaps of rock higher than ever. Rhiainwen in a valley filled with mineshafts and dressing sheds, smoke from a multitude of chimneys filling the sky, hundreds of toiling workers. Eirawen sitting in front of the range, knitting, and beyond grimy windows, the streets of terraced houses in the city of Copperopolis.

Breuddwyd, with a young man. Father? No, someone else. And darkness, hateful, screaming spirits and manifestations obeying her commands. Planets and stars in their orbits, sunrise, sunset, people wielding the power of metals against the servants of the Malevolence. Aurddolen, Tudfwlch, Sieffre, Berddig, Eluned, cludyddau of all seven metals, the people she and the others had known in the Land across the ages from one Conjunction to the next.

She was in the images, seeing, hearing, touching, smelling, tasting. Faster and faster they flashed past. Times and personalities blurred, merged until all became…

Calm. She was neither too hot nor too cold. Sweet, woodland smells filled her nostrils, with birds singing and insects humming. A short distance away was the sound of water flowing in a stream. Soft, springy moss supported her. There was light beyond her closed eyelids, dappled sunlight, not too bright.

She opened her eyes. Ancient woodland surrounded her, leaves falling gently to the ground in a gentle breeze. There was peace inside her, no other personalities fighting for supremacy to commit evil deeds or to recapture their identity. She was herself. Or was she? Her memories as September seemed uppermost but alongside them were those of the lives of Breuddwyd, Eirawen, Rhiainwen, Wenhaf, Dilwen, Gwenda up until and including their period in Gwlad. There too was the recollection of the long death of Mairwen and her brief time directing the Malevolence. The memories were there as if they were her own but the voices of their owners in her head were gone. She was one person but with the lifetimes of the others stored within her. She was September still but with aspects of the others combined. What more had she gained from the other Cludydds and from Malice? There seemed no way to find out until her skills were tested.

September got to her feet and looked down at herself. Her body was still clothed in blue light. She was still here in Gwlad then. What next? The question need not be asked; she knew the answer. There was something else in her. Not a memory or skill from the merged Cludyddau or Malice. She had a purpose that she knew had come from the Cemegwr.

The Dechreuwr had said she would not leave part of herself in September but in initiating the transformation had set her on a new path – her destiny. It spoke, not as a voice but as a conviction within herself: to oppose the Malevolence wherever it could be found, starting here on Daear. Allied with that task was her desire to secure the future of this universe; its rebirth. She felt the determination inside herself but she worried that she had become just a tool of the Cemegwr. Would she ever again feel able to do what she herself wanted?

It was time to find out. The Cemegwr had sent her here: to the woodland on the banks of the Afon Deheuol, in the vicinity of Amaethaderyn. That she deduced from the knowledge of seven visitors to the Land. The village would be a short journey through the wood. The Cemegwr must want her to visit the village again. She would see Berddig and Eluned and then commence her battle to secure the welfare of Gwlad. First she had to travel.

She marvelled at the wonders that had occurred – the principle of arianbyw. She became a panther and set off between the trees.

Running, weaving amongst the ancient trees, she soon reached the bank of the great river. The waters flowed by sluggishly. She turned to the left, instinctively knowing the direction of her destination. Her galloping paws covered the distance in little time. Soon she emerged into a clearing with a few of the familiar round, reed-roofed huts. She stopped and changed into her human form. The village was silent, no hammering of metal, no sawing of wood, no voices. She walked around the buildings, glancing into this one or that. They appeared unused, dusty, decaying, some even beginning to tumble down. She moved on. Even though the Sun was well above the treetops there was a coolness in the air that was unfamiliar here towards the tropics. She reached the centre of the village and the meeting place, the open-sided wood pergola. Still no sign of the inhabitants.

"Hello. Is anyone here?" She turned, looking for signs that her call had been heard. There was no response. Until there came a creak of wood rubbing against wood. The door of one of the nearest huts inched open. A bowed head appeared.

"Who is that?"

The voice, shaky though it sounded, was familiar.

"Berddig?" September ran to the speaker. The door was opened wider. A stooped, silver-haired old man stood there leaning on a stick.

"Cludydd?"

"You're older." Disbelief and horror fought for priority in her. Berddig nodded slowly, stood back from the door and invited her in. September entered the dimly lit hut. It was warmer inside, made cosy by the wall hangings and rugs on the earthen floor. There were few pieces of furniture, just a chair, a low bed, and a table. A figure struggled to rise on the bed. Her hair was as white as Berddig's and her face as wrinkled and thin.

"September? You have returned to us."

"Eluned? What has happened to you both? You have aged so much since I last saw you but that wasn't long ago. A lot has happened and I've been lots of places and times but...but..."

"We have lived ten years since we last met, Cludydd." Berddig lowered himself arthritically into the chair with a sigh. "Yet, we have grown a lot older than our years. The world has aged and decayed."

The aging of the universe must still be accelerating, September thought.

"Where are the other villagers?" she asked.

"Dead," Eluned said. "One by one their spirits have all returned to the centre of Daear. Only the two of us are left here in Amaethaderyn."

"How do you manage?" September could not see how two such frail, elderly people could look after themselves.

"We live still," Berddig said. "Though the Land is dying, trees supply sufficient fruit and nuts for the two of us. But we do not have long left. Soon we will join the other cludyddau on the planets."

"No! I will not allow it."

"Ah, you still have the determination of youth," Berddig nodded and smiled. "It brings delightful memories."

"What do you intend?" Eluned coughed.

"I'm going to restore this universe."

"You will have to drive away the Malevolence from above the stars," Berddig said, "before the Evil achieves its victory at last."

"That is what I will do," September clapped her hands together. "I have changed, Berddig, Eluned. I'm not just one of seven Cludydds called to halt the Malevolence at the Conjunctions. Now I have the strength of all of them to oppose Evil wherever it appears." She spoke with more certainty than she felt. Would the power of Malice, the Maengolauseren and the gifts of the Cemegwr be sufficient to throw back the Adwyth from the boundary of the universe and bring life back to the Land?

"We have confidence in you, September." Eluned's voice had reduced to a whisper, "but we feel the Evil closing in as the restraining power of the planets and stars weaken."

Berddig nodded, his face contorted into an unfamiliar sadness.

"But I don't know what I should do," September cried, "I have all these memories and powers but how do I use them?"

"You are disturbed, Cludydd," Berddig said. "We have watched our friends depart one by one and the Land gradually decay while you, I think, have been caught up in a frenzy of change and re-birth. Come sit, rest awhile. Tell us what has happened to you. Perhaps we can help solve your dilemma." Berddig indicated his chair beside the bed.

September felt weary. The frantic transfers from one time and place to another, meetings with the other Cludydds and the Cemegwr had given her no pause or time to contemplate. Perhaps that was why she had come back here – an opportunity to digest all that happened.

"Thank you. I think I will." September sat down in the chair. Berddig walked slowly to a table at the side of the hut, relying on his stick. He filled a wooden cup with liquid from a jug and returned. September watched every movement that betrayed the frailty of the old cludydd. She took the cup offered to her and sipped it. It was tasteless, tepid water. Once more, it quenched a thirst but had none of the revitalising power possessed by the drinks she had been offered on her arrival in Gwlad. It was a reminder of the failing powers of the universe.

Berddig lowered himself onto the side of Eluned's bed. "Now tell us of your adventures, September, since you last visited us."

She described meeting Heulfryn, their visit to the huge volcano, meeting the other Cludydds at their Conjunctions and the dance that had finally united them all.

"So now the Cemegwr have given you another task. To free us from the threat of the Malevolence for all time."

"That's right." September hadn't explained that the universe of Daear had been a simple experiment of the Cemegwr designed to attract the Malevolence, neither had she mentioned their role in providing the Cludydd o Maengolauseren at each Conjunction or that they had killed her sister before she was born thus consigning her to the Malevolence.

"If I can finally remove the Malevolence from the universe, should I do it now?" September recalled what the Cemegwr had told her. The universe was shrinking as it shed energy and the Malevolence waited beyond the sphere of stars until the universe was reduced enough to swallow up. It would be no use defeating the Evil now with the universe so diminished and Gwlad barely able to support life. What could she do?

"I fear that would be of little benefit to us," Berddig said glumly. "The world and everything in it will surely come to an end soon after your victory."

Eluned coughed to clear her throat then spoke with a weak voice. "But you are not limited to now, are you September? You have drunk of the Gwylib Hoedl Gwyrthiol."

September recalled sipping the liquid from Heulfryn's hands – The Elixir of Life. It had given her a sort of immortality – the ability to exist in all times and places. She had moved to the moment of all the Conjunctions; she could move to any time she wished.

"You're right, Eluned," she said.

"So..." Eluned coughed again and continued, "Would it not be better to remove the Malevolence at a time when the universe was young and full of vitality before the hateful spirits began to molest us?"

"You mean before the first Conjunction." September was

excited by Eluned's suggestion.

"Yes," the old woman said with a glint of hope in her eyes.

September began to think about transporting to that time. The thought of stopping the Malevolence before any of the People could be harmed, before any destruction took place – yes, that would be everything she could wish for.

"Ah, I think you should think carefully," Berddig said. "What would happen if you changed the course of our history?"

September gasped. If she defeated the Malevolence before time had effectively begun then there would be no need to call on the Cludyddau at all. Gwenda and the others, herself included, would not be summoned. She would not exist so she couldn't go back to defeat the Malevolence. It was a paradox. Her thoughts went around and around in the never-ending circle. She held her head in her hands.

"It can't be done, Berddig. If I defeat the Malevolence before anything happened then nothing would be the same. I might even not have been born, so I wouldn't be here to fight the Malevolence. It's impossible."

Berddig chuckled. "No, Cludydd. Perhaps destroying the Malevolence at the start of time is not the solution. But there will be other possibilities."

September struggled to think clearly. There must be a way which did not cause such problems with time but it meant that she couldn't protect Gwlad from the Malevolence throughout its existence. She must act after the seven Cludydds had performed their tasks, when the civilisation of Gwlad had developed through seven Conjunctions and its people and customs had evolved through the successive confrontations with the Malevolence. The Land had still been fertile and fruitful at the time of the last, her own, Conjunction. The people had been happy despite the threat from the manifestations. The cludydds had been at the height of their mastery of metals. That was the time. That was when she should be.

"I know what to do," she said.

"What is it?" Berddig asked.

"When Aurddolen summoned me he said my task was to push the Malevolence back above the stars."

"That's right. That's what the Cludydd o Maengolauseren did at each Conjunction," Eluned whispered, lifting her head from her pillow.

"Yes," September agreed, "but he had forgotten that this was the seventh Conjunction and I was the Seventh Cludydd. There were only ever going to be seven. This was the last. I only did part of my task, and only then at the second attempt. I should have stopped the Malevolence then for all time."

"You mean to go back to your victory over Malice and the Malevolence?" Berddig said, his eyes opened wide with wonder.

"Yes. If I am successful I know it will mean changes to what has happened since the Conjunction. I won't let you become like you are now," September said looking from the bent, shrunken form of Berddig to Eluned who had collapsed back on to her mattress.

"This existence will become a forgotten loop of time," Berddig said.

"Yes, but you'll be young again and the Land will be fertile."

"Go, September," Eluned said. "Defeat the Malevolence and give us our youth."

"I will." September closed her eyes, separated herself from the sad, dismal scene and thought about her destination. Night-time, the desert; her second appointment with the Malevolence.

Part 7

~

Destiny

30

The fused sand was warm and hard beneath her feet. The Sun was high in the sky, a dull orange ball. Its rays burned through the sky which was stained brown even here so far from the northern ice where the Malevolence had descended at the Conjunction. But there was no pain in her hip. The spirits of evil were not here yet. She was standing on a hillock, a sand dune turned to glass, looking across the flat, glassy plain. About a hundred metres away there was a figure standing over an object. Even in the daylight the figure glowed blue. Another figure, identical to the first appeared out of the air. The two busied themselves with the object on the ground. A column of flame erupted from it.

September recognised this scene. It was her mother, Breuddwyd and herself preparing the cauldron of metals for the Toddfa Penbaladr, the Alkahest that would blend the metals, herself and Malice into one.

A black figure, Malice, materialised close to the others. She grappled with one of the blue-lit figures; September herself. She felt her muscles and limbs responding involuntarily, trying to copy the remembered fight with Malice. Although she knew the outcome she felt she had to encourage her earlier self. They wrestled over the bowl until streamers of rainbow-coloured light engulfed them and extended in a column up into the sky. It revolved, swelled and grew brighter until it outshone the tropical but muted Sun. September felt a wind caress her skin. It was a breeze at first but rapidly becoming hurricane-force, her long white hair blown out like the vapour from a steam locomotive. Then the spirits began to arrive. Her birthmark itched, the pain spreading across her hip, but the spirits were not attacking her. They screamed their familiar expletives of hate but were swept into the tornado of light and sucked up into the sky.

Spirits came from all points of the compass, drawn from all

across Daear, spiralling into the column of light, obscuring it from sight. Though each was as insubstantial as a wisp of steam, their numbers were so great that they formed a dark mass of swirling cloud over the land. The sunlight disappeared as their dark shadow covered the ground. The gale buffeted September but she stood firm, watching the myriad evil spirits being drawn from the world. She looked up but could not see through the dense cloud to where the spirits were being despatched back beyond the stars. Their wailing filled her ears and forced her to cover them with her hands. Still in her head she heard their cries of hate for everything in this and every universe. Minutes passed and still they came; the tower of light sucking the Evil out of the Land.

At last the cloud began to thin and once again she could see, across the plain, the column of light. There was no one there guarding or tending it. She recalled being pulled skywards clinging on to Malice and then finding herself back home.

The last wisps of the cloud of spirits were being drawn into the luminous pillar. The hateful screams had dwindled to a whisper. It was time for her to move, to follow the Malevolence off Daear. September transformed into the iridescent blue eagle and flew across the plain. She circled the column and as the last spirit disappeared into the light she followed. A force threw her upwards. She tucked in her wings and transformed to her human figure. The coloured lights dazzled her but she knew she had left the planet behind and was soaring towards the stars. Then as if she had been thrown from a brilliantly lit club into a dark street the light disappeared.

She was floating in darkness. Looking 'down' or at least where down usually was, beneath her feet, she saw the sphere of stars that enclosed the seven planets and Daear. Even as she watched, a dark circle in the sphere closed as the stars returned to their appointed places. Once again the worlds within were shielded from the Malevolence. Life in the Land could return to normal. This time she hoped it would last, that the Cemegwr would restore the fertility of Daear. But first she must prevent the Evil from pressing on the universe. The globe of milky light receded. She turned away and looked into darkness.

The dark stretched forever. There was nothing else in this universe other than the small, vulnerable cluster of bodies orbiting Daear and the guardian stars. Nothing except Evil. She felt the hate pressing in on her. The spirits ejected from the world turned on her, their hate redoubled by their defeat. She had been here once before, inexperienced, unknowing, her skills with the seven metals and the starstone fresh and untried. Her fear then had been overwhelming and the hate had almost consumed her. She had fled back inside the sphere of stars, thankful at making her escape and having learned a lesson about the implacable nature of the Malevolence.

Now she was confident. She had fought thousands of manifestations, defeated the Evil in Gwlad, had faced Malice and now had the combined talents and knowledge of all seven Cludydds. Seven times she had experienced the defeat of the Malevolence. She had the power of the metals, seven times seven, as well as the energy of the egwyddorpum in the Maengolauseren. The spirits could come at her in uncountable numbers but she could not be defeated.

Come they did. A wall of hate surrounded her. Her hip burned to the bone. It was a crowd surrounding her shouting 'Hate!', 'Destroy!', 'Betray!'. There had been times at school when the bullies had circled her ridiculing her name, her hair, her fat, screaming abuse at her. Then she had cowered, covering her ears and eyes, trying to shut out their cries. This was infinitely worse. The spirits weren't just calling her names, they didn't even want her dead as they had no concept of life. They wanted her as one of them, all knowledge and memory of love and pleasure and kindness and beauty lost.

She faced them and summoned all the skills she had learned. Thinking of joy in life and sadness at its passing she shielded her body with chainmail of tin and lead. Anger at the Malevolence's evil armed her left hand with an iron sword, as long as her body, that glowed red hot. Love of all the people she knew, and those that she didn't, gave her a copper helmet with a mouthpiece shaped like a trumpet that would broadcast her voice and her thoughts. Compassion for all those harmed by evil provided her with a silver amulet that fortified her body and protected her from all harm. Excitement at the task ahead of her gave her mercury and the ability to move with incredible speed, and hope for success materialised as a golden breastplate that moulded to her curvy chest and shone with yellow light that filled her with energy. There was still fear, fear of her unknown future, fear of failure, but fear made her cautious and fired up the Maengolauseren within her. She felt its power building and she reached out her right hand. She was ready. The spirits' spears of hate rebounded off her metal armour as she prepared for her attack.

"Be gone!" she shouted and her amplified voice resounded across infinity. A sphere of violet light exploded out of her hand and expanded to fill all of the endless space. The spirits of the Malevolence were swept away. She moved through space as a bolt of lightning discharging her beams of starstone light and striking with her scarlet sword. Space around her was emptied of evil.

She stopped, allowed the light to fade and let her sword arm fall to her side. The hurt in her hip faded. It was done. The Malevolence was defeated. Wasn't it?

The mutterings were distant at first but they grew louder as they approached, the same refrain; 'Hate!', 'Destroy!', 'Betray!'. They pressed in on her as numerous as before. September didn't understand.

"I disposed of you. Cleared space of evil. Where have you come from?"

She unleashed her power again, filling the universe with violet light. Again the spirits were blown away but again they returned, restored and as full of hate. Again and again September used her power but the Malevolence returned undefeated, as strong as ever. Her golden breastplate dimmed, her sword lost its fire.

"What can I do?" she said, though no one listened. "How can the Malevolence be destroyed if it survives even the power that I have? How can I complete my task and save Daear?"

The spirits pressed closer. Her hand was raised to send another blast of power against them but she dropped it. What was the point? The spirits of evil could not be destroyed, she realised that now, recalled it being told to her. Her powers could disperse them, drive them from the universe of Daear, but the infinite vastness of the Omniverse provided them with sufficient time, space and energy to re-group and return. She could continue to fight them and throw them back forever but she could not defeat them. The spirits didn't tire, their only thought was her destruction. If she stayed she would be absorbed by the Malevolence if just once she allowed her defences to slip and during eternity she was bound to do that just once. One slip and she would be a mindless being filled with hate. What was she to do? She couldn't go back to Gwlad with her task incomplete nor could she return home defeated. Her eyes closed, she wrapped her arms around herself, emptied her mind of thoughts. Moved.

31

She was… somewhere. Her appearance had changed. The glowing blue covering was gone. Now she was wearing a pale pink, satin dress, with puff sleeves, cinched in at the waist and generous pleats reaching down to her calves. On her feet were matching pink satin slippers. Her dress was one she had worn as a child when she adored princesses. The grass her slippers rested on was a brilliant green and smooth all the way to the very near horizon. It undulated gently but there was a low hill which seemed also to be a house as it had windows. In the other direction was a wood but the trees were wide apart and the same brightly coloured grass filled the gaps between them. All the trees were apparently the same although September could not identify the type. They looked artificial really, lollipop shaped with smooth, uniform brown trunks and branches and oval green leaves, all the same size stuck on the branches at random. The air was warm and carried a sweet scent of candyfloss. Overhead the sky was a rich blue with cotton-wool clouds that looked as though they really were made of cotton-wool. It was all strange and unreal, and so familiar.

In the distance, near the hill that looked like a house she could see some figures moving. They each had bodies in a different bright colour but were ungainly shapes that were not human. September recognised them.

"They're the …"

"Hello."

She looked down at her feet. There was a rabbit with long ears and a big fluffy white bobtail. Its fur was white with black spots which looked to have been all the same size and perfectly circular once upon a time. Now, though the fur was thin in places and fraying as if it had been through a washing machine many times.

"Spotty!" September bent to pick up the rabbit. It had been

years since she'd held him although he was still stuffed in her wardrobe somewhere, along with other relics of her childhood. For a long period in her early life she wouldn't be parted from Spotty. He was her companion, a confidant and guardian against all the terrors that afflicted an infant. The creature she held now was just as soft and floppy as Spotty had always been except that this one held its head up and looked at her with its large black and white eyes.

"That's my name," the rabbit said.

"You can talk."

"Of course."

"But you can't talk. You're a toy."

"Did I talk to you when you were a child?"

"Only in my head."

"Well, there we are."

It felt strange holding a talking sentient animal. September placed the creature back down on the spongy, bladeless, 'grass'.

"Where am I?"

"Ah, now that's an interesting question. You're here."

"But where is here? What is here?"

"Don't you recognise it?"

September looked around.

"Yes. It looks like the sets of all the TV programmes I watched and picture books I read when I was a kid."

"That's what it is."

"A TV set or a picture book?"

"No, it's what you saw as a child. It is in your memory and your imagination."

"It feels real."

"It is."

"But how can it be? It's made up, fiction, designed to entertain toddlers."

"That is true but it doesn't stop it being real for you, here, now."

September sank to the ground and sat with her legs crossed. The rabbit hopped into her lap and gazed into her face.

"I don't understand," September said, "I was fighting the Malevolence and then I'm here in fantasy land."

"You gave up fighting and wanted to get away, but you

didn't specify a destination," Spotty explained in a manner more authoritative than his soft toy appearance suggested. "You were caught in the interstices of the Omniverse, in nothing, if you like. But the Omniverse won't accept nothing. There always has to be something, so this universe has been created out of your memories. Well, some of them."

"I've created a universe?" September's eyes widened in wonder.

"A small one, a pretty simple one, but yes, this is your creation."

"But how can I make a universe?"

"Oh, it's easy. In your home multiverse it happens all the time. Every decision made brings a universe into being."

September fingered the rabbit's ears like she used to when she was little. They were still endearingly soft despite the years and the washes. It was surprisingly comforting.

"But the world doesn't seem to change when that happens. This is amazing, fantastic."

"That's because you are amazing and fantastic. You are a being of the Omniverse now, like me."

"You?"

"Yes, you don't think I'm just a fluffy toy do you?"

"I was wondering."

"I'm a manifestation of the Brain."

"Oh, you're Cyfaill and the Cemegwr."

"They are other aspects of me."

"Why are you here?"

"To help you, of course."

"Ah, I see."

September looked around. There was movement between the trees, creatures with big round eyes and brightly coloured fur, and tusks or horns. She recognised many of them from the books read to her by Mother or Father, or April. They didn't seem to pay her attention.

"So I came here because I wanted to get away from the Malevolence but didn't want to go anywhere else."

"That's right."

"I can stay here?"

"If you wish, for a while."

"Not for ever?"

"I think it will bore you in a relatively short time, September. These are scenes from deep in your memory. You have a fondness for them, and for me, but you have grown out of them now."

"I suppose so."

"And there are two more reasons."

"There are?"

"You have a task to complete."

"You mean defeat the Malevolence so that you can restore Daear?"

"Yes."

"What's the other reason?"

"The Malevolence will attack this universe soon."

Her heart thumped and she looked around anxiously almost expecting Adarllwchgwin or Cwn annwn to appear immediately.

"Evil will come here?"

"I'm afraid so." The rabbit's eyes took on a cartoonish sadness. "You know the Malevolence is everywhere in the Omniverse and attacks all creations. This universe is small and not at all complex. It has no defence against the Evil so the spirits will soon gain access and aim to destroy it."

The innocently gambolling creatures and the paint-box surroundings suddenly appeared forlorn and doomed.

"What can I do?"

"This universe is not important. It is part of your past. You can dissolve it when you leave."

"Where can I go?"

"Back to the universe of the Maengolauseren. To complete your victory."

"Victory? I fought the Malevolence but each time I thought I'd won and got rid of all the evil spirits they returned, as many as them as before."

"That's because you hadn't worked out how the Malevolence can be defeated."

"I thought I had. I expected that blasting it with violet light would do the trick, but it didn't. It wouldn't would it? You said the Malevolence is everywhere in the Omniverse."

"That's right. Ultimately victory is not possible. The Omniverse must contain evil as without it there would not be any good. Across all the universes and multiverses in the Omniverse we have fought to oppose the Malevolence. All we have succeeded in doing is reach a stalemate. Everywhere the Malevolence threatens but we match it, just. But you have given us a new tool."

"I have?"

"Malice. She provides you with the link to the Malevolence. She had the power to direct the spirits to do her bidding."

"But all she wanted to do was destroy anything good or living."

"Yes, that was her nature as a component of the Malevolence, but she is part of you now. You have her powers but not her purpose."

"But if I let her take over she'll destroy everything."

"It is not like when you were first joined. She is not a separate identity anymore. The Toddfa Penbaladr has combined you and the other six Cludydds along with Malice into one person with the skills and knowledge of all. You just have to use those powers."

September considered Spotty's words. She looked within herself. Spotty was right, she did not have the bickering voices in her head or feel a presence trying to submerge her as she had before. Instead she could easily access the memories of Gwenda, Dilwen, Wenhaf, Rhiainwen, Eirawen, Breuddwyd – and Mairwen. She recalled how the other Cludydds had fought the Malevolence seven times with all the powers of the seven metals and the starstone at their disposal. Tentatively she delved into Malice's recollections. She had a glimpse of Malice triumphant at the fall of the Arsyllfa.

Crashing and cries came from the picture-book wood, drawing her back. September looked up and leapt to her feet, tipping the rabbit onto the ground. Trees were swaying, falling. Smoke rose on the horizon and drifted towards her. Creatures fled in all directions.

"What is it?"

"The Malevolence, a manifestation," Spotty called from her feet. "Pick me up, let me see." September leaned and lifted the fluffy creature up in her arms.

"But what manifestations can there be in fairytale land? In my universe."

"There were things you feared even in children's stories. Can you remember what scared you back then?"

"Scared me?" September thought. "Yes. The giant. I never liked the idea of something wanting to eat children like me."

A roar reverberated through the wood. The figure towered over the trees, humanoid with straggly hair and beard and rough-cut clothes which he threatened to burst out of at any moment. A tree torn from its roots was grasped in his right hand and a cow tucked under his left arm shrieked 'Help me!'

"It's him. The Giant," September cried. It reminded her of the re-born Tudfwlch, her friend who she had killed.

"A manifestation created from your own memories," Spotty said.

"I have to destroy it to protect these creatures," September said as a mixed herd of deer, pigs, unicorns and wooden puppets ran passed her. "How do I do it?"

"You know the way," Spotty said. September held out her spare hand. A pink wand with a glittery star on its end appeared in it. September gasped but gripped the wand firmly. She raised it up pointing to the Giant.

"Be gone!" she shouted. The Giant looked surprised for a moment then disappeared in a puff of pink smoke. A rain of sparkling glitter descended to the ground disappearing as it touched the grass. Peace returned to fairyland. The creatures ceased their flight and returned to whatever they had been doing before the arrival of the Giant as if they had no memory of the danger they had been in. A cow with a straw hat on trotted by mooing quietly.

"There. That did it." September dropped the hand that held the wand.

"They'll be back," Spotty said, "the Giant and other wicked characters that you feared."

"They will?" September knew that Spotty was right. The Malevolence never gave up, was never truly defeated, however many times it was beaten back. "This happens everywhere?"

"Yes, every universe is threatened by the Malevolence.

Many have defences such as the sphere of stars and the seven planets that shield Daear except at the Conjunctions. The larger, more complex multiverses withstand the Evil but it infiltrates and destroys from within."

"You mean like home? The bad things that happen are because of the Malevolence?" She recalled being told something about the evil in her own universe.

"Yes," the rabbit said, nodding, "the Malevolence manifests in the evil within the universe."

"If it's everywhere and indestructible, what can I do?"

"As I said before we were interrupted, September, you are different. You are the key, a new and unexpected but nevertheless very welcome, key that maybe will shift the balance in our unending struggle with the Malevolence. Malice gave it direction, could order the actions of the individual spirits that make it up. Malice directed her hate against Gwlad and against you but now you have her powers. You can use them to your, our, purpose."

"Can I stop the evil spirits hating and destroying?"

"No, but you can direct their hate."

"Against what?"

"Themselves."

September looked down at the fluffy rabbit cradled in the crook of her arm. The frown that creased the brow of the creature indicated a determination and an intellect not normally associated with small, furry animals. What would people at home think seeing her discussing the struggle between good and evil with a toy she discarded years ago? That was the thing wasn't it. She wasn't at home, she wasn't with people she knew and she wasn't the person she once was. The diffident, lazy, teenager addicted to cake was gone. Instead she was the person who had existed trapped inside the dim, thoughtless fat-suit that the world saw. She always knew that she could be someone special but had never known how to become it. The moment she had found the intriguing pebble that turned out to be the Maengolauseren had changed all that. She had learned that hidden in her genes were the traits that made her the Cludydd and now after all her experiences she had a new identity. She liked her new self – the quick thinking, the knowledge, the powers – but she now knew that she had left her old existence behind. Maybe she would get back to life at home with Mother and Father and attending school and so on, but the core of her destiny would now be this other self – living in the Omniverse, battling the Malevolence, conversing with Brains and visiting strange and unusual places.

A cackling laugh above her head made her look. The broomstick made a 'swoosh' as it shot through the air over her. September got a glimpse of a crouched creature in black with a pointed hat.

"An evil witch," September cried.

"Another manifestation," Spotty said.

The witch banked above the hill-house and flew back towards her. A loud crash of jaws snapping made her look in the other direction. In the wood was a gigantic crocodile, its jaws dripping seaweed and foul smelling saliva. A tick-tock sound came from within it. September shivered.

"I always hated that crocodile and others. They just seem to kill without any emotion."

"Just like the spirits of the Malevolence. You must act before they destroy all your creations."

The witch approached skimming above the ground. September raised her hand that was still holding the fairy wand. She was going to send the Malevolence the deterring spell when she remembered what Spotty had said. Destroy them and they'll come back but Mairwen/Malice wielded her power by using the manifestations. The wand fell from her hand.

September focussed her eyes on the witch. She looked into the memories she had from Malice; how she had manipulated the destructive urge of hundreds and thousands of spirits. She saw how she channelled her hate. Hate surged through her veins, her skin burned, her nostrils flared.

<Spirit of the Malevolence, listen to me.>

The broomstick stopped in mid-air. The witch looked down at September.

<You are my servant. Direct your hate at my bidding. You will obey me because I am your mistress.> Power filled September. She was the controller, the wielder of this instrument of evil. She could direct it in any way she wished.

The witch nodded her head in acknowledgement.

<Now do what I command. That crocodile is your enemy. It is a hateful thing. Destroy it.>

The witch leaned on her broomstick, turned and accelerated towards the crocodile. The cartoon reptile waddled through the trees snapping its jaws at the terrified creatures that froze in its path. The witch swooped towards the crocodile. She raised her wand and sent a blast of black magic at the gigantic creature. The animal howled in anguish when its side erupted in flame. The witch passed over its head sending a jet of black fire down the length of its body and the long, long tail, but the crocodile raised and twisted its head and its massive jaws crashed together on the witch's legs. The crocodile shook the witch who held on grimly to her stick while firing burst after burst of dark light at the beast. The mortally injured crocodile gave one final mournful roar and disappeared in a cloud of rainbow coloured tinsel and streamers. The witch disappeared too.

September sucked in air, struggling to breathe, her muscles trembling. She wanted to destroy more, turn her powers on the weak and innocent creatures that ran around her. One part of her fought with another though they were both herself. The destruction must stop. The evil was gone. There was no more need for Malice's destructive power she told herself. Gradually control returned. Sweat broke out on her forehead and slowly her cheeks cooled.

"There," Spotty said, "you did it. You persuaded one manifestation to destroy another."

"I feel terrible," September said lowering herself to the ground and setting the rabbit down beside her, "I felt the hate burning inside me and I wanted to destroy that crocodile more than anything else."

"But you controlled it. It wasn't as if you were handing yourself over to Malice. It was you that commanded that witch not Malice or the Malevolence."

"Yes, I see I have that power within me, but what use is it?" Her heart still thumped and her breath came in gasps.

The picture book and children's TV creatures gambolled around her unconcerned by the attacks by the Evil.

"You can set the Malevolence against itself. It has always

been a swarm of individual spirits acting alone but behaving as if there was a common purpose. You must have watched those birds in your world, starlings, which take flight in huge numbers and weave incredible patterns in the sky. They look as if they are moving with one mind but in fact each bird is following its own instincts. The spirits of the Malevolence are the same. All they want to do is destroy. It appears as if the Malevolence is deliberate and controlled but it isn't. At least it wasn't before Malice appeared and exerted her influence over the evil spirits on Daear. Now you can use her power to make the spirits war with each other."

September listened to Spotty's speech with a growing conviction. She had experienced the power of hate. She didn't like it but could see how she could use it to make the Malevolence fight itself.

"A civil war," she said.

"That's right. It won't destroy the Malevolence throughout the Omniverse, but in individual universes it should set the evil against itself and distract it from destroying the good."

"I don't know if I can do it," September said. "The hating was awful. What if it takes over and I become like Malice?"

"That's why you needed the knowledge and powers of the other Cludydds. Their strength and dedication will protect you."

September sat up and gazed around taking another look at the characters and scenes she recalled from her childhood.

"What will happen to this when I go? The Malevolence won't return and turn them all into its servants will they? I can't imagine an evil Bambi."

"It is only your imagination that keeps it in existence. When you leave it will disappear."

"And you, Spotty?"

"Me too, but I'm sure you will meet another aspect of me soon."

She stood up and brushed the creases out of her satin dress.

"I always wanted to be a fairytale princess. I wore a dress like this day after day when I was about four. Now I suppose I've been one."

Spotty bent his head back to look up at her. His ears almost touched the grass. "You're not a princess. You are the queen."

"The Good Queen or the Bad Queen?"

"The Good of course."

There was still doubt in September's mind. Could she trust herself if she gave herself up to Malice's powers? Perhaps she would end up leading the Malevolence instead of setting it at war with itself. She wanted someone with her to hold her hand, pull her back from evil.

"You will return to complete your task?" Spotty said.

"Yes," she said, but first she would collect her guardian.

September closed her eyes and thought of Mother.

32

"I know you need me," Breuddwyd said. "It's alright, Em, you can let me go, now."

September released her arms from around her mother. It was dark and a cold, damp wind blew into her face. They were standing under the aerial on the top of Penybryngolau.

September stared at her. She recalled this moment. What Mother had said had been in reply to something she had said. September remembered saying, "I need you." Then they had gone to the centre of Daear. No time had passed here, in this universe, while they had been away, and they had returned to the positions they had been in when she had performed symudiad, but Mother was reacting as if nothing had happened in that moment.

"What was that you said about Mairwen?" Breuddwyd went on. "What do you mean control her? She died before you were born."

The look in Mother's eyes told September that she didn't understand. She had no recollection of all that had gone on in that missing instant.

"Did you come with me, Mother?"

"What do you mean? I've only just caught up with you. The woman in the pub said you'd shown a lot of interest in this place and that you set off up the path hours ago."

"You don't remember going to the centre of Daear with the five other Cludydds and Malice?"

"What are you talking about, Em? Have you got cold? Perhaps it's hypothermia. Let's get you down to the car, get you home." Breuddwyd wrapped her arms around her and guided her along the path away from the summit, the Roman fort and the aerials.

September let herself be led but she was confused. Surely she had come back at the moment that they had set off for the ceremony that had unified them, but Mother didn't seem to recall that happening. She pushed herself away from Mother. The arms released her reluctantly. September stopped, glancing back at the dark silhouette of the summit.

"I've got to go and defeat the Malevolence so that Gwlad can be restored. Will you come with me Mother?"

"You're talking nonsense, Em. I don't understand you. We're going home."

"But I've got to, otherwise Berddig and Eluned and all the other people of the Land will die."

"Have you got a fever or something, September? You're rambling."

"But you must remember Mother. You were there. The Maengolauseren, the manifestations, the Malevolence."

Breuddwyd shook her head.

"You're not making sense, love. Look we must get down to the car as soon as possible and get you home. You're ill." She took September's hand in hers and dragged her off down the hillside. September stumbled along beside her. How could Mother have forgotten everything, her own visit to the Land as Cludydd and then their joint return to defeat the Malevolence?

"I know you've had a difficult time, Em. Those bullies in school have upset you. But running away doesn't solve anything."

"I wasn't running away."

"Why did you come here? There aren't many places further away."

"This is where it all started. Gwenda was the first, then Dilwen and Wenhaf..."

"What do you mean, Em? Who are these people?"

"Our ancesters, our great grandmothers. They lived here."

"Oh, I see. That talk with Emlyn about your great-grandmother and the previous generations has gone to your head. I wondered if that was what had happened and remembered that Emlyn mentioned this place. That's why I decided to come here to see if I could find you. What's happened to you, love? Have you been dreaming about our ancestors, Em?

But it wasn't a dream was it? She was the Cludydd and now had the powers of all seven Cludydds plus Malice. The

Gwylyb Hoedl Gwyrthiol had given her the ability to go anywhere or anywhen in the Omniverse to destroy the Malevolence. She hadn't imagined it, she was sure.

They reached the road. The Volvo was parked in a layby. A hundred metres away, across the stream, the lights of the Moon and Stars Inn still shone from the small windows. Breuddwyd unlocked the car doors and helped September into the passenger seat. She hurried around the car and got in, started up and pulled away.

September peered through the windscreen up to the ridge. Had it all happened as she remembered? Finding Cyfaill the Brain, the symudiad to Amaethaderyn, meeting Heulfryn and the Cemegwr, the gathering of the Cludydds, battles with the Malevolence, talking to Spotty in her picture-book universe. There were so many memories and it had all happened so quickly, but it was all too real to be a dream.

The warmth of the car and the monotonous drone of the engine made her sleepy. She dozed for most of the journey home. The quiet when the engine died as Mother turned off the ignition stirred her. She opened her eyes and saw the driveway of their house.

"Here we are, Em. Let's get you inside and into bed. It's late."

September opened the car door and put her feet on the concrete. She hadn't expected to come home. Her future had seemed to involve battling the Malevolence and flitting from one universe to another, conversing with the mysterious Brains who needed her and encouraged her.

She pushed herself on to her feet as the front door opened and Father emerged. He gathered her up in a hug.

"Oh, Em. We were so worried about you. Why did you go off on your own?" Together they walked into the house. There wasn't anything she could say as a response. Gus was on the stairs.

"You're back then. What did you run away for? How sad is that."

"Shut up, Gus," Father said, "Em doesn't need you having a go at her."

September shrugged and climbed the stairs, squeezing past

Gus. An adequate retort didn't come into her mind and she wasn't going to explain herself to him. She reached her room, pushed the door open and went inside. As the door swung closed, she went to the chair in front of her desk and looked through the open curtains, out of the window. The sky was dark, the Moon and stars obscured by clouds. She sat, staring, thinking through all that had happened since she had taken herself off. When had she left? Yesterday in this timeline, a little longer as far as she was concerned but really only a couple of days, nothing like as long as her extended trip across the Land. She struggled to recall everything she had done, everyone she had met, all the things she had learned about the Omniverse, the battle with the Malevolence and the role of the Brains. Perhaps it did seem too fantastic to be true, but she had lived it, she knew it was true, even the last episode in the universe built from her own memories.

She stood up and went to her wardrobe. Burrowing in amongst the hanging clothes, behind the boxes of shoes and games, right at the back she found what she was looking for – a black bin bag. When she had hauled it out she tipped it up on the floor. A host of soft toys tumbled out. She grabbed a black and white rabbit and hugged it to her chest.

"Speak to me Spotty. Tell me it's all true."

Spotty said nothing.

There were other things mixed up with the assorted cloth animals. There were dolls and a dress in pink satin. She had forgotten she still had it. It was tiny when she held it against herself. She screwed it up and tossed it on the floor.

There was a tap on the door and then it opened.

"I've brought you a hot chocolate, Em. You used to like … Oh, what have you done?" Mother paused on her way into the bedroom, a steaming mug in her hand. An irritated look crossed her face when she saw the pile of old toys in the centre of the floor.

"I wanted Spotty." September cradled the rabbit.

Mother's expression softened into a smile. "Oh yes, love. I'm sure he'll comfort you. Do you want this?" She held the mug out. September took it and put it on the desk.

"Thanks."

"That's alright love. Get to bed and have a good night's

sleep. Don't worry about school tomorrow. Let's get you right."

September nodded and Mother withdrew, pulling the door closed behind her. There was whispered conversation outside her door then footsteps on the landing.

September held the rabbit up so that they were eye to eye, and spoke to it as if it were alive.

"She's forgotten it all, Spotty. She doesn't know anything at all about the Land, or the Malevolence or the People and their amazing metals. But I need someone to guard me when I make the evil spirits fight each other. Who else can I get?"

There was just one other person who she knew well. They'd shared a head. September closed her eyes and thought of Llelluched and Gwenda. The chair disappeared from beneath her.

Her bottom landed on hard earth. It wasn't night-time anymore. There was light coming through the poor fitting shutters over the windows and the door. The bed compartment, the single bed, the rolled up sleep mats, the hearth, all were familiar. This was the home of Gwenda and her family.

"Who are you?" a voice asked from the shadows beside the single bed.

"Gwenda?"

"Yes."

September stood and took two paces towards the voice. A girl with white hair sat beside the low bed that Tadcu usually occupied. Someone lay motionless in the bed. Was it Tegan? She crouched down close to the girl.

"It's me, Gwenda. I'm September."

The girl shuffled back against the bed frame.

"I don't know you. Are you a ghost come to torment me? Go away."

"I met you at the Conjunction, then I was in your head. I was there when Malice made you attack your sister. We climbed Penybryngolau and went to Daear."

Gwenda shook her head.

"Your words are madness. Tad says I hit Tegan. Pedr found me wandering by the fort. Go away. I must care for my sister and atone for what I did in my madness."

"But Gwenda, don't you remember Gwlad, the mountains, the forests, the ocean. You must remember the Malevolence and the manifestations, the Ceffyl dwr, the Adarllwchgwin, the Draig tân."

Gwenda held her hand up protecting her face, hiding her view of September.

"Your words are nonsense. I know nothing of what you speak."

She too had forgotten her time in the Land, forgotten her role as Cludydd. September stood up, stepped back.

"Are we related?" Gwenda asked. September looked at herself. She had left her flab behind and wore the slim, fit body she had grown to love on her journey across Gwlad. She was wearing a simple calf-length woollen shift like Gwenda and the other women. Waves of white hair flopped over her shoulder.

"Yes, Gwenda, we are." September pushed the door open and stepped into the yard. There were the noises of activity in the dressing shed, and a figure was approaching beside the stream. She gathered up her skirts and ran upstream away from the mine works. After a hundred metres or so she felt she was out of sight so settled to a walk thinking about what had happened. Both Gwenda and Mother had lost all knowledge of the Maengolauseren and forgotten all their experiences in the Land. Presumably the same would apply to the other Cludydds. She was alone, the one and only tasked with bringing civil war to the Malevolence to relieve the strain of the evil on the Brains. She sniffed and tears came into her eyes. Alone with no-one else to share her story.

She reached the horseshoe shaped dell where the waterfall fell over its three steps. There was a figure in a rough woollen smock and leather sandals standing by the pond. Despite the different clothes she recognised him.

"Cyfaill!"

He looked at her sternly. "You haven't returned to do battle with the Malevolence."

"How do you know? Time is different there and I've been back and forth so much, how do you know I haven't gone and done it?"

"Because it is you we are concerned about, September. It is your timeline we are following not that of this world or Daear."

"You're concerned about me?" Her tone expressed her disbelief. "Is that why you've left me all alone?" She flung herself at Cyfaill and beat her fists against his chest. For a moment he stood still absorbing her onslaught, then he grabbed her wrists, forcing her into immobility.

"What is the matter, September? We thought you were heading straight back to the universe of Daear to bring civil war to the evil." Cyfaill dragged September to a moss-covered outcrop of rock He sat down with September at his side. She slid off the rock and slumped on the ground in front of him, sobbing.

"I was afraid."

"Afraid of what?"

"Becoming evil."

"Ah. Why do you fear that?" Cyfaill put his arms around September and hauled her up beside him.

"Because the feeling of hate was so strong when I commanded that witch. I felt I was going to be swallowed up by hate."

"But Spotty told you that the experiences of the other Cludydds that you have absorbed will protect you."

"Yes, he did say that, but I didn't feel safe. I thought that if Mother could come and be by my side she would be able to slap me out of it if I started to become evil."

Cyfaill placed his hand tenderly on September's. "You discovered that wouldn't be possible."

Tears trickled down September's cheeks. "She's forgotten everything. She doesn't know she was a Cludydd anymore. She thinks I'm mad."

Cyfaill pulled her head onto his chest and caressed her thick white hair.

"There, there, September. I understand."

September pushed herself away from him and stood up. She faced him, glaring angrily.

"Do you? You're a Brain. You say you know everything but do you know what it's like to be alone, to know that the universe is filled with an evil that wants to destroy everything and not be able to tell anyone without them thinking you're round the bend?"

Cyfaill sighed. "No, I don't suppose I can understand that feeling."

"You haven't tried to understand. Ever since you created that universe you've used the People that live there to die fighting evil and you engineered me and my great grandmothers for your entertainment and to keep the Malevolence occupied. You even killed my twin who appeared by accident and then she nearly spoiled your plans."

September knew she had scored a hit by the wounded look that was on Cyfaill's face.

"I'm sorry September. You're right. We have used you and your predecessors but it hasn't been a game. We may have given the impression that we didn't care about the People of Gwlad and it is true that we haven't been interested in each individual. We made a mistake with your sister; we're not perfect. We can't predict or control every occurrence in the Omniverse." He shook his head sadly, "You weren't supposed to know about us."

"Things got out of control did they?" September snapped.

"Yes, September, they did. You and your sister were not supposed to be identical but instead of your mother having two embryos, she had one which split in two. You were always meant to be the seventh child, the Cludydd, but Mairwen was a complication. We thought that terminating her existence would solve the problem."

"And so her spirit was thrown into the darkness." September shivered at Malice's memory of her timeless exile.

"That was an unfortunate waste of a spirit but spirits of darkness have no memory of a past existence. We hadn't allowed for the powerful link that Mairwen retained with you."

September sniffed. "So your wonderful plan fell apart."

Cyfaill nodded. "That's right. We hadn't reckoned on the Malevolence getting direction. It was a surprise to us when Malice became a leader of the evil. We had no idea what effect that could have but it worried us greatly. When Malice prevented you from defeating the Malevolence at the

Conjunction we feared for the whole Omniverse. We had no idea what to do but you pointed the way."

"I did?" September looked at Cyfaill with her eyes wide.

"Returning with Breuddwyd showed that the Cludydds together could overcome Malice and the might of the Malevolence. You gave us the hint and now we think that you can be an important ally in the battle against evil."

September recognised that Cyfaill was treating her as an equal to himself and the Brains but she wasn't prepared to stop feeling miserable yet.

"When Mother joined me it was wonderful to have someone else to talk to who knew what had happened to me. Now she doesn't, but it's not just Mother is it? Gwenda and all the others have forgotten too, haven't they?"

"Yes, September. I thought we had explained this. When the union took place, the spirits of the other Cludydds returned to their bodies in their own times. It was their experiences and skills with the Maengolauseren that became embedded in you along with Malice's powers. You are unique, a child of the Omniverse. Having drunk the Gwylib Hoedl Gwyrthiol you are able to move freely in time and space and insert yourself into any universe, and, as you have shown, you have the unique ability to manage the spirits of the Malevolence without being dominated by hate."

"I just wanted to be normal," September sobbed.

Cyfaill chuckled. "That is no longer an option, September. You are extraordinary."

"But I can't go back home ever again."

"You can, if you wish. You can go back to the exact moment when you left whenever you like and continue your life."

"But it'll be a lie. I'll never be able to act normally when I know that with a flick of my hand or a twitch of my nose I can be somewhere completely different."

"That is true, but there are many individuals who when they grow up find they are playing a part while they live a different life inside. Your mother, father, brother and sisters still love you. You can have fun with your friends and then go off and save a universe."

September gave a small laugh. "You make it sound so easy."

"Oh no, September. It's not going to be easy. There is no

certainty that your battles with the Malevolence will be successful. As I said we don't control everything in the Omniverse. Your spirit is in danger but you are our best hope for an advantage in the eternal war and we will be with you at all times and places."

"So you want me."

"Of course. We need you. This first trial with the Malevolence at Daear is crucial. It is a test of whether you can direct the evil spirits to battle with themselves. We will be watching."

"The Land will be restored?" September sat beside Cyfaill again on the outcrop.

"Yes," he replied replacing his arm around her shoulders. "Once the immediate threat of the Malevolence is removed. We shall rejuvenate and regenerate it."

"And if I don't?"

"The universe of Daear will weaken until the Malevolence can enter and complete its destruction."

"So to save Elunded and Berddig and the rest I have to get the evil spirits to fight each other. But I don't know how."

"You found a way in your make-believe universe."

"The witch and the crocodile weren't allies."

"Neither are the manifestations of the evil that appear in Gwlad."

September sat up straight. "Really? I thought they were united in wanting to destroy everything in the world."

Cyfaill smiled. "United is the wrong word. If they have no direction they attack the good like wasps are drawn to jam. But hate is their only emotion so they feel no affection for or unity with their own sort."

September jumped to her feet and faced Cyfaill. "So I just have to direct one manifestation to fight another."

"That's right."

"But there are billions of spirits. I couldn't direct every single one."

Cyfaill nodded. "That's right but you won't have to. Think about what you know of the manifestations on Daear."

September pondered. "They give form to the four elements that constitute the matter of the universe – earth, air fire and water."

"Very good," Cyfaill said, "and what else do you know of these elements?"

September scratched her head. Aurddolen and Heulfryn had told her more about the elements… What was it? They have qualities.

"That's it!" she shouted gleefully. "Each element has two qualities, hot or cold, wet or dry. Each of them is the opposite of another."

"You've got it," Cyfaill replied.

September's mood turned sombre. "But if I want to get the manifestations of the elements fighting each other they'll have to be in Gwlad. I can't let that happen; the People might be killed or turned to evil."

"You are right. The type of manifestation is a consequence of the structure of the universe. Your fairy-tale-land had giants, wicked witches and crocodiles; Daear, built from the four elements, has its own set of manifestations derived from the culture we modelled the world on."

"I need a decoy. A world that is built like Daear, that isn't inhabited but will attract the same manifestations."

"Ah. Now you are thinking," Cyfaill agreed. "Remember we are with you. Whatever you require can be provided."

"I suppose I had better get on with it then." September realised that Cyfaill had guided her to the answer and in doing so had given her encouragement. Her resentment at the Brains' manipulation of her life had subsided and in its place she felt a new confidence. Fear of the Malevolence and of falling under the spell of Malice's hate remained but was subdued by the knowledge that even though Mother couldn't be at her side the Brains would be.

"Well done, September. Take a deep breath, puff out your chest, put a smile on your face and think of all the goodness you will be doing by destroying the power of the Malevolence. Think of all the people who will be able to live good and happy lives, the plants and animals that will grow, the planets that will continue in their orbits."

Determination filled her. She would be the Cludydd who removed the threat of the Malevolence forever. It was time to complete her task.

September moved.

33

There was just one point of light in the dark. The only matter, and possible source of light in this universe, was contained in the sphere of stars, the seven planets orbiting within it and immoveable Daear at its centre. It was a small lonely solar system floating in an infinity of darkness occupied by evil. That bright mote was so tiny and insignificant that it might as well not be there. The dark pressed in all around her, featureless, empty. Except, by the itching in her hip, it wasn't empty. September looked longingly at the distant speck of light. How she wished she was there amongst the trees on the banks of the river and beside the lake with the people of Amaethaderyn, or even on the freezing slopes of Mynydd Tywyll or deep in the dark forests of Coedwig Fawr. Anywhere but this cold, loveless place. But this was where her task demanded she must be. Among the spirits of the Malevolence.

They were amassing around her now, drawn by her energy of life. Their incessant moans of hate and threats of destruction resonated inside her. She felt them with her heart and stomach as much as she heard them with her ears. She trembled with fear. What terrors would happen to her if she fell prey to them? How agonising could it be to become a servant of the Evil as her friends, Tudfwlch and Arianwen had done? The power of the Maengolauseren was ignited inside her by her fears, urging her to release the violet light that would disperse the Malevolence. Allowing the spirits to approach her was almost unbearable and grew more painful as their numbers built and built. But she had to resist. Unleashing the starstone fire was only a temporary respite, she knew now. It was Malice's skills that were the key to a real victory. With an effort that strained her willpower she held the Maengolauseren in check.

She waited for the spirits to gather, allowed them to come

close, forming rank upon ragged rank all around her. Their cries of hate were monotonously identical but she heard every single individual though there was an uncountable number of them. They had no plan, no strategy. They did not cooperate or form alliances but in their intention they were single-minded. Their sole purpose was to destroy all matter, living and inanimate; to tear down the structures of the universe, whatever local laws or forces applied, and rid the Omniverse of its inhabitants. They had no understanding of what it was they sought to destroy. It was existence itself that was anathema to them.

September reached deep into her mind, searching for the memories of Malice that she had assimilated. Finding the hate gave her a shock. It was raw, unfocussed, powerful. It was made up partly of anger at being denied life, partly of envy for those that had what she had been prevented from sharing, and partly of fear of what had been to her the unknown. Within that core of hate was the memory of directing the manifestations of the four elements as the spirits materialised in the Land. There was no joy but there was satisfaction in wielding the manifestations as they destroyed and converted the good folk of Gwlad to evil. Malice's memories and feelings conflicted with her own but they were hers now. She felt the hate grow in her.

The Malevolence did not attack her. Why not? Did the spirits sense the part of her that was Malice? Perhaps they were confused, their hatred for her living soul held back by the recognition that she held within her a part that was, like them, consumed by hate. This was her chance, the opportunity to take control, to turn the spirits on each other. But while directing one evil witch had been easy, now she had to command multitudes of spirits to do battle with many, many more. She was worried. This task required much more of her than controlling one spirit had done. She would have to give herself almost totally to Malice's power in order to manage a sufficient portion of the Malevolence. She feared being seduced by the power of evil, of her own identity being overwhelmed by the arrogance of rule. There was just Cyfaill's assurance that the memories of the other Cluydydds and the seven-fold strength of the Maengolauseren to hold onto would prevent her descending into a kind of hell. Malice's skills were hers. She knew what she had to do.

The senseless hate of the hordes of spirits had to be re-directed from her and the distant glowing universe and onto other representatives of the Evil. How could she make them destroy each other? The witch had done her bidding and attacked the crocodile but she couldn't guide each of the spirits under her power to its target. There were simply too many. She must be like a general directing armies. In the darkness of infinite space the spirits were invisible and unconfined. They needed a battlefield to line up against each other, but not their former battleground of Gwlad. That must remain safe within the protective orbits of the seven planets. Cyfaill's words came to her. She was a being of the Omniverse now. Spotty had explained how she had created a universe out of her childhood memories and imagination and Cyfaill had said that the Brains would respond to her requests. It was time to build a sister world of Daear.

A shell of dark grey rock formed around her. It was the essence of the element Earth; pure, uncontaminated with any other element. The structure of this world would be unlike Daear. There would be no core of Egwyddorpum, the quintessence, the fifth element, to be a source of the world's life force. She was that, the Cludydd o Maengolauseren. She felt the layer of Earth grow to form a cold, dry globe, thousands of kilometres in diameter. Then a change. It rained. Huge drops of Water fell on the surface over all the world. A torrent of cold, wet rain covered the world to a depth of many kilometres. The rain stopped and the surface stilled. Then a breeze of Air, warm and wet, blew over the surface. The wind strengthened as the Air thickened and it blew all around the world. Finally, above the Air, lightning flashed and auroras glowed as Fire, hot and dry, encircled the globe forming the last elemental sphere. The four layers were complete; Earth, Water, Air and Fire, perfect in their sphericity. But she didn't want perfection. Perfection would not be vulnerable to the Malevolence and she needed vulnerability. In her hollow at the centre of the world she raised her hands pushing against the layer of Earth. A point on the sphere of Earth swelled, became a hump, and thrust up through the Water above the Earth. A great mountain burst through the ocean that covered the world and continued to grow up into the Air and into the Fire above.

Her world was complete. She moved to the side of the mountain where it sloped gently into the ocean.

She stood on dark, smooth rock, unweathered by time or by any living thing. Before her was the ocean unbroken by any other land mass. Small waves disturbed the surface raised by a gentle breeze in the clear air. The sky was bright above her head but there was no Sun. There were no clouds either, just the uniform, unnaturally bright blue, except for one spot directly overhead. It was a white globe smaller than the apparent size of the Moon from Earth. This wasn't the familiar satellite, but the sphere of stars that enclosed Daear seen across the darkness of space. A space filled with the spirits of the Malevolence. Now she had to call them to this new world that had popped into existence in the space-time of this universe.

The call had to be similar to that inadvertently sent out by the People of Gwlad. That call had been transmitted since the universe had been made by the Brains and had continued through seven Conjunctions and seven summonses of the Cludydd. How could she copy that call to make it appear that this new world of four elements was the same as Daear? The answer was within her of course. The Brains had linked Daear to Llelluched on the Earth of her universe. The first Cludydd had spoken the language of the Celts as had four that followed. The old tongue used by the People had mystified September when she had arrived in Gwlad but now she delved into Gwenda's memory. She lifted up her head, raised her arms and shouted out.

"Deuwch! Deuwch gweision o Adwyth. Deuwch amlygiadau o Pridd, amlygiadau o Dwr, amlygiadau o Awyr, amlygiadau o Tân. Deuwch!"

"Come! Come servants of the Malevolence. Come manifestations of Earth, manifestations of Water, manifestations of Air, manifestations of Fire. Come!"

Her words rose into the sky and beyond, radiating out into the realm of the Malevolence. Deep in Gwenda's recollections she found songs. Songs of love, of joy, of friendship, praising the land, birds, flowers, and other living creatures. She sang them all, feeling the excitement of expressing the emotions. The ground echoed her words, the ocean carried them around the world, they carried through the air and the fire. The world sang with its Celtic inheritance.

September paused and waited and listened.

At first it was like a breeze disturbing a field of grass or bees in a bush. It grew louder, like waves crashing onto cliffs, rocks tumbling down a mountainside. She turned to face the mountain. The noise became that of a road drill hammering into concrete. The ground around her erupted, rock was thrown up into the air. From the holes that had formed emerged small human-like figures with bent backs and heads sitting on neckless shoulders. Their arms stretched to the ground and ended in massive hands with mole-like claws. Hundreds of the Coblynau crawled out of their tunnels and onto the surface of the ground around her. Behind them came the grey, slender but crooked figures of Tylwyth teg, hissing and spitting their acid from their thin, lined faces. Amongst them were dozens of bent grey hags, Gwyllian, that came staggering towards her. The hordes of manifestations approached her, and stopped.

September looked at the creatures. The Coblynau and Tylwyth teg she had rarely seen above ground and the Gwyillian she had only experienced at night. Now they stood blinking in the bright diffuse light looking up at her with their dark and emotionless eyes as if they expected something from her.

Of course; the manifestations looked on her as their leader and their guide. They had come to destroy the world she had created but had found one of their own, the spirit of Malice. They began crying, 'Hate, hate, hate,' not as one, but as a million individuals. Her body responded to the gales of emotion, wanting to join in. It must be like the supporters at a football match, all wanting their team to win and pouring their collective disgust onto the opposition team and followers. She didn't want to be part of it but she found herself exhilarated by the wave after wave of raw hate. She raised her arms acknowledging herself as the manifestations' leader. The cries grew louder in response although the same chorus was endlessly repeated. She felt the heat of the hate within her, hate that anything other than herself should have existence.

In a corner of her mind September thought, *I have to turn them on themselves, but how? They are united in their hate and will follow any instruction I give them. How do I turn one on another?* These were all manifestations of Earth and shared the qualities of dryness and coldness. That was why they were found underground or at night.

She had a plan, or at least the beginning of one. This would be her army and they would destroy the manifestations of an opposing element. Which was it to be? Here she stood at the boundary between Earth and Water. Water – cold and wet. She turned to face the ocean.

The sea that had been flat calm was now disturbed. Huge breakers were forming and roaring towards the land like a tsunami. September watched the approaching wave. Its shape was changing. No longer was it a straight, monstrous roller. It was splitting up into many separate forms. From the foam emerged the sea-green tossing manes, prancing legs and flapping wings of Ceffyll dwr and the frog-like heads, bat-wings and scorpion tails of Llamhigwyn y dwr. The water manifestations reached the shallows and September was reminded of how huge the creatures were. Each was as high as a house, as big as a tyrannosaurus rex. They approached the land.

September turned back to face the assembled Earth manifestations. Her outward appearance turned as black as her heart.

"There are your enemies," she screamed. "Creatures of the wet. Hate them. Hate them with all your passion and destroy them." The hate swelled inside her, a dark and cold emotion that swamped almost all other feelings and thoughts. All she wanted was for her forces, her servants of Earth to destroy the creatures of the Water. The power of her hate spread out of her and flowed over all the assembled Earth manifestations.

The Coblynau, the Tylwyth teg and Gwyllian took up her

cry, shouting their hate. September urged them forward to meet the water manifestations on the shoreline. They began to move, not in formation like an army but as a rabble. But though they were ill-disciplined, they were determined. The hordes of manifestations flowed around September leaving her standing, throbbing with hate. They crawled, stumbled, staggered, towards their foes, the manifestations of Water.

The creatures of Earth and Water met. The Tylwyth teg spat their acid, the Coblynau tore at their foes with their clawed hands and the Gwyllian reached out with their long, skeletal fingers. The Ceffyl dwr stamped their feet and tossed their heads and the Llamhigwyn y dwr lashed their coiled stings. Where one manifestation met another the conflict was short as each exploded into a cloud of dust or a deluge of water, but more and more servants of evil joined the battle on both sides. Manifestation destroyed manifestation but yet more of the monsters appeared to continue the battle.

September was exultant. The thrill of the destruction filled her and she urged the warring creatures on. She had no other thought but of wreaking vengeance, of bringing about the destruction of her enemies.

Almost no other thought.

A tiny part of herself stood apart, watching, waiting. *This isn't you, September*, it said. *This is Malice. Don't let her dominate you. Don't let her memories and her powers overcome you. Remember why you are doing this – to remove the threat of the Malevolence from Daear, and from your friends across Gwlad. Remember love and joy and compassion and sadness and anger and surprise and hope, the emotions of the metals and the planets, and fear, the emotion of the Maengolauseren. Remember that you are the Cludydd o Maengolauseren, the One, the Unity of Seven.*

She remembered. She leapt into the air, transforming into the violet eagle and looked down on the two armies. From high above the isolated island September could see the battle raging along all the coastline. Dust and spray obscured some of her view but there seemed no end to the battle. As fast as Earth manifestations were destroyed more erupted from the mountainside and took their places in the fight. Meanwhile out at sea, wave upon wave of the water manifestations swam to the shore to replace their dissipated fellows.

September circled the mountain, flying higher and higher. Now the battle she had ignited seemed small and distant. Had she done enough to occupy the Malevolence in this universe? She was approaching another boundary – that between the spheres of Air and Fire. She knew her task was not complete. She had occupied part of the Malevolence in conflict with itself, but there was more she could do.

September looked around the sky and saw a squadron of Adarllwchgwin, manifestations of warm, wet air, soaring through the air towards her, squawking and beating the air with their wings while their red-skinned riders brandished their tridents. Despite the roar of beating wings and screaming riders she heard another noise, a piercing whistle. A Cyrhyraeth, invisible as the wind, was moaning towards her, a miasma of decay. There was one other air manifestation, the Pwca, difficult to spot as it could change its shape at will. September almost smiled as she recognised it, a great black cloud that had appeared on the horizon and was blowing towards her. Already flashes of lightning illuminated it and thunder rolled around the curve of the globe.

She looked above her, beyond the air and into the glowing blue of the sphere of Fire. Bounding towards her were the fiery hounds that were Cwn annwn, baying and coughing gouts of flame. Above them were Draig tân, incandescent globes with luminescent tails looping around the curve of the horizon.

September changed into her human form and faced the Air manifestations that had gathered around her. Once again she summoned the memories of Malice and hate grew in her. Her outer covering turned from radiant violet to the darkness of a black hole. Confidence in her power grew as she contemplated the destruction of her enemies.

"Spirits of the Malevolence," September cried out above the din of the Adarllwchgwin, Cyrhyraeth and the Pwca mustered around her. "There is your enemy." She pointed to the Cwn annwn and Draig tân that fell towards them. "Air must oppose Fire. Wet against Dry. Direct your hate at the manifestations of the dry. Destroy them!"

Her army responded immediately. The manifestations turned away from her and faced their enemies that approached them. The Adarllwchgwin soared to attack, the riders unleashing their lightning bolts. They found their targets in the flaming dogs which exploded into fireballs that faded as they expanded. Other Cwn annwn locked their jaws on the giant birds which then burst into a cloud of vapour that evaporated and disappeared.

Now the great cloud of the Pwca was overhead and forked lightning speared upwards into the sphere of fire as well as downwards. Where the lightning met a Draig tân, the comet was riven into many pieces that rained down through the air, guttering as they fell. The whining wind of the Cyhyraeth blew around the forces of Fire, extinguishing the flames. Meanwhile other Draig tân ripped through other clouds of Pwca and the moaning Cyrhyraeth and turned them to mere gusts of air.

More and more manifestations of Air and Fire were arriving as the conflict spread around the globe. September looked around and saw that the armies were evenly matched as yet more Fire manifestations descended from on high and more Air manifestations climbed through the air to meet them. She grew flushed and excited as she watched one army follow her command to destroy the other. September urged the foes to the fight feeling her hate burn hot within in her. But there remained a coolness at her core. There resided the memories of the seven Cludyddau who had witnessed so much death and pain during their Conjunctions. The memories reminded September of her task, that the hate wasn't hers.

She took a deep breath willing her heart to slow its frenzied beating. This battle between opposing elements would last indefinitely now, perhaps forever. The battling manifestations did not need her presence to keep them at war. Now that they possessed something to focus their hate upon they would fight without ceasing.

Her black gown took on a violet radiance as she regained her self-control. This small universe that she had seen created was now a cauldron of war and destruction. All four elements had been brought into conflict drawing in the spirits of the Malevolence. Nevertheless she saw that she could do more to ensure that the evil remained focussed for all time on destroying itself, like a snake consuming its tail. She must ensure that no accidental alliances were forged between elements even though there was no intelligence directing the spirits that inhabited the manifestations. Each element must fight every other, hot against cold, as well as wet against dry.

She moved to the peak of the mountain that thrust above the sphere of Air into the sphere of Fire. Overhead already there appeared first one flaming Draig tân, then another. The balls of fire and flaming tails grew as they approached, every one directed towards September. Across the mountain top, to her right and left, raced the fiery hounds, the Cwn annwn, flames flickering into the air above their charging bodies.

Then from the rock beneath her erupted Coblynnau, and Tylwyth teg and Gwyllian. Once again September allowed the hate to boil up from the buried memories of Malice deep within her mind. Again her dress turned black. She exulted in the feeling of power it gave her over the monsters of the Malevolence. Raising her arms she shouted, "Sprits of Earth. You are mine to command. You shall have your war. You shall have enemies to vent your hate and your spite upon. See? They come." She directed the manifestations of Earth to do battle with those of Fire. Fireballs and clouds of dust exploded and dissipated around her. She urged her army on, its fallen instantly replaced by more manifestations and its opposition similarly reinforced. The hate swirled through her and she exulted in the mayhem.

She descended to the surface of the ocean and commanded the forces of Water to engage with those of the Air. Adarllwchgwin dived onto Ceffyl dwr. Pwca, in the form of swarms of locusts, fell on Llamhigwyn y dwr. All were destroyed in waterspouts and whirlwinds but more manifestations arrived to continue the fight.

On the almost vertical flanks of the huge mountain, Earth manifestations grappled with creatures of Air that swept over them. Coblynnau plucked Adarlwchgwin from the air as vulture shaped Pwca grabbed Tylwyth teg from their lairs and whining Cyrhyraeth whistled amongst moaning Gwyllian. The air was filled with dust and vapour.

Creatures of fire and water met in hissing, boiling eruptions. Fires were doused and water evaporated but there were more creatures arriving to take their places. Ceffyl dwr climbed into the sky to meet the falling Draig tân. Their battles ended in explosions of super-heated steam. Thunder rolled across the sea as the vapours dispersed. More fiery orbs appeared in the heavens and more of the water horses sprang from the ocean. Cwn annwn pounded across the shallows to meet the Llamhigwyn y dwr. The flaming dogs leapt at the throats of the giant chimeric creatures. The scorpion stings of the Llamhigwyn y dwr lashed at their attackers. Both manifestations burst into geysers of scalding vapour which spread out, thinning until it was invisible. Yet more creatures appeared to fight to their mutual destruction.

Filled with the exhilaration of battle September flew around the world from one sphere to another urging manifestation to fight manifestation. Her excitement was uncontained. She screamed hate at the manifestations driving them on to their fiery, watery, dusty, gassy ends. Each percussion as a pair of creatures was destroyed gave her a thrill more powerful than she had ever felt. She urged the elements to endless war.

Now she soared into space and looked down at her handiwork. The world she had brought into being was a pulsating, convulsing, festering globe of eruptions and explosions. No part from North Pole to South, from beneath the bed of the oceans to the flaming firmament, was not seething in conflict. Around her the spirits streamed from the infinite darkness to continue the fight with their fellows.

Realisation came that she was no longer needed to maintain the civil war within the Malevolence. The war had its own momentum now. Her hate died and she saw her body and limbs take on a violet glow. The breadth of emotions of the Cludydds pushed out the single-minded hate of Malice. Nevertheless, there was no compassion for the spirits of evil committed to fight with each other forever. Instead she felt joy that their hate had been diverted from Daear and its attendant planets and stars.

She became aware of a presence near her. The figure of a woman appeared in the darkness, at first ghostly pale but slowly acquiring substance until she seemed solid. She was dressed all in white and had white hair and white skin but September knew her. She was the Cemegwr she had met in Coedwig Fawr and at the centre of Daear, the one who called herself the Dechreuwr.

Her voice came to September across the emptiness of space. "Congratulations, September. You have succeeded in your task and saved yourself. You have proved that the seven bearers of the Maengolauseren are more than a match for Malice."

"Perhaps, but hate is such a simple emotion," September replied. "It needs no explanation, no justification. It is just there."

"That is true and it is good that you have learned the nature of hate. You will control it more easily in the future."

"There is more to do in the future?"

"Of course, September. Here, in this small universe you have set the Malevolence at war with itself. The spirits of evil cannot be destroyed but will set upon each other for eternity in the battleground that you have established. Elsewhere in the Omniverse the Malevolence is still raging, still spreading its hate, still set upon destruction. There will be need for your skills in other universes."

September was unsure about how she felt about the Cemegwr's revelation. She wanted to return home to peace and normality, to grow up as the woman she wanted to be; and yet, she did not want to let go of the feeling of power she had as the embodiment of the Maengolauseren. The memories and experiences drawn from seven conjunctions and even Malice's power over the spirits of the Malevolence made her feel strong and special. Could she be both a normal woman and a superhero?

"So you will summon me again?"

"Yes, September. You will be called."

"But I can go home and live a normal life?"

"If you wish. You have the freedom of time and space now that you possess the Gwylib Hoedl Gwyrthiol."

September remembered that there had been something else she wanted. She turned to see the distant glittering jewel that was the sphere of stars and thought of the people who lived in Gwlad on the world of Daear at its centre, those she knew and the many who she did not. She looked at the Cemegwr's face and wondered how she would respond to her next question. Would she answer truthfully?

"Is the Land protected and refreshed now?" September asked.

"Yes, September. The Malevolence is now fully occupied with fighting itself and we have re-energised Daear and its system of planets and stars. It will run indefinitely now. The people of Gwlad will live their lives free from the terrors of the Malevolence."

"Can I visit them?" she asked, eager for the answer.

"Of course, September. You can go whenever and wherever you like. Your presence is no longer needed in the war between the elemental manifestations."

"Right. Let's go." September stood still, closed her eyes and prepared herself for symudiad.

34

Her eyes were squeezed shut. What would she see when she opened them? She had chosen the when and where of her arrival carefully. It should be about a week after the last Conjunction, a few days since she and Mother had driven the Malevolence from the Land and Malice had been absorbed into her. The place was where she had arrived in Gwlad before. On her first summons it had been clean and fresh but on the other two occasions the depredations of the Malevolence had been obvious.

There was warmth on her face, the heat of a tropical Sun in winter, but the air smelt fresh as if it had recently rained. It was a pleasant odour, not the stench of decay which the Malevolence had cast over the land. The ground felt soft and springy beneath her feet. She stood still for a minute or two listening to the sound of birds calling. The Land seemed alive.

At last she opened her eyes and looked around. Most of her arrivals had been at night. Now she could take in the configuration of the landscape more clearly. She noticed how much the ridge on which she stood resembled the ridge of Penybryngolau above Llelluched. The two sides of the ridge sloped gently down into wooded valleys. To her right there was a gentle rise up to the summit. At Penybryngolau it was where the Roman fort and the modern aerials were. Here it was the site of the Cysegr, the Refuge. It still showed the effects of the fall of the Draig tân; all the trees had fallen, snapped like matches. The vegetation covering the ridge and the slopes also displayed the signs of the Malevolence. The top grass was dead and grey but beneath it September could just see fresh green shoots sprouting. The Land was recovering.

Down below in the valley was the river, the lake and the clearing in the woodland where Amaethaderyn was situated.

A few wisps of smoke rose into the air above the village. The fires she hoped were a sign of people at their occupations and not of smouldering ruins. She would have to take a closer look.

The transformation into the iridescent blue eagle took just a moment of thought of unpredictable and unrelated words and she launched herself into the sky. She circled around the hilltop taking in the view of forest and hills and the river meandering towards the distant ocean. Then she swooped down, skimming above the hillside meadow, across the river, up and over the trees lining the banks and down into the village. There were ruins, wood and thatch, huts collapsed and burned, but there were people amongst the few intact buildings. She flew down to the open space between the houses and workshops and landed gently. People were already running towards her as she changed back to her normal self. Normal that is for Gwlad; she found herself clothed in a blue glow.

"Cludydd! You have returned to us," Berddig said between gasps. His appearance pleased September.

"Berddig! You're…you're young!" Although he looked tired, a little thin and out of breath he was the young, smiling man she had known at the start of her prolonged period in the Land leading up to the Conjunction, not the older or the aged man she had met on her last two visits.

He looked surprised. "We have been through many trials while you fought the Malevolence, but only a few days have passed since we last met, Cludydd. I do not think I would have aged much."

"No, I mean you look well. You all do." Each face in the crowd that surrounded September was smiling. There was Catrin, the copper bearer, but there was one particular face she searched for. The familiar features appeared among the throng. Eluned stepped forward, flung her arms around September and hugged her.

"This is a wonderful surprise, Cludydd," Eluned said when she had released September and stepped back. "Never before has the Cludydd o Maengolauseren returned after the Cysylltiad, but we know you are different because you returned with the sixth Cludydd to drive the Adwyth back beyond the stars."

"It was my failure to defeat the Malevolence at the Conjunction that made this time different."

Berddig responded to September's regret. "But it was Malice that stopped you then. Already the storytellers are developing the saga of the Conjunction with the twin sisters. We will tell it to our children and their children."

"It will be the last Conjunction they have to compose a song for. The last time when you had to face the threat of the Malevolence." September hoped that the promises made by the Brains would be kept.

"That is good news," Eluned said. "Some prophecies said that there would be just seven comings of the Evil and therefore seven Cludyddau. But why are you here with us now, Cludydd?"

September looked around the smiling throng. "I wanted to see how you were coping after the Malevolence had gone."

Berddig pointed at the ruins. "The Evil caused great destruction which will take a long time to put right, but we are making a start. Come, let us show you." He held out his hand. September took it and he lead her through the crowd with Eluned by her side and Catrin close behind. The villagers followed. They reached the edge of the lake. A gentle breeze stirred ripples on the water.

"It has refilled," September said.

"Yes, but most of the reeds died during the Evil," Berddig said. "We will have to wait for more to grow before we can put roofs on more homes."

"I saw that you have rebuilt some."

"We needed shelter for everyone. There is a lot more work to do to ensure that we live. Our crops must be replanted, and that is difficult without tools of haearn."

"Iorwerth?"

"Iorwerth died in the battle," Eluned said. September remembered and felt sad. She had put a lot of things right but still many of the People, and cludyddau in particular, had died defending their homes from the manifestations of evil.

"Oh, yes, I remember now. Arianwen was killed too."

"Yes, it was a cause of great sadness," Berddig said looking unusually glum.

"What about Padarn?" September asked. She recalled him being very ill while the Malevolence reigned and during a visit to a future that she hoped would not now take place, she had learnt he had died soon after.

"He is weak, but he lives," Eluned said. "Come and visit him." The party turned away from the lake and headed towards one of the timber-framed huts. Berddig held the curtain aside for September to enter. She hurried to the bed on which Padarn lay under a blanket in dim light. His face was grey and surrounded by straggly silver hair. He opened his eyes and when he saw September leaning over him a thin smile creased his cheeks. The lead-bearer's voice came in a whisper.

"Cludydd, this is an unexpected joy."

September held his hand in hers. Compassion filled her and she summoned the power of arian.

"You don't have a silver bearer here but perhaps I can help you." She poured her sympathy into the old man, wishing him renewed strength and vitality. A pink glow slowly came into his cheeks.

"Ah, Cludydd. I feel your healing power. Thank you." Padarn's hand squeezed her own with some force. He released it and pushed himself up onto his elbows. Eluned stepped forward with a cup of water.

"Padarn! You have strength again. Drink this to aid your recovery." She held the cup to his lips and he drank thirstily. "Oh, Cludydd. You have revived him," she said filled with joy.

September stood up and faced Berddig. "I don't know what else I can do but if there is any way I can use my powers to help you, please tell me."

"Thank you, September," he answered. "Restoring Padarn is a wonderful gift to us. Catrin has regained her power of communication so we have requested tools from our neighbours along the River Deheuol. We will survive and rebuild. Our future is a joyful one, I am sure. Let us celebrate."

He stepped out of the hut and began issuing orders. September heard feet rushing away to perform whatever tasks Berddig had assigned to their owners and cheerful, excited voices. Catrin flung apart the shutters at the windows and the sunlight brightened the single circular room. Eluned moved a chair from the far side of the hut to beside Padarn's bed and insisted that September sit down. The lead-bearer was now sitting up and despite his elderly appearance was filled with energy and with happiness at his recovery.

"You have given me new life, Cludydd," he said, his voice much stronger than before. "I will be able to provide the people with the protection my skills can offer once more."

"That's great," September said, filled with delight at seeing the quick results of her healing.

"You said we wouldn't be threatened by manifestations again," Eluned said, sitting herself on the rug at September's feet.

September nodded. "The Malevolence is being kept busy elsewhere. You will be safe in the Land."

"That is good news, Cludydd," Eluned said. "Now our powers can be used to help the People lead healthy and comfortable lives."

"How will you cope without a bearer of silver?"

Padarn answered in his grave voice. "Perhaps a cludydd o arian will visit us from one of the other villages not too far away. Maybe a new cludydd will come and live among us. Without the Malevolence taking cludyddau we should be able to increase our numbers."

People entered the hut carrying trays of bread and cheese, bowls of fruit and jugs of fresh water. They crowded into the hut until it was filled to bursting and September was quickly supplied with samples of the food and a goblet of water. She wasn't hungry or thirsty but she took a morsel and a sip of everything she was offered. The delightful flavours reminded her of her arrival in the village but she noticed that there was much less food on offer than before.

"I hope you will not run out of food before you can harvest more," September said between nibbling a small piece of tasty hard cheese.

"It will be difficult," Berddig said, "but the forest provides us with nuts and fruits. The Malevolence did not have time to destroy all the trees and we were able to preserve some of our animals."

"That's good," September said, at last feeling confident that the futures she had seen of the Land dying and the People reducing in number would now not become reality. She felt relaxed, perhaps for the first time since she had been drawn to this universe. Her task, which had seemed straightforward, to throw the Malevolence out of the Land, had been complicated by the appearance of her twin, but was now complete. She could return to her home and resume life as a teenager, finish school, start a career. Or she could stay here, using the powers of the seven metals to help the People. Both had their attractions, the humdrum life she had grown up in with its daily problems and this new and still unfamiliar environment where she had status but would always be unique and alone.

September chatted to Berddig, Eluned, Padarn and Catrin and listened to their stories of how they had survived the days of vengeance by the Malevolence and how they had begun to rebuild when the power of evil was removed. She heard of their plans for the future, how they would overcome the difficulties that they had been left with by the destruction and death. People started to leave the hut as they finished their meals. There were jobs to be done that couldn't be put off any longer. Gradually September realised that while the people were pleased by her presence they had other concerns to occupy their time. She would be a passing novelty if she stayed.

"I must let you get on," she said rising to her feet. "There is one other person I would like to see before I leave."

"Aurddolen?" Berddig guessed.

"Yes," September said. "His daughter is dead but I hope he is better."

"He is still at Mwyngloddiau Dwfn," Catrin said, "from where he sends out messages of encouragement across the Land and announces plans for the recovery."

"I shall travel to him there, then," September said. She stood up. "Thank you for your welcome again. I hope your future will be happy." She leant over to hug Padarn and then each of the other three cludydds took their turn. Berddig was last.

He released her saying, "Thank you, Cludydd. If you are

able to visit Gwlad again, please come to us."

"I shall," September said thinking of towering, snow-covered mountains and tall, dark buildings.

The houses crowded in on her, the alleys between them filled with snow through which narrow paths had been cut. The snow was pure white, clean and fresh, not discoloured by the Malevolence's filth. From the footmarks in the snow September could tell that people had been moving about although no-one was in sight. There were noises of activity though; the clashing of hammers and the rattling of chains, the sound of metals being worked at the top end of the town. It was cold but the air was still and the sky overhead bright blue. The dome of gossamer-thin tin-lead she had placed over the town had gone, its protection from the attacks of the Malevolence no longer needed.

As she had hoped, she had arrived outside Aurddolen's house. She took a step towards the door. It opened and the blonde haired man looked out. He saw her and his face broke into a smile.

"It is you, Cludydd. I sensed your arrival. Come in."

Although the cold did not affect her, September was pleased to enter the warm and cosy house. Aurddolen was alone but signs of his work were visible. The low stone tables were covered with large leather-bound books and sheets of rough, yellow paper. His golden staff and orb stood beside the fireplace in which golden flames flickered.

"Your presence is a joy, Cludydd, but you have not been summoned to our aid," Aurddolen said.

"No, I'm here because I want to be," September said, "I came to see how you were now that the Malevolence is gone."

Aurddolen sat on one of the large cushions beside a table and invited September to join him. She settled down and crossed her legs.

"The Malevolence caused great destruction and many people died or were taken by the Evil, but we survived and we will re-build. I am planning how we can use our resources and the powers of the cludyddau to the greatest effect. Already the miners and the metalworkers are at work."

September nodded. "So I heard."

"And I must plan for our future," Aurddolen continued.

"But you know there will not be another Conjunction, at least, not one that lets the Malevolence through."

"Ah, yes Cludydd. I had suspected that our world had changed. Hedydd reported that there is a new star on the sky.

"There is?" September was mystified.

"Yes, Cludydd. It appeared only yesterday, close to the Pole Star, indeed over the site of your first meeting with the Malevolence at the Conjunction. It is a strange star, different in appearance to all the others in the sky."

September was still not sure what Aurddolen was referring to.

"How is it different?" she asked.

"It is not the pure white of the other stars but has a mottled, twinkling appearance. Its colour changes from blue to yellow to red. It is troubled. Hedydd says that it appears more distant than the sphere of stars, as if it is beyond our universe."

Understanding dawned. Aurddolen was describing the world she had brought into being, the proxy for Daear where the Malevolence was currently and eternally fighting itself. Of course from this distance the battles between the manifestations would appear as changing colours as they exchanged energies and destroyed each other in bursts of Earth, Air, Fire and Water. Its position in the sky of Gwlad was a puzzle however. When the Cemegwr had responded to her commands for the world to form it must have amused them to arrange it so that it appeared on Gwlad to be where the Malevolence had descended.

Aurddolen was continuing. "The appearance of this star, and of Malice, your return with the sixth Cludydd, your mother, and your victory over the Evil are signs of variation from the prophecies and the records of previous incursions by the Malevolence."

"And now you will be free of the Malevolence for ever. The Cemegwr, have seen to that," September said, eager to convince the Mordeyrn that the future would be different to the past. Was she right? Would the civil war between the spirits of the Malevolence last for evermore and leave the Land unmolested by manifestations? She only had the Cemegwr's and Cyfaill's word for it.

"Ah, the Cemegwr. It seems I was wrong. They do exist, and show concern for our well-being."

"They do, but not really in the way people here thought they did. I don't think they will interfere in the Land again."

"Perhaps they should remain as mythical beings in our stories, Cludydd."

"That's probably a good idea."

Aurddolen sighed. "It will be strange to be planning a future without the threat of the Malevolence. My whole life and time as Mordeyrn was spent preparing for the Cysylltiad. The work of the Arsyllfa was solely to find out as much as we could about the peril that was to come. Now it is destroyed, much of the knowledge lost, and its purpose has disappeared."

"There will be other challenges," September said, "such as making sure all the People have enough food and places to live."

"You are correct of course." Aurddolen sounded almost wistful.

"What about yourself? I'm sorry you haven't got Heulwen." As soon as she had spoken September regretted mentioning Aurddolen's daughter. She was sure he must be hurt by her death.

Aurddolen bowed his head. "She is gone and her end was not what a parent would want for their child." He looked up at September and there was a glint in his eye. "But that is a past that cannot be changed. I must look to the future. Heulfryn is like a son to me and he will be my successor as Prif-cludydd o aur. His powers are strong."

"Good. So will you stay here?"

"For a time, while we are getting supplies to those who need them. But that will not take very long. We must identify young people who can become cludyddau and train them. That is my biggest task. For that I shall travel the length and breadth of Gwlad visiting as many communities as I can. I shall even return to Amaethaderyn. Perhaps I will end my days there."

"That's good. I have just come from there and Berddig and the others will welcome you I am sure."

Aurddolen smiled. "And what of you, Cludydd? The

seventh and last. You are different to your predecessors; your ability to re-visit us for example." He spread his hands.

"I am the last, the only one if you like." September sensed an ending. "I think my time here has finished. I'd like to stay but I'm not sure I could fit in to ordinary life."

"Hardly ordinary given your power to wield all seven metals."

"True, but I'm not sure I want to be the special one that everyone knows about. I don't want to be a celebrity."

"I think I understand, Cludydd. So you will return to your own world?"

"Yes, although I think the Cemegwr, have plans for me."

Aurddolen frowned. "They will leave us alone but still have interests elsewhere?"

"That's one way of putting it."

"Well, good luck, September, and remember there will be a welcome here for you for ever."

"For ever is a long time."

"Hardly long enough to express our thanks to you."

"Now you're making me blush."

"You have no reason to be embarrassed, Cludydd. You have changed since the Maengolauseren brought you at my summons. You have shown yourself to be adaptable and a quick learner. You have borne the starstone and wielded its powers with skill and you have overcome all the perils that have been placed in your way. When you arrived you were unsure of the part you had to play, uncertain of your own strengths. I hope you can now return to your world with the knowledge that you can succeed at whatever you desire. I hope that is our gift to you."

September considered what Aurddolen had said. He was right. She had changed. If 'growing up' meant learning about yourself and finding that you had abilities that you didn't know you possessed, then yes, she had grown up. The fat, lazy, silly teenager was gone. It would take a while at home, to achieve the fit, toned body she had here, but now she knew what she could achieve.

"Thank you, Aurddolen. Farewell."

"Good bye, Cludydd."

September closed her eyes and thought of home.

35

She was sitting in her chair, the starless night in front of her beyond the window. Steam from the hot chocolate rose from the mug on her desk. Spotty was in her hands.

"I'm back, Spotty, as if I haven't been away. Again. But this time I've finished the job. I think." Fatigue swept over her. Fatigue from the journeying from one universe to another, from one time and space to another. Fatigue of dealing with the Brains, of opposing the Malevolence, of wielding the powers of the Maengolauseren.

"Such a lot has happened," she said to the unresponsive rabbit, "but there's no-one I can talk to about it except you. Mother has forgotten and won't understand. My head is buzzing but I need to sleep." She lifted her mug and took a sip. It was still too hot for her so she put it down again and placed Spotty beside it. She stood and undressed, leaving the clothes she had worn for her two-day trip to Wales in a heap on the floor, then pulled her nightshirt on. It was so comforting to clamber into the top bunk and slide under her duvet. Despite all the images of warring manifestations and the people of the Land that flickered behind her eyes she soon drifted into sleep.

"I spoke to your school yesterday," Mother said at breakfast. "They don't understand what happened in Biology on Monday, and I don't either. Miss Hargreaves is upset about what you did."

September paused with a spoonful of muesli halfway to her mouth. Malice's attack on her Biology teacher while she controlled her body had seemed like a dream from the distant past but here it was still fresh in everyone's minds. Previously, Mother had known what was going on in September's head but now she was as mystified as everyone who knew her. She had no memory of Malice.

"I...I don't know what happened," September said, a hollowness forming in her stomach. "Everything went black. I found myself standing over Miss Hargreaves. She was cowering as if I was going to hit her."

"You were; with a broken glass tube. You terrified her," Mother said.

Gus looked up from his phone with his mouth full of toast. "You turned mental, or something."

"No. It's... I don't know. I can't explain..." September couldn't think of any words that would make any sense to Gus, Mother or her teachers. "I don't know what I did. I didn't mean it." That would have to be her defence.

"Well, that's what I said," Mother said and got up to collect another two rounds of toast for Gus. "I told them that you'd been under a lot of strain recently; that the bullying had got to you. They accepted that. They know they've let you down in the past." Mother seemed satisfied that it was her history of persecution that was the reason behind her outbursts.

"Yes...I suppose..." September muttered.

"They realise they should have done more to help you, so they won't be punishing you for Monday's incident." Relief washed over September. "But they want you to see the Counsellor this morning. I'll take you in. You won't have to go to classes until you're ready."

Was she ready? Would she ever be? She was the Cludydd o Maengolauseren who had faced hosts of manifestations of evil, who had conversed with Brains, who saved lives. Of course she was ready. Ready to be a hero, but to face her friends, teachers, other students – and a Counsellor; that was different. That was much, much more daunting.

"You will do it, Em? You won't run away again?" Mother looked at her with a mixture of concern and sternness.

"Of course not," September said wondering how bad it could be.

"Did you enjoy your little trip to woolly Wales?" Gus asked.

"Shut up, Gus," September said.

"Yes, be quiet Augustus," Mother added. "Go and get yourself ready. You've eaten enough toast."

Gus hauled himself up and slouched out of the kitchen.

Mother looked at September, her head tipped tenderly to one side. "I hope you're alright, Em. It would be dreadful if there was something wrong with you."

"There's nothing wrong with me," September replied a little firmer than she intended. She softened her tone. "I'm sure that whatever it was has gone now."

"I hope so, darling. Come on we'd better go."

September was relieved that they arrived after the bell had rung. The entrance foyer was almost deserted as they crossed from the school entrance to the administration suite. September looked at her surroundings. Apart from the few days between her trips away she felt as though she had spent little time here in the last three months of her life. The buildings hadn't changed but she had.

Mrs Philips, the Deputy Headteacher, stood by the door and ushered September and Mother through. They entered a small waiting room.

"Please sit down Mrs Weekes, September," Mrs Philips said in her kind voice. "The Counsellor, Sally Roberts, will see you very soon." She left them and went through a door with the label 'Counsellor' on it. Mother sat on one of the straight-backed chairs.

"Come and sit down, Em," she said pointing to the seat next to her.

"I need the loo, Mother," September said. She discovered that what she said was true. Anxiety had caused the muscles in her abdomen to contract.

"Oh, Em, really. Is there one nearby? Have you got time?"

"There's one just around the corner. I won't be long." September went back into the foyer and keeping the wall on her left followed it round till she came to the girls' toilets. She pushed the door open carefully, stretching her neck to look around it to see if there was anyone there. She didn't want to meet anyone, neither friend nor foe. Often, there was someone lurking, taking a few minutes out of a dreaded lesson, but surprisingly it was empty. She stepped inside, let the door close behind her and headed towards a cubicle.

"Hello, September."

She span around, astonished at the male voice. Standing by

the sinks was a young man. He wore chinos and brogues, a polo shirt under a brown cord jacket, and thick, dark-rimmed glasses. His brown hair was combed neatly to one side.

"Cyfaill!" She recognised the Brain instantly. "What are you doing here?"

"I needed to meet you, September, and this seemed a moment when we would not be disturbed."

"But I've got to go and meet the Counsellor. Mother and Mrs Phillips are there."

"This won't take a moment of your time here. You know that."

"What won't?"

"Your assistance is needed, September."

"My assist…Gwlad isn't being attacked is it? Berddig, Eluned, Aurddolen…"

"They're alright, September. At least I imagine they are. That universe is free from the Malevolence thanks to you."

"What then? Why do you need me?"

"Your powers are needed elsewhere and elsewhen."

"Where? When?"

"I'll explain when we go. Take my hand. I'll be your guide." He stretched out a hand towards her.

"But…"

"Your hand please, September."

September paused, thinking. Which would be the most difficult – explaining herself to the Counsellor or facing the hordes of the Malevolence in a strange universe? Before her sixteenth birthday the first was the only, if unlikely, prospect. Now she had both in her future. She remembered Cyfaill telling her before that many people had two existences, the self they presented to the people around them and the one in their heads. Hers was different because she existed here as a teenage girl and in the Omniverse as some sort of super-hero. She couldn't refuse either path and, she realised, she didn't want to.

She reached out her hand towards Cyfaill's. Their fingers and palms touched. His hand grasped hers. She watched a spark of violet light grow out of their entwined hands. It expanded till it enclosed them. The wash-basins and toilet cubicles and the tiled walls disappeared beyond the dazzling light. September felt a familiar dizziness as her feet lost contact with the floor and gravity stopped. They moved.

…ooo…

Acknowledgements

Having published the first two volumes of *Evil Above the Stars* I am delighted that Peter and Alison of Elsewhen Press agreed with me that there were still questions unanswered and that a third volume was not only possible, but necessary. Thank you Peter and Alison for maintaining the faith. Of course I must thank Peter for all the work pre- and post-publication and Alison for the design. Another special thanks goes to Deirdre for her expert copyediting which sorts out my grammatical and punctuation errors, and to Sofia for proofreading. Thanks also to CPI group for, I expect, some excellent printing.

Unity of Seven is a little different to *Seventh Child* and *The Power of Seven* in that more of the action takes place at real (some renamed) places in this world. I would like to acknowledge my debt to Michael Brown, author of "*A History of the Dylife Mines and surrounding area*". Dylife, between Machynlleth and Llanidloes in mid-Wales is Llelluched in September's story. It is an area that has intrigued me for many years and Michael's book both increased my fascination for this remote mining community and gave me some useful information that I have made use of. I must note however that there is no detailed record of mining there between Roman times and the early seventeenth century. My description of Gwenda's family's mine is pure imagination based on drawings from *De Re Metallica* by Georgius Agricola published in 1556. I would like to take this one and only opportunity to thank Tom and Roy of Lloyd's Hotel in Llanidloes for providing a wonderful base for our exploration of the area. I apologise to the new owners of The Star Inn at Dylife in that I ignored their excellent refurbishment and based Doli and the Moon and Stars on what the pub may have been like some years ago.

As always it is my pleasure to acknowledge my wife,

Alison, as both greatest support and first critic. She has also, very willingly, accompanied me on a number of visits to Dylife, and we have picnicked a couple of times in the grotto where September first meets Cyfaill.

Finally my thanks to readers of vol.1 and vol.2 for having stuck with the story this far. I hope you enjoy this addition to the series. This is the final part of *Evil Above the Stars*, but not the end of September's story.

Elsewhen Press

an independent publisher specialising in Speculative Fiction

Visit the Elsewhen Press website at elsewhen.press for the latest information on all of our titles, authors and events; to read our blog; find out where to buy our books and ebooks; or to place an order.

Elsewhen Press

an independent publisher specialising in Speculative Fiction

Volume 1 of Evil Above the Stars

Seventh Child

Peter R. Ellis

September Weekes is accustomed to facing teasing and bullying because of her white hair, tubby figure and silly name, but the discovery of a clear, smooth stone at her home casts her into a struggle between good and evil that will present her with sterner challenges.

The stone takes her to *Gwlad*, the Land, where the people hail her as the *Cludydd o Maengolauseren*, the bearer of the starstone, with the power to defend them against the evil known as the Malevolence. September meets the people's leader, the *Mordeyrn Aurddolen*, and the bearers of the seven metals linked to the seven 'planets'. Each metal gives the bearer specialised powers to resist the manifestations of the Malevolence, formed from the four elements of earth, air, fire and water, such as the comets known as *Draig tân*, fire dragons.

She returns to her home, but is drawn back to *Gwlad* a fortnight later to find that two years have passed and the villagers have experienced more destructive attacks by manifestations. September must now help defend *Gwlad* against the Malevolence.

Seventh Child is the first volume in the thrilling fantasy series, *Evil Above the Stars*, by Peter R. Ellis, that appeals to readers of all ages of fantasy or science fiction, especially fans of JRR Tolkien and Stephen Donaldson. If old theories are correct until a new idea comes along, does the universe change with our perception of it? Were the ideas embodied in alchemy ever right? What realities were the basis of Celtic mythology?

ISBN: 9781908168702 (epub, kindle)
ISBN: 9781908168603 (256pp paperback)

Visit bit.ly/EvilAbove

Volume 2 of Evil Above the Stars

The Power of Seven
Peter R. Ellis

September Weekes found a smooth stone which took her to *Gwlad*, the Land, where the people hailed her as the *Cludydd o Maengolauseren*, the bearer of the starstone, with the power to defend them against the evil known as the Malevolence. Now, having reached Arsyllfa she is re-united with the *Mordeyrn Aurddolen* with whom, together with the other senior metal bearers that make up the Council of *Gwlad*, she must plan the defence of the Land.

The time of the next Conjunction will soon be at hand. The planets, the Sun and the Moon will all be together in the sky. At that point the protection of the heavenly bodies will be at its weakest and *Gwlad* will be more dependent than ever on September. But now it seems that she must defeat Malice, the guiding force behind the Malevolence, if she is to save the Land and all its people. Will she be strong enough; and, if not, to whom can she turn for help?

The Power of Seven is the second volume in the thrilling fantasy series, *Evil Above the Stars*, by Peter R. Ellis, that appeals to readers, of all ages, of fantasy or science fiction, especially fans of JRR Tolkien and Stephen Donaldson. If old theories are correct until a new idea comes along, does the universe change with our perception of it? Were the ideas embodied in alchemy ever right? What realities were the basis of Celtic mythology?

ISBN: 9781908168719 (epub, kindle)
ISBN: 9781908168610 (288pp paperback)

Visit bit.ly/EvilAbove

Elsewhen Press

an independent publisher specialising in Speculative Fiction

THOMAS SILENT

or

Why there are no more mermaids

BEN GRIBBIN

When widower Angelo found a small baby on the beach twelve years ago, he decided to bring him up as his own son. A sign around the baby's neck said 'THOMAS SILENT', so that was the name he was given. Apart from other people's curiosity about his name, Tom's life so far had been happy and uneventful. When he wasn't at school Tom would help Angelo run the café in his beachside shack. One sunday morning Tom was in the café on his own when a tall, thin, old man called Phillimore came in to escape from the rain. He showed Tom seven bright blue-green stones that he claimed came from a mermaid's necklace. When Tom held one of the stones he could almost feel the rise and fall of the ocean. Phillimore left and Tom thought no more about the stones or the strange old man until Angelo died and the café shack was closed.

Six months later when Tom visits the deserted shack, he finds an envelope from Angelo and discovers what else had been found with the baby on the beach. Tom's simple life suddenly becomes a mysterious adventure that starts with a magical night-time swim to the shore of a strange land. He meets Coralie, a girl hiding in the caves on the beach with Phillimore. The people of the land are held captive to the will of an evil tyrant whose power comes from more of the blue-green stones, which he has been hoarding in the city of Murmur. Tom realises that he, Thomas Silent, is the only one who can defeat the tyrant and save the people of Murmur. But first he must understand the power of the sea-stones and discover his true self.

This delightful tale of real mermaids and mermen will enthrall any teenager who knows that they are special and have a great destiny waiting for them. Those of us who have left teenage years behind will equally relate to Tom's personal journey. We have all looked out from a beach and wondered what is over the sea, but so very few of us find out like Tom.

ISBN: 9781908168931 (epub, kindle)
ISBN: 9781908168832 (144pp paperback)

Visit bit.ly/ThomasSilent

About the author

Peter R. Ellis would like to say he's been a writer all his life but it is only since retiring as a teacher in 2010 that he has been able to devote enough time to writing to call it a career. Brought up in Cardiff, he studied Chemical Physics at the University of Kent at Canterbury, then taught chemistry (and a bit of physics) in Norwich, the Isle of Wight and Thames Valley. His first experience of publishing was in writing educational materials, which he has continued to do since retiring. Of his fictional writing, *Evil Above the Stars* is his first published speculative fiction series.

Peter has been a fan of science fiction and fantasy since he was young, has an (almost) complete collection of classic SF by Asimov, Ballard, Clarke, Heinlein and Niven, among others, while also enjoying fantasy by Tolkien, Donaldson and Ursula Le Guin. Of more recent authors Iain M Banks, Alastair Reynolds and China Mieville have his greatest respect. His Welsh upbringing also engendered a love of the language (even though he can't speak it) and of Welsh mythology like the *Mabinogion*. All these strands come together in the *Evil Above the Stars* series. He lives in Herefordshire with his wife, Alison, who is a great supporter.

www.ingramcontent.com/pod-product-compliance
Lightning Source LLC
Chambersburg PA
CBHW062009190726
48283CB00002BA/620